BORN A VIKING
BLÓT

RICCARDO POLACCI

ISBN: 978-1-7380458-0-8 (Paperback)
ISBN: 978-1-7380458-1-5 (eBook)

First printing edition 2023.

riccardopolacci.com

Contents

Preface

The world was collapsing around me when, during the peak of the Covid-19 pandemic, I had an irresistible urge to open a blank document and write. I felt this voice asking, begging me to write his story—the story of Sigurd, a Norwegian child and his family during the Viking Age.

The story would continue to unfold and come to me while daydreaming. I simply couldn't stop writing and researching. After sharing the first drafts with my family, I thought it worthwhile to share Sigurd's story with the world. This book is the first part of a saga that is still alive and evolving.

I've studied Old Norse, Norse mythology and history for the last eight years. My focus has been to try to understand how they lived and interacted with the world. How did they pray? What did they eat? How did they interact with their loved ones?

While reading and studying the material produced by leading experts and prominent scholars is the best way to absorb as much knowledge as possible, something about the tangible is irreplaceable. And so, following my research, I travelled to Norway, Denmark, Sweden, Finland and Iceland. This allowed me to feel, touch and see the contents of my studies, apart from harassing local historians with my questions.

We know so little about the Viking Age, yet we're fascinated by this historical period. Norsemen didn't write down their lives, beliefs or stories. Apart from some scattered runestones, all we know about them comes from scarce archaeological finds, testimonies of other contemporary societies and what authors centuries after the Viking Age period wrote. Authors like Snorri Sturluson (Iceland, 1179-1241), who wrote the Poetic Edda and the Prose Edda. Two of the most important sources we have of this historical period. Because of this scarcity of sources, most of what scholars do while researching the Viking Age is guess and interpret.

This book should not be viewed as an accurate historical representation of facts and events but as a personal interpretation of what could have been plausible. I've freed myself from the shackles of accuracy in specific domains, such as dates and historical characters, to allow the story to unfold more freely and enhance immersion.

An exact date of when the story takes place is not provided for several reasons. The first is that Sigurd would not have known exactly which year it was since Norsemen didn't follow the Gregorian calendar but rather followed an agricultural-centred lunar calendar. The second is that I didn't want to bind my story to a specific point in time. There might be instances where certain events would have happened much sooner or later than what is recounted or hinted at in this book, or perhaps they happened but have never been recorded, making them plausible.

While the characters and events are fictional, the places aren't. In this book, we find Uppsala, in Sweden, which was one of the most important spiritual centres of Viking Age Scandinavia, and Hladir (*Hlaðir*), modern-day Lade, in Norway.

I make very specific and limited use of Old Norse, mostly limited by two recurring words, *völva* and *blót*. The meaning is inferred by the context in which they first appear. I don't apply the proper plural form of these words in Old Norse but rather anglicise them as *völvas* and *blóts*.

For better readability, I used the terms Scandinavia and Scandinavians loosely even though Norsemen didn't use these terms. They would refer to themselves by their country or ethnic groups, such as Norwegian *(Norðmenn* or *Noregsmenn)*, Danes *(Danir)* or Swedes *(Svíar)*; or by where they came from, Westmen *(Vestmenn)* if they came from the west, such as settlers from the British Isles, or Eastmen *(Austmenn)* for Norsemen coming to a settlement from Scandinavia, from the east.

Setting aside boring historical clarifications, I would like to take this opportunity to thank the people who have enabled me to succeed in writing, editing, formatting and publishing this book. First, my wife, to whom I owe over two years of weekend mornings. Her patience, support and sacrifice give me the strength and time to further pursue this insane endeavour. Her help in marketing and publishing the book is invaluable.

Second, I would like to give special recognition to my parents. Not only have they read every single draft with the utmost urgency and passion, but they've provided me with thorough and sometimes ruthless feedback that helped me further improve.

It has been an exciting and unprecedented journey, albeit not as intense and life-defining as the one Sigurd Eiriksson, our protagonist, will have...

Chapter 1

Pilgrimage

The journey had proven difficult due to Grandmother requiring constant rest. Father was grumpy. He was always murmuring apologies to the gods, fearing that we would be too late. After all, almost a moon had passed since the spring equinox.

We spoke little during our long walking days. We had to think of what was ahead of us, and what we were going to ask them. Every time that I sensed I had a chance, I would ask Mother and Grandmother questions.

"Why don't we ride a horse or a carriage?" I asked Grandmother.

"The journey is part of the process," she said.

I didn't understand how walking rather than riding could be part of the process, but whenever I'd complain, Father would give me one of his ice-cold looks.

"Why is Father so grumpy?" I asked Mother during one of our resting stops.

She gave me a sweet look, as if I understood nothing, and then explained to me he was always like this during these events.

"He's talking to them, clearing his head and preparing himself," she said.

We were sitting under an oak tree near a stream. Grandmother was playing with my four-winter-old sister. Mother was organising our travel food and our bags, making sure that everything was in order. Father was far away from us, on top of a small mound, sitting alone, immersed in his thoughts. Ever since we started planning this trip, he started behaving this way. I was counting fish and trying to stab them with my spear, but I could hardly graze them. Some fish would have been nice for a change. I was growing tired of mushrooms, bread and berries.

Like Father, I was also immersed in my thoughts. Why was he behaving this way? What was ahead of us? I knew we were going to a famous temple, but what was the big deal? Why didn't we go there before?

Grandmother said that we need to do this every nine winters, that everybody needs to get closer to the gods and, as she said, "get naked in front of them." I had already been to our temple in Hladir many times, and I had already taken part in many *blót*. Last winter I was even responsible for fetching our goat for sacrifice. There must be something different this time, something bigger, and it bothered me that nobody was telling me anything.

We finally seemed to be arriving at our destination, The Great Temple of Uppsala. We were half a day away from getting there, and I already saw a change in Father's behaviour. He seemed worried, almost nervous. I had never seen him showing any emotion at all. Unexpectedly, while we were preparing our bags after our last resting stop, Father called me. It was the first time that he directly spoke to me during the voyage. All that time he had been like a mute, with little more than some mutters and murmurs pronounced.

"Sit," he commanded.

And, of course, I obeyed and sat right where I was standing, on the ground. A weak simper appeared on his face.

"There is a rock near you, you can sit there," he said with almost a sweet voice.

I started laughing, but immediately he changed back to his serious and almost menacing look. I had a knot in my throat. Maybe this wasn't a time for laughs. He sat near me, with the same focused expression on his frowned face.

"Do you know where we're headed?" He asked while breathing deeply.

"Yes," I replied, "A Great Temple. We're in Uppsala, right?"

"'The' Great Temple," he corrected, "and yes, we're in Uppsala. Do you know why we came here?"

I thought I knew the answer, but I didn't want to risk it. The depth in his voice, the ice-cold eyes, his frown, the scar on the left part of his face… Sometimes he could be very scary, other times gentle, but today he was both at once. I didn't dare to answer. I just shook my head. Without a moment of hesitation or any type of reaction, he explained.

"We're here to meet people from different backgrounds, some might say. We're here to meet Swedes, Danes and Norwegians, some might say..."

A huge disappointment and rage could be read on his face.

"We're not here for those things, Sigurd. We don't care about the living, we don't care about the dying. We care about the gods. That's all that matters and that's all that should matter."

While pronouncing these last words, he gasped and turned his head to the side. For a moment, he looked enraged. I couldn't quite understand why. I noticed that for him this was a big deal, but, apparently, for others, it wasn't. While turning his head back to me, looking me straight into my eyes, I could feel his look piercing me. He could look right through me. I felt like he could read my mind. He then continued with his explanation, talking slowly and deeply, as if his life depended on every word that would come out of his mouth.

"We're here to expose ourselves to the gods. We'll build a bridge of blood to reach the gods that will act like the Bifrost. They'll see right through us, they'll evaluate us, and they'll decide what our fates will be."

He then paused for a moment. I sensed he wanted those words to sink in.

"Sigurd, we need to prepare ourselves to be in their presence. This is not Uppsala, this is not Sweden or even Scandinavia. At least not these days. These days this place is Asgard. And we're the gods' guests now. Behave accordingly."

I was so focused on absorbing, understanding and deciphering every syllable out of his mouth that I didn't realise that I was gasping, holding onto the rock on which I was sitting with both hands as if it was a cliff. During this whole time, Father had his left hand closed into

3

a strong fist and his right hand, the one missing a finger, was grabbing his Mjölnir pendant, the Hammer of Thor.

Probably I showed some signs of worrying, after all, I thought we were just going to a bigger temple to take part in a bigger *blót*. The moment Father noticed my concern, he placed his left hand on my shoulder. I was shaking and sweating.

"You're over eight winters old now. You're a man. You're my son. Whatever happens, whatever you see…" he paused, took a deep breath and then grabbed me gently by my neck with both hands while going down to his knees in front of me. Putting his forehead against mine, he whispered, "It's the will of the gods. We're nothing without them. Just remember that."

Immediately after pronouncing these last words, he kissed me on the head and without even looking at me; he stood up, grabbed his bags, spear and axes, and walked away.

I returned to grab my bags and prepared to resume the last stage of what now I understood was a pilgrimage. I was repeating the entire conversation over and over in my head, trying to find hidden meanings to all the things that Father said and how he said them.

While grabbing my things, I noticed that Mother and Grandmother were standing there, waiting for me. My sister was there too, nibbling on a piece of bread. They looked at me, then looked at each other, nodded and started walking. I didn't want to talk to them. It was a good thing that they didn't ask me anything about what happened with Father. I honestly needed time to be with myself, in my head, with my thoughts. Was I ready to be "naked" in front of the gods? Would they like what they saw? If the gods could look through me half as much as Father did, then I needed to be prepared.

"Am I worthy? Am I really worthy of being in the gods' presence? Strong enough for Thor? Knowledgeable enough for Odin? What will Tyr think of me? And Freyr? And Frigg? Which gods are we going to meet? We can't possibly meet all of them… "

My head was spinning. I was analysing myself as best as I could. And whenever I wasn't doing that, I was trying to understand Father's words, his reaction, his attitude…

Looking at my feet while walking always helped me forget about the world and focus on my mind. I never understood why. Maybe it's the constant and yet predictable movement. I could walk for days immersed in a sea of thoughts and ideas. Sometimes, a dream would pop into the stream of thoughts that I navigated.

While I was diving into the depths of my mind, I bumped into Grandmother. She had abruptly stopped. So did Mother with my sister in her arms. We had arrived.

We were on top of a hill, in front of us I could see a woodland with many clearings. Groves and clearings were intercalated, almost as if put there by some giant. It looked ancient, very ancient. The groves looked like they were still the giant Ymir's hair, dropped after being slain by the three brothers, Odin, Vili, and Vé. This place felt different already.

Father was headed towards the biggest clearing of all. It was as if he knew perfectly every part of this landscape. In this clearing, I could see a town. It was surrounded by a wooden palisade and had three gates, one north, another west and last, the closest to us, east. We had to take a detour and approach the town from the east to avoid some uneven terrain that would have slowed us further.

Inside the town, I noticed a compound of buildings, of which one was huge. The primary structure was forming a triangle with two other buildings slightly smaller. In between and surrounding these three buildings, there were smaller ones. Yet, the smallest of them was as big as our temple back home in Hladir.

The compound was between the northern and western gates. On the other side of the palisade, I saw the biggest grove of all, formed with tall, strong and ancient trees. There were plenty of houses and buildings across the town and in all the other clearings that I could see from the hill. It looked like a lot of trading happened in this place, at least from what I could see. The landscape was fairly flat, there were some hills here and there, and the biggest one was where we were standing.

Chapter 2

Uppsala

We descended towards the town. Father was ahead of us. I was very nervous. Grandmother was silently crying, my sister was very agitated and Mother was trying to calm and comfort both of them. Father had almost reached the base of the hill when he stopped under a huge beech tree located right in front of the eastern gate.

When we got to the tree, I saw he had dropped his bags and was sitting on an unearthed root with his head leaning back on the trunk, his eyes closed and both hands crossed in his chest. Just as we arrived at the spot, Mother gently dropped my sister and grabbed her chest with one hand, while watching him she teared up. Grandmother broke the silence by just whispering, "Harald…" and then followed by hugging me by the head and kissing me.

I knew my uncle was called Harald. He was Father's twin brother and died almost a winter before I was born. I didn't understand what was happening with Father, my uncle, the tree and Uppsala. But I didn't have time to think much about it because he stood up as soon as he sensed our presence, picked up his bags and signalled with a head motion that we had to go.

The *Thing* was in the southern part of the town, right in the middle. It was slightly elevated with a couple of steps, which wasn't strange for such an important town hall. In front of it, there was a crossroads leading towards the three gates, forming a small clearing. Next to the main building, I could see a smaller one, probably the Earl's residence.

The guards that were posted outside the town hall had different shields, armour and clothes, which made me think that probably several chieftains were feasting in the hall, leaving their escorts outside. In our town, our *Thing* is guarded during special events and feasts by the chieftain's guards, easily recognizable by their shields, bearing a bear's claw.

All around the town, I found people from many places. I could hear Swedes, Danes and Norwegians from different regions than mine, and even other people speaking in a foreign tongue that I never heard before. They were trading, talking politics and about conflicts, marriages, and battles. Most of these traders had many ornaments, and they didn't seem battle-scarred at all. They all carried pouches with pieces of silver, some of them even pieces of gold and precious stones.

They looked nothing like Father. He was of average height but strong as a boar. He was inked all over his body and had plenty of battle scars, the most obvious ones are the one on the side of his face and the missing finger. He also had huge scars all over his back, legs, and arms. His beard was decorated with beads and he shaved the sides of his head, exposing his most precious inscriptions and, of course, some battle scars, like his bitten-off ear.

Even though we were poor and Father wasn't a chieftain, some of these prominent men would respectfully nod their heads when they encountered him, and salute him, showing the utmost respect.

On a couple of occasions, men stared at Mother and whispered between them. She was a very beautiful woman. She was tall and strong, had green eyes and dark blond hair tied in a nape bun. The only times that I saw some warmth in Father's eyes was when he looked at her.

I lost track of time and space while walking in this place. I was too absorbed in observing and trying to make sense of it all when, suddenly, Mother called. We arrived at the entrance of a small house. Father entered, and we stayed behind, waiting. I sat on a pile of straw with Grandmother, and just watched and waited.

Many people arrived in horses and carriages, and some of them brought their slaves. Wealthy men, looking like earls and chieftains alongside poorer men, formed an amalgamation of people never seen before.

"Are you struggling to make sense of all of this?" said Grandmother. The look of confusion and overwhelm must have been quite evident.

It was refreshing hearing these words. I nodded effusively.

"You see," she said, "in the *Thing*, right now, most probably there are leaders, earls, chieftains and maybe even kings discussing politics. There you have traders going about with their business. You see families like ours walking around too. All these people came here from many places."

"I see," I replied, thinking that she was stating the obvious.

"How much time do you think it took for most of these people to come here?" she asked.

"Riding horses? At least half the time that it took for us!" I promptly replied.

She laughed, throwing her head backwards.

"You got that right! And tell me, how many of them really came to settle their business with the gods? And how many came here to settle their business with politics and silver?" she said while caressing my head.

I gave those questions time to sink in before answering. I thought they deserved some meditation rather than an impatient answer.

"I believe, the less people care about being comfortable during the trip or obtaining some rewards out of it, the more they're thinking about settling their business with the gods," I finally replied.

Grandmother laughed again. "You truly are your father's son…" she said with a smile.

At that moment, Father peeked out of the house and called us in. We entered this dark house that was near the palisade somewhere between the town hall and the western gate. There was a small window where the light could get in, but most of the light came from a fireplace in the middle of the room.

An enormous man greeted us. I recognised him even though I had never seen him. Mother and Grandmother spoke about him often. He had saved Father's life at least half the times Father had saved his. The huge and fearsome man was taller than Father with long red hair and a big beard tied in several knots. He looked more cordial and warm than Father.

He grabbed my shoulders softly, or at least that's what he thought. I thought he was going to break me in half.

"So, you're the young Berserker that your father always talks to me about!" he yelled.

Now that was a surprise. Father talking about me? I looked at Father, sitting at the table near the fire, and he didn't even blink.

"I guess so," I replied to the giant, feeling courageous after knowing that Father talked about me. "I know who you are, you're Olaf Ragnarsson. They call you 'The Bear', right?"

Olaf laughed hard, and when I say hard, I mean back in Hladir, our town in Norway, they probably heard it.

"Not only do you have the looks but also your father's smarts! And what are they going to call you then? The Great Sigurd Eiriksson? You look like a wolf to me. You could be known as 'The Wolf'!"

At this point, I realised he wasn't shouting. This was how this man spoke. My thoughts were promptly interrupted by Father's intervention in the conversation, "Let him be called by whatever deeds he's able to perform if it'll be the will of the gods."

Olaf then turned around and, while joking with Father about how 'social' he was, offered beer to all of us, including my sister. We all drank beer, except for my sister, of course. During the conversation, Olaf explained how Father was the most fearsome warrior he ever saw in his life and the most devoted to Odin. These conversations carried on for a long time. Grandmother knew Olaf since he was a child, and Mother knew him also from the 'old days'.

Father didn't talk. He sat close to the fireplace and stared at the flames. I couldn't help wondering why Father was behaving like that. What was going through his mind? Without realising it, I was doing the same thing that he was doing, but I was staring at him instead.

I was surprised by Olaf, who sat near me violently, forcing me to come back into reality after spending most of the time sitting away from everybody, staring at Father; wondering what happened to him, what life he lived and what deeds he performed to earn the respect shown by all the men earlier that day. Mother and Grandmother were in a corner talking with my sister sleeping on their laps. And Father was still near the fireplace. The few times he moved were for sipping his beer.

Olaf then whispered to me, well, it wasn't quite a whisper, but more like a normal person talking. "You wouldn't want to be in his head."

I looked at him with wide-open eyes, thinking this man could read my mind.

"Your father is hardly in this world, Midgard, but he's not in Valhöll either. Or at least not yet."

I worried. What did he mean by 'not yet'?

"You see, men like him are rare to find. He can be the dearest and greatest friend, which would suggest that he's part of this world. But on the battlefield... He's not from this world. You need to understand that the path that your father treads is a sacred path, a hard path. He doesn't fear death more than he fears life."

I didn't know what to think about this. Initially, I thought he was drunk, but then I recalled the stories about Olaf needing more mead than Thor to get drunk, so that couldn't be it.

"I don't understand," I replied. "Aren't you both warriors? Shouldn't you be like him?"

Olaf smiled, "If a man picks up a shield and a spear and is willing to use them, does that make him a warrior?"

"I guess so."

He smiled again. "Does that mean that your grandmother is a warrior if she picks up a shield and a spear?"

"No," I said, "She's strong, but she's not like Father, nobody is."

"On that, we agree, boy. Nobody is like your father."

I couldn't help thinking that each time that I was about to get some answers, I only got more questions in return.

"But Olaf, aren't you a great warrior too?"

Some pride could be seen in his eyes.

"I am indeed a warrior, and not bad at it according to my age and the fact that I still breathe. But, you know, I'm not like your father.

He has a fire inside him that I don't have. I'm a brute, a skilled brute I might add, but still a brute," said Olaf with a deep voice.

"And Father?" I immediately asked.

"Eirik is a Berserker," he replied, "like the old ones, like the ones from tales and stories. He has a special connection with the gods."

At that moment, a question popped into my head. I didn't even know why or how it had formed, and I just heard the words coming out of my mouth.

"And Uncle Harald?"

The moment I asked that question, Mother and Grandmother stopped talking. Olaf immediately looked at Father and held his breath. Father deeply exhaled, placed the beer cup on the table and turned his head towards us for the first time during that evening.

"Harald was a true son of Odin. A true brother of Thor. A proud disciple of Tyr. A true warrior that belongs in Valhöll," he said while standing up and going outside.

I felt I shouldn't have said anything, but Olaf put his huge hand on my shoulder.

"Don't worry about your father. There are many things that you don't understand now but you'll understand them in time. For now, you should rest. Tomorrow is going to be an intense day."

We went to a small room in the back. There were four beds, a small niche on the wall with some gods' figures and a small window. I couldn't stop thinking about that last day of our journey. All sorts of thoughts, ideas and theories were crossing my mind at lightning speed. I couldn't sleep, I couldn't think. So I decided to ask.

I took a small pouch from inside one of my bags. In this pouch, I had my gods. These were small wooden carved figures of the gods. Father would carve them while returning from raiding seasons or battles. "Each time the gods allow me to return, I'll carve one for you," he used to say.

I had Odin, the all-father. Thor, the thunder god, the strongest of all. Tyr, mighty and skilled in battle. Heimdall, with his Gjallarhorn.

Loki, the sly one, master of shadows and mischief. Frigg, Freyr, Baldur, and many others.

By placing them near the oil lamp that was lighting my side of the room, I formed my own sanctuary, or *hörgr* as Grandmother called them. I then asked Odin to clear my mind so that he could show me the path to truth and knowledge. I asked Thor for strength, feeling I was going to need it. And asked Frigg to protect me and my family. I wanted nothing bad to happen to them.

I kept talking to the gods until I fell asleep. I slept like never before. It almost felt like I slept for a hundred winters. I dreamt about the Great Hall, where Odin's warriors fight each other until Ragnarok. Then I dreamt of Ragnarök. I dreamt of how Jörmungandr surrounded Midgard, how Thor defeated the monster, how Loki was imprisoned…

It felt like during that night I went to the origin of it all; I saw the sacred cow feeding the giant Ymir, the formation of the nine worlds. I saw every single event that led to that very moment when I woke up and saw Father standing by my side. He had already cleaned himself and probably had already eaten something.

"Welcome back to Midgard," he said.

I looked at him, still confused about my dreams and wondering what he meant by that.

"Up. Move," he commanded. I obeyed.

Chapter 3

Odin's Wolves

That morning Olaf's house seemed different from the previous day. It was brighter. The small window and the door were completely open. The fresh summer breeze came in alongside the warming sunlight. There was an incredible day outside, with a clear sky, and a strong and warm sun.

While I was eating some porridge with berries, Mother told me that Father went out with Olaf to attend some business. She couldn't tell me more about it even if I kept asking. Grandmother was sewing some of Olaf's worst clothes, maybe to repay him for his hospitality or maybe because that's just how she was.

After getting cleaned with the house's water pot, I decided to roam the town. As soon as I got out of the house, I saw a group of kids fighting with sticks, maybe practising for future battles. Father told me I'm a man. I couldn't play those games anymore. I needed to understand more of what this was all about. Why were all these people gathered here? What was so different here?

I passed a group of families near Olaf's house. They were Danes. They were also poor. I couldn't see any horses, carriages, expensive brooches, jewels or clothes. Amongst these people, a man got my attention. He was bald, short and had a long beard tied in a thick braid. He was only wearing his pants. Being shirtless, I could clearly see his very muscular body full of scars and inscriptions. He was sharpening a sword a few feet away from his family. He also looked like he was living inside himself, just like Father.

After a walk, I sat down near some benches, just to observe. I liked to do this a lot whenever I would be in a new environment, sit back and observe the interactions between people. Mother used to say that I was like an owl, watching with wide-open eyes.

Suddenly, I picked up a conversation of two men drinking and talking, sitting on one of these benches. They looked like wealthy men, not chieftains, but not simple farmers either. Maybe they were traders. One of them had long black hair tied in a ponytail, a short curated beard and expensive clothes. He didn't have many jewels though, but the clothes I could see were fairly new and of good quality. The other man, an older man, had long white hair and a long beard. Even though he didn't have his hair combed nor his beard taken care of, his clothes were also of good quality, and he had several bright beads around his neck.

"Have you seen 'The Bear'? He looks bigger than what I remember!" the older man started saying.

"Yes. I wouldn't want to be on the wrong side of an argument with him. But, have you seen who joined him yesterday?" replied the younger one.

"No," said the old man, "Who joined him?"

"One of those crazy berserkers. The craziest of all, if I might say. The twin that's alive."

Hearing that, the old man reacted surprised and offended, "One of Odin's Wolves?" he asked.

"Yes, one of the 'Crazy Twins'. I always wondered who was the hungry one and who was the greedy one!" said the young trader while giggling.

At that moment, the old man slapped the other man's hand, the one holding the mead cup. I could see a fire in his eyes. He was probably as enraged as I was. They were talking about Father and Uncle Harald after all!

The old man grabbed the younger man by his throat with beastly strength, transforming into an enraged animal. He was a pleasant and polite man when I first saw him and now looked like one of Loki's creatures.

Getting closer to the young man's face, he started speaking very calmly while suffocating him "Never talk about things that you don't understand. Most of all, this is the worst place and time to talk about these things. If you talk again about Odin's Wolves and their brothers in this way, I will slit your throat myself." And then he released him.

The young man started coughing. He had a red face and blue lips. His eyes looked like they were about to jump out of their sockets.

14

The moment he recovered some air, he looked extremely angry but scared. "Screw you and that band of fanatic criminals!" said while running away.

I was so enraged and confused. Why would these people know who Father and Uncle Harald were? Why were they known as Odin's Wolves? And their brothers? And why did the young man hate them?

I didn't realise that I was standing in front of the old man, exactly where the other man had recovered his breath, watching the man run away, getting smaller and smaller in the distance while holding my axe. Visualising myself killing him, I could feel the rage that started to build up the moment I picked up the conversation. Went from my lower stomach to my upper stomach, then to my chest. From there, it just transferred to my legs and arms, wanting to wield a weapon and run towards him. And then, finally, to my head. I wanted to kill that man and I was thinking of a hundred ways of doing so.

"Hey! Boy! Put that away. You'll end up hurting yourself with that thing," said a voice from behind me.

It was the old man. He regained that pleasant look that he had the first time I noticed him. I wanted to reply something polite as Mother taught me to, but only these words could come out of my mouth "I will kill him".

The old man didn't laugh at me, as I expected, he instead took me seriously and replied "And perhaps one day you will, but right now you can put that thing away, take a deep breath, and sit here for a while until your rage flies away."

I complied, putting away my axe and sitting near him. I couldn't notice earlier from where I was standing while listening to the conversation, but this was a tall and strong man. Winters had passed, but you could see that he must have been a fearsome warrior in his youth.

He had his hair covering half of his face, so I could only see one of his eyes, and he had a very cold and deep eye, a piercing eye, just like Father. "Are you feeling better now?"

"Yes, I feel nothing right now," I promptly replied to my surprise. Indeed, I wasn't feeling enraged at all.

"Good," he replied, "Good... Now you're able to think. Aren't you?"

"Yes, sir. I am. Clearer than ever."

"So, you wanted to kill that serpent. How would you do that right now?" he continued.

"I wouldn't. I'm not old enough. He would kill me before I could even get close. I'll have to wait, and whenever the gods decide to put me in front of him again, I'll end him," I replied with no effort. Words were simply coming out of my mouth with ease.

The old man laughed, "The gods... You sound like a smart man trapped in a boy's body!"

I laughed as well. I'm not sure why. Then, I felt confident enough to ask, "Sir, who were these Odin's Wolves that you two talked about? And why does he hate them so much?"

The old man looked at me like Father sometimes does, a serious and deep look, like reading my mind. I felt as defenceless with him as I felt with Father.

"Well, Odin's Wolves were Geri and Freki, of course. And that man probably doesn't like wolves. What do you think?" replied the man.

I wanted to tell him that, obviously, I knew who Geri and Freki were and that I knew that Odin's Wolves referred to Father and my uncle. I also wanted to tell him I knew he was trying to trick me by hiding the truth of what he really knew. But, at the same time, I didn't know this man. He was a total stranger and after what I had seen and heard previously, I didn't really know if I wanted people to know who I was.

"I'm just devoted to Odin. We came here to settle our business with the gods, not amongst men. I was angry because of that," I heard myself saying.

When the old man heard these words, he smiled, as if he was expecting them somehow. "Well then, go prepare yourself for settling your business with the gods. I'm sure your mother is probably worrying right now."

"Yes, I'll do that now. Thank you, sir. May I ask what your name is?"

"My name is 'the old man on the bench', boy. Now go!" he said while signalling me to go with his arm. And so I did.

I started running towards Olaf's home, already thinking about how I could extract some information about what had happened; probably my best bet was asking Grandmother or Olaf.

Suddenly, amid my run and my thoughts, I heard a voice that said from a distance, "I'll see you soon, Young Sigurd!"

I froze. Could it be possible that the old man knew the entire time who I was? And if so, how? Never had I seen or heard of that man. I turned around and looked at the bench as many people crossed in front of me carrying animals in cages, bundles of straw and clothes. There was a lot of buzzing in that street at that moment that didn't allow me to see the bench. The moment the crowd cleared a little, I could finally see it, and it was empty.

"Well, that means nothing," I thought to myself while walking towards Olaf's house. I had run for a bit, during that time the old man could have gone away. Also, Sigurd is a very common name, and some kids were playing with sticks earlier, so probably one of them was this 'Young Sigurd'. It was probably nothing. My priority was to go home and figure out what the deal was with what the young man was saying.

Chapter 4

Preparation

Upon arriving at Olaf's house, I found Grandmother was still sewing. Near her, a pile of patched-up clothes had formed. Mother had laid out white gowns on our beds and was preparing some bread while my little sister played with the fireplace's ashes. She had half her face black and the other half white. I think she had played with Mother's flour previously.

"Where have you been?" asked Mother the moment I stepped foot into the house.

"Around," I replied, "What's the deal with Thrúd? She has half her face covered in ash and the other half covered in flour. She looks like a *völva* during *blót*." Mother laughed.

"Maybe that's her fate. Who knows? She could be a priestess someday..." replied Grandmother.

"It is as if she already knows," added Mother.

"Knows? She knows what?" I asked.

"Well, today is the first ceremony. We'll go to The Great Temple," said Mother.

At that moment, the door opened. Father and Olaf came in and they paused at the entrance, assessing what was going on in the house. "Let's get ready," said Father as he went to the back room. Olaf followed him, but first, he kissed Grandmother on the head. I guess he noticed the pile of patched-up clothes.

I looked at Mother, not quite knowing what I had to do, and she signalled me with her eyes to go to the back room too.

Father was in front of Olaf's sanctuary, which had been carved into the wall. It had several gods figures, not as many as the ones that I had on mine near the bed though. He then murmured something to them, and after that, he removed his clothes.

I was always impressed when I saw Father's naked body. The number of inscriptions and scars that he had were very shocking to me, and whenever he showed any part of his body to other grown men, they would react surprised too. Olaf didn't seem to be bothered or surprised though. He also went to the sanctuary and murmured some words for a while. It was strange to see him this serious, focused and committed. He looked like a joker the night before, but today he was a different person.

He also removed his clothes, and the number of scars had nothing to envy Father's. He had a considerable scar crossing his chest, almost as if caused by a huge battle-axe. His arms and legs were full of scars too. He also had a lot of inscriptions inked, but not as many as Father. He had more drawings of animals than Father, especially bears.

As they started to get dressed in the white gowns that Mother had laid out on the beds, I kneeled in front of my sanctuary. Because I didn't hear what they had said to the gods, I just asked them for protection and guidance, feeling lost and afraid of the unknown.

I then removed my clothes. The only scars that I had were on my knees from when I fell while running on rocks and on my shoulder, from when I played with my neighbour with sticks. I tried to make them notice my scars, as few as they were.

Luckily, Olaf noticed the scar on my shoulder. "Well, I'm sure that scar didn't come from falling, right?"

"It was while fighting with my neighbour, after all the evening fighting, he managed to hit me once," I proudly answered.

Olaf smiled and gave me a pat on my back. I felt like my chest was going to explode. This man's hand was like my entire back.

Before heading towards The Great Temple, we had to paint our faces with black paint made of ash and white paint made of something else that I don't know what it was, it might just have been whiter ash or even flour.

While painting us, Father was serious, murmuring words as he had done since we left home. Olaf also murmured. It was still strange seeing him so committed and serious; it made me feel the obligation to do the same.

When Grandmother stood in front of me to paint my face, she said while smiling, "White for clarity, knowledge, clairvoyance, memory, love and affection." She then changed the bowl, took the one with the black paint, and with the same deep tone but with a more serious face said "Black for strength, decisiveness, responsibility and courage."

When it came to my sister, she already had her face painted from when she was playing, it wasn't quite the same paint but Grandmother said "Let her keep her own paint, we can't teach a master when is born with the gift."

After we had readied ourselves to encounter the gods for the first time since we had arrived in Uppsala, we left the house and headed towards The Great Temple.

Chapter 5

The Great Temple

While we were heading towards The Great Temple, all the people that I had seen previously were now dressed in their white gowns and also had their faces painted.

Nobody had any ornaments on them, except for some pendants, rings and bracelets, but mostly everybody had removed all jewels and clothes. We were all wearing the same long white gowns, painted with the same colour and made of the same materials and walking towards the same place. You couldn't tell who was a chieftain, a farmer, an earl or a king at first glance. But you could still identify them if you looked closely.

Prosperous people still had some bracelets or pendants that showed their wealth. Also, some of them had guards around them. Even though the guards were dressed like all of us, I could still recognize them from earlier in the day.

Be it as it may, it was humbling to see all these people blending together under the will of the gods. It made me think again about the purpose of this trip. It made me think again of what Father had told me on that mound.

I started getting nervous. The more we got close to the temple, the more anxious I got. I started asking for forgiveness from the gods. I felt like I got too distracted with other things since I arrived without preparing myself for this moment, and I knew they could see right through me.

As it often happened, I found myself looking at my feet while walking, apologising to Odin, Frigg, Freyr, Tyr… When suddenly we stopped. We had arrived.

The Great Temple, the compound actually, had been lit with hundreds of torches all around. In front of us, there was a tall wooden building. Mother picked my sister up, and Grandmother started explaining to me, finally.

"That big building is Odin's Temple. The one on the left is Thor's. That one on the right is Freyr's. Do you see what they form? You've seen that shape on your father's body."

Indeed, I saw it on Father's body. He had a shape inked in his left chest like three triangles intertwined. The big temple with the two other big ones, but smaller than the first one, was forming a perfect triangle. Between these bigger buildings, there were another three temples, smaller ones, like the one in our town. They were also forming a triangle.

"Grandmother, the smaller ones are also forming a triangle, right?"

"Yes, Sigurd. The one between Thor and Odin is Tyr's. The one between Freyr's and Odin's is Frigg's. And the one we just passed in the back is Heimdall's."

I didn't even realise that we had already passed in front of one. I was so immersed in my conversation of apology with the gods that I forgot to look in front of me. "Now," I thought to myself, "most probably Heimdall is angry at me. He controls access from Asgard to Midgard, guarding the Bifrost. He is very powerful. I'm in trouble."

"Don't worry about Heimdall, child. He won't be mad at you. I'm sure you were already talking to him, is that right?" asked Grandmother as if she could read my mind.

"Yes!" I almost yelled, "I swear I didn't mean to miss his temple," I added in a lower voice.

"Don't worry. They can see through you and inside you. They know your intentions and how you feel. Heimdall knows you didn't mean to be disrespectful."

That reassured me. And promptly I realised we counted two triangles, but the shapes and symbols that I saw in many places, including Father's chest, were three triangles, not two. "Grandmother, where's the third triangle?"

"You don't remember Sigurd?"

"No. Did we already see those temples?" I asked, wondering how distracted must I have been.

"You weren't paying attention. Probably your father scared you. What shape did the three main clearings of these woodlands have?"

"Well, there was this one, the biggest one at the top. Then two other smaller at-..." I immediately realised the clearings were forming a perfect triangle when seen from the highest mound, the one we came from.

"There you go, Sigurd. There you go..." she said while continuing to walk and signalling to me with her head to pay attention and to walk.

We continued walking and positioned ourselves in a circle in the centre of the compound. It was still bright when we had left Olaf's house, but now night had silently fallen upon us without even realising it.

The only lights were the ones from the torches and the sky. Many stars could be seen, the smell of fat burning in the torches, the grass from the surrounding fields, the mud under our feet, the wood, the ash on our faces... I was feeling like I was entering another world. Nobody spoke once we had formed the circle. Even my sister was quiet.

From inside the temples, *völvas* and temple assistants came out, also dressed in white with their faces painted. But the colours of their faces were different, each temple had a different colour.

It looked like the *völva* from Odin's temple had a red colour; I guess blood. From Thor's, red and blue. From Frigg, white and black. And so on. I couldn't quite focus on all of them because my attention had focused on Odin's *völva*. She had similar eyes and expression as Father's. A more focused and intense look that gave the impression that it could pierce your being.

The priestess from Odin's temple took a step forward. "We're all gathered here tonight to reunite ourselves with the Æsir. Today, we'll dedicate ourselves to them. We'll show ourselves to them as we are, and not as we think we are. They'll see us for who we really are, and not for who we want to be perceived as." She paused and looked at some of the easily recognizable wealthy men from the crowd.

I didn't quite understand the entire speech, but Father's words resonated inside me, and they started to make more sense.

The *völva* continued, "Every nine winters, we gather here. And every nine winters, the gods cross from Asgard to Midgard and talk to us, listen to us, but, most importantly, reveal us for what we are, for who we are." People started to tear up, and some women started crying.

I looked at Father; he was clutching his robe at the height of his chest. It looked like he was about to tear it open. He was looking up at the sky for some reason. And he was moving his heels up and down. His eyes were watery as he kept closing and opening them while breathing deeply.

Olaf had his eyes closed. His arms were crossed and his eyebrows frowned. Mother was crying silently, hugging Thrúd in her arms. Grandmother was grabbing my hand, eyes in tears, looking at the sky.

The speech continued "Before addressing our own fears, confessing our deepest secrets to the gods and asking our most precious wishes to them. We must ask for permission from the All-father." During the first part of the speech, the other *völvas* and temple assistants were looking downward, at their own feet. The moment the *völva* said these last words about asking permission from Odin, they all simultaneously raised their heads and looked forward.

"Odin had to sacrifice his eye in Mímir's Well for knowledge. He had to offer blood for knowledge," after Odin's *völva* said this, all the other temple people murmured something incomprehensible at the same time.

"Odin had to sacrifice himself by hanging for nine days and nine nights, in order to obtain knowledge of the nine worlds and the knowledge of the magic runes. He had to offer blood for knowledge," and again, the same incomprehensible murmur was outed by the *völvas* and their assistants.

Right after this was said, the assistants of Odin's temple brought forward a cow. I wouldn't know what colour it was because it had been painted in black and white, with the same paints we had used for our faces.

"With this blood, Odin, All-father, we ask your permission to wander amongst you and all the Æsir. May it be enough payment for our intrusion," solemnly said the *völva* while lifting a ceremonial sword.

Right after pronouncing these last words, they restrained the animal, grabbing it strongly from the horns and some ropes tied around the neck. Promptly the *völva* stabbed the animal in the lower part of the neck, near the heart. The animal moaned and a jet of blood splashed into the ground. The *völvas* and the temple assistants secured the animal so it wouldn't move much, and placed a big bowl under the blood fountain coming out of the cow's torso. Soon after, the animal collapsed.

The crowd then went one by one towards the *völva*, to get a sip of the blood.

As we got closer, I could finally see what the process was. The person would get in front of Odin's *völva* while an assistant would hold the container with the blood. The chief priestess would immerse a smaller bowl into the bigger one, and the person in front of her would drink a sip while she murmured some more incomprehensible words.

Soon enough was Olaf's turn. The *völva* looked at him with a sign of recognition. And in addition to making him sip the blood, she immersed two of her fingers in it and passed them through his forehead.

Then it was Father's turn. The moment he stood in front of the *völva*, time seemed to stop. They stared each other straight in the eyes. Nobody moved. The *völva* had his same ice-cold look, that deep piercing look. I had never seen anybody looking into Father's eyes like that. That moment seemed like it lasted forever. Even though people in the queue were impatient, nobody even dared to breathe loudly.

After what seemed an eternity, the *völva* gave the small bowl to Father, until now she and the other *völvas* were the only ones who touched the bowl. He immersed it in the blood, and drank the whole bowl, without dropping a single drop, without changing the expression on his face and, all of this, without stopping to stare at each other's eyes.

The *völva* opened her hands in a tray position so that he could place the empty bowl in them. After immersing her entire hand inside the blood container, she passed her fingers on Father's forehead, dragging them down until reaching his chin. She then placed her hand on Father's chest, where he had the triple triangle inked, and placed the same hand on her chest.

After that, she lowered her head, looking downwards, and Father continued walking.

Now was Mother's turn. She sipped the small bowl. Then the *völva* looked at my sister and offered the bowl that still had some blood in it. Almost looked like daring her. Thrúd immersed one finger in the bowl, then put the finger in her mouth, watched the *völva* and smiled. The spirit woman then briefly and gently nodded, and Mother kept walking.

Then it was Grandmother's turn. She also had blood on her forehead, just like Olaf.

And finally, it was my turn. I didn't know why, but I couldn't stop staring at those ice-cold eyes behind the face paint. I stared at them the same way I sometimes did with Father. The *völva*'s look felt as if I was completely naked in front of her. She could see my body, my heart, my thoughts… After this first impression, I knew I should have looked away, or simply gone ahead with the blood-sipping, but I couldn't, something inside me couldn't stop staring at those ice eyes.

She intensified her look as I noticed that silence around me had formed. I felt challenged, almost threatened. But I couldn't let go. My first instinct was to intensify my look too, but then I remembered the 'old man on the bench', and I relaxed and breathed.

I stood there, relaxed, breathing, staring into the *völva*'s eyes, in peace and full of confidence.

After a while, she also relaxed, deeply exhaling. Almost relieved. She then offered me the bowl, as she had done with Father and my sister before me. I took it, immersed it in the container, acting without thinking, and drank the blood. It felt like drinking warm iron.

I didn't particularly like it; I didn't dislike it either. As I felt the warmth get into me, I felt differently. I felt connected.

After returning the small bowl to the *völva*, she placed her hand on my chest, and then on hers.

I didn't get any blood in the face, and I felt that whatever had to happen, it already did. At this stage, I knew we would have to break eye contact. And the same force inside me that insisted on me staring into her eyes so deeply, now made me respectfully lower my head, and walk away.

Once I walked a couple of steps, I looked in front of me and saw that my family and Olaf were waiting for me after they had carefully witnessed my interaction with the *völva*. Mother and Grandmother teared up.

Father and Olaf were standing tall, strong, partially covered in blood and proud. They had watery eyes, almost teared up. They looked at me, nodded, and started walking towards the temples. I followed them.

Chapter 6

Talking to the gods

The first temple where we entered was Thor's temple, the mightiest god of all. These temples were enormous, with logs going all the way up to the roof and huge beams crossing the ceiling. At the sides of the entrance, outside, there were long tables with all types of food and drinks.

Once I passed the door, the temple was dark, lit by a few torches in the walls and several bowls with fire on the floor, leading towards a gigantic statue of the god himself. It was a long room, just like a longhouse. On the sides, there were benches and tables. More drinks and food could be found on these tables.

I couldn't quite see the god from the entrance, just the shape. I started walking through the dark room. Many people were walking around, murmuring, drinking and eating. We arrived in front of the god, Thor. It was a massive wooden statue, with pieces of gold, stone, precious stones, silver and iron. He looked so alive!

Near him, there were piles of offerings of every kind: clothes, food, drink and some jewellery.

I stood there without knowing what to do. I was used to our temple back home in Hladir. It was just a simple small wooden building with a few medium-sized statues and a tiny room where the *völva* would live.

Grandmother placed her hand on my shoulder and whispered into my ear "You're in front of Thor. Be strong. Talk to him." Then she walked towards the statue and started praying to herself.

I took a couple of steps and placed my hand on the wood. It felt warm and dry. I was expecting to feel the god's extraordinary power and might. Maybe lightning passing from the statue to my fingers. But I just felt wood. Slightly disappointed, I proceeded to pray, asking for strength and protection for me and my family.

In the beginning, it felt a little strange. For me, talking to the gods had always been something very private. I never tried it in a vast temple filled with people. But, after deciding to give it a better try, I closed my eyes and started talking to this statue... I felt as if someone was listening to me, even though I didn't hear any responses. I felt courageous; I felt strong. As my confidence built up, I intensified my praying. I wasn't even sure I was pronouncing all the words properly. But I paid no attention to that. I was just talking to Thor.

Once I finished, I opened my eyes and turned around. Mother was standing nearby, proudly looking at me. She was carrying my sister, who had become mute since she entered the temples' compound.

I then went roaming the temple, observing what people were doing, as always.

Some men were talking to each other as if they were in the market or the *Thing*. Others were even getting drunk with all the mead that they were drinking. They started shouting, jumping and hugging each other.

It angered me. I almost felt like a holy man after my "conversation" with Thor. I felt so empowered, so enraged. But then, at that very moment, I realised that one of the loudest men was Olaf. Our Olaf! I couldn't believe it. How could he desecrate that place?

While I felt the rage boiling, I heard a laugh near me. It was Grandmother. She had finished her prayer, and now was laughing, watching Olaf going crazy with the other men. She hugged me with one arm and raised her mead horn with the other. At this point, I didn't understand anything anymore.

She stooped and spoke to me, close to my face, "Cheer up Sigurd! We're in the presence of the gods!"

"Precisely," I replied in all seriousness, "Shouldn't we show some respect?"

"What do you think we're doing, boy? Cheer up! And show your gratitude to Thor for him joining us today!" she yelled, then drank more mead and went towards a table to refill her horn.

This wasn't for me, I thought. I decided to step back a little and stay close to the statue. I almost felt the need to protect it.

While watching all that was happening, I noticed Father was behind Thor, in the gap between the wall and the god. It was probably the darkest place of all, for torches weren't meant to light that part of the room. He had his arms crossed, grabbing his elbows, and his head was pointing upwards as if he was looking at the god's head, but his eyes were closed.

"You're so much like him," a gentle voice behind me said.

I turned around and saw Mother. My sister was jumping around with Grandmother, Olaf and the others.

"What do you mean?" I asked, intrigued.

"He also struggles to understand other people's feelings. You see Sigurd, every person is different, and every person feels differently."

"What has this anything to do with-"

"Look at those men," she interrupted my immediate reply, gently placing her hand on the side of my face, "they're talking as if nothing was happening but, do you really know what is in their minds and hearts? Are you certain that none of them feels the same rage you feel? Or even the same love?"

I didn't know what to answer. I never stopped to think about what those men felt. I just felt that their behaviour was wrong.

"You don't know what their life was like. You don't know what are the reasons for their coming here. Maybe these men haven't spoken with each other since the last time, since nine winters ago…" she said while caressing my face. She had a nostalgic tone when she spoke about the last time.

"Now look at your grandmother!" she said while pointing at Grandmother.

At that moment, I started seeing her differently. Her grey hair had flowers and leaves in them, and many braids. I didn't notice them earlier. How could I have missed them? She was jumping and dancing, looking younger, more beautiful, and stronger. She was throwing my sister around, patting Olaf in the back with fast and strong blows.

"Do you see now, Sigurd?" whispered Mother, "Do you see how Grandmother feels Thor? How is she grateful for his presence?"

I was speechless. "But…" I tried to reply immediately while looking at Olaf but she didn't allow me to finish.

"But Olaf? Does it surprise you he would act loudly?" she said while laughing. "You need to observe more, Sigurd. Allow your mind to understand what your eyes see..." she said while caressing my face and drying invisible tears from my cheek. And, at that moment, I noticed it. I could see it clearly now.

While Olaf was dancing, jumping, yelling, drinking and laughing, he was feeling. I could see everything moving slowly at that moment, very slowly. Every little jump lasted an eternity. I could see the drops of mead coming out of his horn, slowly falling to the wooden floor. I started noticing his scars, slightly shining in the light of the torches. His face was hard to read. He was smiling, but, at the same time, he was crying.

Now and then he would pay attention to one of his scars, then he would yell and jump, scream and sing. His hair was flapping, and his knotted beard too. Tears were coming down his face and I couldn't understand if they were tears of joy, sadness or both. I didn't know what to make of this.

"Sigurd, usually, there is always more to something than what meets the eye," said Mother, probably sensing my overwhelming confusion.

Her comment was met with utter silence. I just wondered, what else was there with Father? I stared at him, hoping that maybe Mother would comment something about him. But she looked at him and then looked at me and started walking towards the temple door, signalling me with a head motion to do the same. I followed her, leaving Thor and Father behind.

The moment we stepped out of the building, I was surprised by how busy The Great Temple had become. Thor's temple was slightly elevated. It allowed me a better view of the compound. In the middle of the circle formed by the temples, people were coming and going, groups of people talking, others drinking, singing and dancing.

"Where are we going next? When will we visit the All-father?" I asked Mother.

"Whenever you want. I'll have to go to Freyr for next season's crops. And then to Frigg."

"Shall I come with you, Mother?"

"Do what you feel like, Sigurd. This evening, do what you feel like," she said heading towards Freyr's temple.

Feeling overwhelmed by the overall experience, I wanted to stay close to Mother, but, while we were passing right in front of Odin's temple, I felt this strong need to go inside it. I stopped. I couldn't resist it.

"Mother," I called, "I really would like to accompany you, but... I feel I need to go see Odin."

She smiled and nodded, almost as if she was already expecting that I wouldn't go with her.

The entrance of Odin's temple had been brushed with the remaining blood from the cow's sacrifice. This temple was a couple of steps higher than Thor's and Freyr's. It was definitely taller and had some sort of tower in the middle part of it. It was decorated with carved golden inscriptions and knots all around.

I found myself at the top of the steps, right in front of the wide entrance. Also here I could find several tables with food and drinks on the outside, and I could already see that at the beginning of the temple, on the inside, there were more tables with drinks and food.

I wanted to go in but, for some reason, I couldn't find the courage to do so. This feeling, this initial impulse, desperately asked me to go inside but, at the same time, I felt I couldn't take another step. I felt scared. People were coming and going, some involuntarily hit me while getting in and out of the temple. I just couldn't move. The two temple assistants who were at the entrance were staring at me, making me even more uncomfortable.

Suddenly, I heard a strong and deep voice "Welcome to the home of the All-father, Sigurd." It sounded partially like a familiar voice, even though I never heard it before. But the moment I heard it, I felt protected, as if nothing could ever harm me. I felt courageous again.

While I was taking my first step, I felt a firm hand on my shoulder. It was Father. He was standing near me, very close to me, looking forward, towards the black hole that was the entrance to the temple. He then looked downwards with those ice-blue eyes, "Welcome, son, to Odin's house."

It was the same voice that I had heard earlier. It was Father's voice, but still I didn't recognise it. He looked different, more gentle, more loving and relaxed, like at home. He didn't have a frown anymore.

We entered the temple. It was longer and taller than Thor's. On the sides, there were also benches and tables with food and drinks. The ceiling and the walls were decorated with inscriptions, symbols and other ornaments. I could see better in this temple because of the higher number of torches. Everything had been smeared with blood. Walls, benches, floor and even part of the ceiling were soaked. The smell of smoke, blood, mead and herbs was overwhelming.

I was following the path formed by the fire bowls on the floor. Suddenly, the lights divided widely, forming a circle, and then returned to the initial form and continued straight. In the middle of this circle — a big circle I might add — there was a huge stone table. It didn't look like it had been moved there but looked like it had always been there. It seemed to me the temple had been built on top and around this huge rock.

The stone was large enough that a big horse could fit on it, also the huge entrance would allow an animal that size to fit in. The middle of the stone was slightly hollow, inclined towards us. I believe this stone was used for sacrifices, and the blood would slide towards this side, falling into what looked like a wide groove on the floor. The groove was divided into two other grooves that went towards both the entrance and the back of the temple, following the fire bowls.

As I got closer, I saw the stone resting on top of a small mound. The boulder had been painted in black and golden colours. It had many carvings. Some were familiar and newer, others seemed ancient, and I didn't understand those symbols and inscriptions.

Father stared at the rock as if it could stare back at him. He said nothing nor did anything, just stood in front of it. I looked into his face, thinking that maybe he was reading the inscriptions, but he wasn't. He was simply staring at it.

I was desperate to go see Odin, but I didn't want to interrupt Father in whatever he was doing. He then slowly exhaled, totally emptying his chest of air. It seemed to me that it took forever. It was a calm and long, very long, focused exhale. Once all the air was out of his body, he started deeply inhaling again. Again, extremely slowly. Taking his time to allow the air to fill any gap in his body. While doing this, he was lifting his head at the same pace as the inhale, until his gaze fixed whatever was in front of him. I looked in that direction too and saw the shape of a colossal statue. Father was still inhaling. His chest was bigger than ever, his muscles felt even bigger, and he looked stronger. His stare was as ice-cold as I had ever seen.

Eventually, he stopped inhaling and kept the air inside. He stared at the statue's shape in the dark for a while. Then he released all the air again in a slow exhale. It wasn't as slow as the first one, but from my impatient point of view, it seemed very slow. Once all the air was out again, he looked at me and said "It's time."

We passed the sacrificial boulder and went towards the end of the temple, following the fire bowls on the floor and the grooves on the sides. And we finally stopped in front of it.

What a work of art. It was a giant statue, carved in rock and wood, with many details. It had gold, iron, precious stones, silver, and every other material that you can imagine. Odin was in a frontal position, holding Gungnir, his mighty spear. He had a raven on each shoulder, Huginn and Muninn, Thought and Memory. At his feet, he had his two wolves, Geri and Freki, Hungry and Greedy. The statue was surrounded by what looked like water. It looked like a well, but it wasn't deep at all. The grooves from the ground would end at the tip of the water. This structure was enormous. There was a small bridge to cross over this water and get closer to the All-father, who was standing on a small island.

We crossed and stood in front of the statue without pronouncing a single word. I felt so small in front of the High one. I talked so often to him, carrying him in my pouch, and now he could carry me in his pouch! He felt so real…

Father crossed his arms over his chest, each hand touching the opposing shoulder and he closed his eyes and started to inhale and exhale deeply and slowly again. The pace was faster than the first time he did it, though. It seemed like he was talking with his breathing. It had a rhythm. He closed and opened his eyes several times and lowered and lifted his head several times.

I decided to stop looking at Father, give him his privacy and started focusing on myself. I stared at the colossal figure for more time than I can recall, and couldn't feel much at all. Disappointment started growing in me. I had great expectations for this moment.

After some more time passed, I started getting bored, waiting for Father to finish so we could go. I didn't want to leave before he finished. I didn't want to disappoint him. So I kept admiring the statue, all the details, the ravens, the wolves, the water... Wait a moment!

I looked back at the wolves, Geri and Freki, and I noticed something familiar. They had a pendant hanging around their necks. Geri, the hungry one, had a rounded pendant with the three triangles entangled, the same symbol that Father had in his chest. And Freki, the greedy one, had a similar rounded pendant, but this one had a cross-like symbol. It comprised a perfect cross, with the same distance from all ends to the centre, and a second one, exactly the same as the first one, but rather than pointing towards North, South, West, and East, it pointed towards the cardinal points in between. In the middle of it all, a circle surrounded the centre of these crosses. Alongside each arm of the crosses, there were three perpendicular marks and, at the end of each arm, a curved shape, making it so that each arm ended with three different points.

I had heard of this symbol; it was known as The Helm of Awe. I had heard that Uncle Harald had this symbol inked on his forehead, but I had never heard this from family, just rumours.

While I was looking at these symbols, focusing on them, and thinking about the false rumours about my uncle's forehead; I heard a deep laugh. It sounded like it came from a distance but yet it felt close. Like it came from a cave or a well, but I was pretty certain that it came exactly from in front of me, even though that wasn't possible at all.

Several people were drinking, dancing, talking and jumping in Odin's temple as well. So, most probably, the laugh must have come from one of them, and somehow I heard it like it was coming from in front of me. While I was having this very thought, I heard it again. It clearly came from this figure in front of me, or maybe it simply was in my mind. I decided to look upwards, towards Odin's face, but I was feeling the same way I felt in front of the temple, afraid. I had disrespected the All-father with my boredom and childish attitude during this whole time in front of him.

I gathered all my strength and looked upwards towards his face. Nothing changed in the statue, but everything changed inside me. I felt like I was being held in the air by some force, even though I could still feel the floor beneath my feet. I felt like my thoughts weren't my own anymore, but rather that this force could control my mind, and read through it. It vaguely reminded me of the feeling when Father or the *völva*, earlier that evening, pierced me with their look. But this was more intense, brutal and careless.

I felt like I couldn't breathe, my heart was pumping strongly, and I didn't feel my legs or my arms anymore. I could still see the statue in front of me, but I began to see through it. After a while, a bright shape started taking form. It wasn't quite a human shape, nor a known object. I just knew it wasn't that statue and it wasn't in that room. It was as if somehow my eyes could still see the statue in the dark room of the temple, but my mind was ignoring that and seeing something else, superimposing it.

I started to breathe slowly, trying not to panic. Soon enough, I felt more comfortable. The oppressing force didn't feel that oppressing anymore. The panic and fear transformed into curiosity. I had completely forgotten about the people in the temple, the floor beneath my feet, my arms, legs... Even Father near me. I felt completely exposed and naked in front of this shape, this figure, and I was starting to understand it.

Slowly, the more I relaxed and accepted what was happening, the more the figure started taking the shape of an old man with an aquiline nose, white long hair, a white long beard and a missing eye with a huge scar. His only eye was ice, the most piercing look ever.

36

I didn't talk; I didn't need to. He already could see through me. He moved his head ever so slightly, like inviting me to look in that same direction. And so I did.

I saw a big ball of blue ice. It started getting smaller. Soon I realised the ball wasn't getting smaller, but rather I was getting farther away from it, even if it didn't seem that I moved at all. The ball transformed into a very recognisable eye. It was Father's eye. We kept getting farther away, higher, and we could see Father. He was very young and strong, his face and body were covered in blood spatters. Around him, dozens of killed and mutilated enemies. Father was gasping. He looked tired. He was looking around, almost as if he was searching for more enemies to slay. Suddenly, his head turned, and he looked me straight in the eyes. As soon as our looks met, he started relaxing, slowing his breathing evermore, and I felt like we were getting closer and closer to those ice-cold eyes again, to the point where I could only see both eyes, then one eye, then a big ball of blue ice... All of a sudden, we moved back again, but this time extremely fast. The blue ball transformed into an eye, then into two eyes. The sequence was as fast as Thor's lightning. We kept moving back and promptly from the eyes I saw my face, then my body, here, standing in front of Odin in this very temple.

I stared at myself. Then, my other self looked at Odin's figure, looked back at me and I suddenly felt slammed down, back into my other self, in the ground. And everything went dark.

Chapter 7

The Twelve

I started hearing some noise from a distance and slowly opened my eyes. I was sitting in a corner of the temple. Grandmother was sitting near me, still drinking mead and talking to Mother and Olaf.

"Welcome back, boy!" yelled Olaf while raising his horn and spilling half of the mead in it.

"For how long did I...-"

"Not much, Sigurd, just a little," interrupted Grandmother.

Looking around, I saw Mother talking to other women and my sister sitting down on the small bridge that leads towards Odin's statue, wetting her feet and playing with the water.

Suddenly, I saw Father talking to a strong bald man, with a long beard tied in a thick braid, shortly realising that he was the Dane that I had seen while roaming the town. The Dane had the same blood marks that the *völva* had marked Father with.

There was also a third man amongst them. A robust and strong man, taller than Father, and definitely taller than the Dane. He had blond shaggy hair and a thick beard, with some precious stone beads in it. It seemed to me he was a wealthy man since he had a big and thick golden arm ring, a silver Mjölnir pendant and some crystal beads. He also had the same blood marks that Father and the Dane had.

Standing near Odin's statue, on the side, as far away as possible from the people and the torches; they weren't drinking nor singing, but calmly talking.

"Grandmother, who are those men talking to Father?" I asked.

She looked at them and changed her face completely. She went from smiling and careless to serious and concerned in an instant, "Ask Olaf, he can explain better than I can."

Olaf had heard the conversation, so I just looked at him, expecting an answer. He sat down on the bench with me, took a huge sip from his mead horn and said with a melancholic and sad voice "They're what's left, Sigurd."

"What's left of what, Olaf?"

"Of The Twelve, boy… Of The Twelve…" he answered while taking another big sip of mead.

I stared at him, with the face of someone that needed more details and was starting to get annoyed. He looked at me and sighed with a mixture of understanding and annoyance.

"Sigurd, don't believe what people say. When times change, people try to change things that should always remain the same, that are sacred. And when they can't change them, they aim to destroy them," he said as he paused to sip more mead, "and boy, the best way to destroy people is not by killing them, but by destroying their legacy and letting them live to see it being destroyed."

"I understand," I replied, "I want to die in battle and go to Valhöll, and feast with Odin and the other champions. But I want to do so only if I know that my sacrifice will be remembered. Is that what you mean, Olaf?"

"Something like that, boy, something like that…" he replied. After that, he emptied his horn with a huge sip, stood up with a jump and cheered up, "Enough of that for tonight, Sigurd! We're here to rejoice amongst the gods!"

He then grabbed me from my chest, pulled me up in the air and launched me into the middle of a group of people who were dancing with animal masks, bear hides and wolf skins.

I jumped my way out of the dancing and returned to Grandmother. She was staring at Father. She looked sad, serious and nostalgic. I then grabbed two horns, filled them with mead, took a wooden bowl and filled it with bread, some pieces of meat from the cow that had been sacrificed and then cooked, and some mushrooms. I went back to the bench and offered it to Grandmother, who greeted me with the biggest smile and the strongest hug. We then spent the rest of the evening drinking, eating and, I'll admit it, maybe dancing a little.

The next morning, I woke up and helped Mother with some chores. I was surprised by how the day was presented before me, simple and dull. I couldn't help feeling disappointed that nobody asked me about what had happened. Everybody acted like it was a normal thing as if it never took place.

"Is everything alright, Sigurd?" asked Mother as I helped her clean the fish.

She must have noticed that I didn't speak during the morning and struggled to even make eye contact, which was extremely odd for me.

"I don't know," I replied.

"Do you want to talk about it?" she insisted.

Where was I supposed to start? How could I ask? I didn't even know why I was angry. I didn't know what exactly happened to me, nor if it was real. Yes, that's it...

"Was it real, Mother?" I asked.

"How did it feel?" she quickly replied, as if she didn't need to think about the question.

"Real, very real. But some parts... In Odin's temple, they couldn't have been real at all!"

She laughed, reminding me of her laugh from when I tried beer for the first time. I was about six winters old and Father allowed me a sip of beer. I hated it but, at the same time, wanted to try more. It was a laugh of understanding, of experience and love. Or at least I perceived it that way.

"But Sigurd, why do you say that it couldn't have been real? I don't want to know what you saw unless you want to tell me. That's between you and Odin. But one thing I know, if the All-father wanted to tell you or show you something, he must have had his reasons. After all, he's the wisest of all," she said while separating the fish's skin from its flesh, "not everything needs to make sense right away. Sometimes we're revealed with knowledge for which we don't possess the answers, yet."

I needed to think. I felt my mind moving at the wind's speed. After a while, I couldn't resist it anymore, and I broke the house's silence.

"Why didn't you warn me? Why didn't you explain what would happen? Why do I always have to figure out things on my own?"

She smiled, which irritated me, and then she quickly started talking, knowing that if she kept smiling, it would keep irritating me even further.

"Sigurd, my child… You always have so many questions. It's in your nature…" She suddenly stopped working and raised her eyes towards me, giving me more attention than the fish, finally! "We don't tell you everything that is going to happen because you need to experience it yourself. That's the way it has to be," her attention turned back to cleaning the fish, "and besides, where would the fun be in telling you everything?" and laughed again. This time, I laughed too. I've always felt a sense of comfort when talking to her.

At that moment, Grandmother and my sister entered the house. They had gone for a walk earlier that morning. We finished the remaining chores together, then I sat down near the fireplace. I was looking for the best opportunity to ask Grandmother about The Twelve.

Soon enough, she sat near me. She usually could read my face and knew that I needed to talk to her.

"What's in your mind, little one?" she asked.

"Grandmother, yesterday, when I saw Father with those men, Olaf told me that 'they're what's left of The Twelve', what does that mean?" I asked, trying to be as direct as possible.

She exhaled slowly, her smile disappeared and was replaced with a worried, sad and melancholic face, "What do you know about berserkers, Sigurd?"

Tough question, I thought. I had heard of berserkers from people around. They were these very strong men, half animals, half men. They would not fear death nor pain, they would go to battle without armour, biting shields, howling, roaring… They were violent criminals, I heard; who would steal women and kill for pleasure. They were outlaws, without honour.

But then, when we got here, Olaf said that Father was like a Berserker, and he said it full of pride and admiration. He even joked with me saying that I was the 'young Berserker'. How could these two concepts be true? I fully trusted Olaf, but then, how can all the people be wrong?

Suddenly, I felt Grandmother's hand over mine. She grabbed it.

"Don't worry Sigurd. I know you must feel confused, and even more with all that has happened these last days. But let me tell you something..." she said while moving in the chair, making herself more comfortable as she usually did before telling us one of her magnificent stories.

"In times of old, the gods would walk, talk, sleep, eat and live amongst us. They would come from Asgard all the time. We also had frequent visits from Giants too. Sometimes Thor and Odin had to help us get rid of some of the most violent and problematic of them. We used to be close to the gods, and they were close to us. At that time, a group of formidable warriors was formed. Amongst the most devoted and skilled warriors, twelve were selected by Odin himself. Twelve warriors to fight for him, for his name, for his people, our people. These warriors were so close to the gods that they had some magic powers themselves. They could talk to the gods the same way I'm talking to you now. They could resist pain like no other man, and they had a powerful connection with the elements of the world, including animals."

At this point, I was hypnotised. Mother had stopped doing chores and sat down near us, with her hands full of flour. My sister was sitting near the fireplace playing, but since Grandmother started talking, she stayed still, listening and paying the utmost attention, as if she were an adult.

Even though it wasn't even noon, the house was dark. The small beam of light from the tiny window was at our back. Most of the light that we had at that moment, in front of us, came from the fireplace. Grandmother was very old, around sixty winters old already. She still had some leaves and flowers from the previous evening's celebration on her hair. She was a strong and beautiful woman with ice-blue eyes, just like Father's. The light of the fire would reflect on her face, making it look magical, mysterious, almost ancient.

"These men," she continued, "could not be commanded by men, only by the gods. They would often fight the Jötuns, the Giants, alongside Thor himself!"

She now paused, staring at the fire, as if she was getting lost in her thoughts, as if her mind was a storm trapping her in, not letting her go.

With no movement, still staring at the fire, she resumed, "But men always want more. Men need to command, need to possess. And these warriors, chosen by the All-father himself, were the best weapon! For one of these berserkers could slay fifty of the best warriors of any earl or chieftain!"

She started raising her voice while accelerating her breathing, "In the beginning, men started to have more faith in silver than in the gods. And that made the high ones retreat to Asgard and Vanaheim, and never come back. Then, men in charge would start having power over temples and *völvas* so that they would answer to them and not to the gods. And this led to The Twelve, the mighty warriors, chosen by Odin, to be finally commanded by men."

Her eyes were filled with tears. I couldn't understand if they were of sadness or rage. Her hands were closed in fists.

"The Twelve were tasked with the hardest challenges of all," she continued, "Initially, they were used to fight foreigners that would invade our lands, protect our people, our beliefs, our gods. Then, they were used to invade the invaders, the foreigners, releasing the gods' wrath on anybody who had the misfortune of standing in front of them.

"But then... Then they were used for invading the earls' or chieftains' political rivals, fighting amongst neighbours, amongst brothers. They were slaying the same people they were born to protect," she then lowered her face to the side, almost with shame.

She stayed in that position for a while, trying to recover the strength to continue with her story. When she raised her head again, staring at the fire, a tear of fire could be seen rolling down her face.

"With the passing of time, many of these warriors lost their lives. The most fortunate died and went to Valhöll, joining their brothers and Odin in the Great Hall. Others, less fortunate, lost their ways and lived in misery..." she continued while both her cheeks were now wet from tears.

"Thanks to these warriors, many men expanded their territories and their wealth. Many lands were conquered, and many battles were won. But slowly, these men were not accepted anymore. Their old ways were too hard to understand, to accept. They were outcasted by the very lords who benefited from them. Stories spread about how these men were evil, savage, bloodthirsty monsters in search of riches and women. Sadly, a few of these stories were true. Some of these men travelled far away to serve in foreign places as mercenaries in search of blood. Others, those who weren't able to renounce their land, stayed here and tried to survive as best as they could. Most survived without harming others."

As soon as these words were pronounced, the door opened. It was raining outside, there was a tremendous storm. Lightning struck right when the door opened, and there stood Father. His clothes were the same as the night before. He was soaked, the blood from the ceremony had dissolved with the water, tainting all of his clothes. He looked at us, as if he knew what had been said in that room a moment ago, and then went directly towards the backroom to get changed. Right after him, entered big Olaf, also soaked. He had new clothes, though. It almost looked like he spent the entire morning out looking for Father to bring him home.

After that, silence reigned in the house. Father and Olaf dried themselves and changed their clothes. Mother finished baking bread. Grandmother, my sister and I stayed in front of the fireplace, in silence.

Chapter 8

Berserkers and Ulfhednar

We finished eating as silence still reigned in the house. The weather changed, the storm had passed and now there was a light rain.

Father and Olaf went outside and sat on two tree stumps that were adjacent to the house wall, below the small window. I was inside, looking out the window, thinking about what that vision at Odin's temple meant and about The Twelve when I suddenly heard Olaf's strong and deep voice talking to Father.

"You know Eirik, you'll have to start treating Sigurd as a man now."

Father replied with a grunt of assent.

"You'll have to take him with you these days. You cannot shield him anymore. He'll receive his arm ring pretty soon," continued Olaf.

"I know, I know, Olaf. Time passed by too fast," said Father.

For a while, there was silence. I could hear them breathing deeply as if they were worried about something.

"I'm here for you, Eirik, you know that. We're brothers," said Olaf, breaking the silence. Father exhaled deeply after hearing these words.

"We'll always be brothers, Olaf, always, no matter what happens..." said Father with a sigh, "Promise me that you will-"

"Don't even say it. You know I will," interrupted Olaf.

They stayed there a long time in complete silence. I was wondering what was Father shielding me from. It never appeared to me he treated me softly. I also didn't like where the conversation was heading, like if Father would have to go away. Maybe he was about to go raiding again.

"Do you remember, Eirik, when we used to go fishing? The peace of the rivers in the mountains," said Olaf with a deep nostalgic voice.

"The salt of the sea..." replied Father.

"Carving holes in the ice…" added Olaf, "there wasn't a fish in all Scandinavia safe from us!" They both laughed.

"Do you remember Harald?" said Father, "He used to steal fish from my basket so that he could say that he caught more fish than me."

"Harald the greedy, eh?" replied Olaf with a titter, "He always made us laugh so much. For the gods! I miss him…"

"He always made us proud," replied Father, "now he's probably making fun of us while getting drunk with the others in the Great Hall."

"Well, one thing is for sure," said Olaf, "If someone can get kicked out of Valhöll that's him! Who knows if he doesn't return one of these days!" and they both burst out laughing.

After hearing that I went to my bed. I didn't mean to eavesdrop, but once I heard the beginning, I couldn't resist staying there and hearing more.

Soon after, Father came into the backroom to rest. After all, he spent the entire night out. I took my chance and went outside, seeking a conversation with Olaf. He was still sitting on the tree stump, his head against the wall and his eyes closed. I didn't know if perhaps he was resting too, so I just sat near him in silence and waited.

"Hi there, young berserker," said Olaf the moment I sat down, still in the same position, without even opening his eyes.

"Hi Olaf, do you want me to leave and let you rest?"

"I rested enough all these past winters, boy. You can stay."

We stayed there in silence for a while. I was looking for a way of asking questions without being too direct or annoying. I would try by just mentioning Grandmother's story, and seeing if he cared to add any more details, maybe details concerning Father and Uncle Harald.

"Earlier today, right before you came back home, Grandmother told me a story. A story about The Twelve. About how these men were born as Odin's best warriors, devoted to him, commanded by him. And then men slowly started taking possession of everything, even of The Twelve, and they fell in disgrace. Or something along these lines," I said.

46

I tried to make a vague argument, intentionally leaving out as many details as possible, hopefully prompting him to jump in and add more details. Maybe, if he was feeling talkative, he would fill in all the gaps that I had.

He smiled, still with his head against the wall and his eyes closed.

"You remind me of your uncle Harald, smart as he was, and also of your mother, a cunning woman. You know Sigurd, my father was killed in battle when I was a boy around your age. My mother had to marry another man, and he took her to Sweden. He was a wealthy man. She wanted to take me with her, but I didn't want to leave the land. I wanted to follow in my father's steps. So she talked to your grandmother, and I was adopted by her, she became my step-mother," he now opened an eye, the one closest to me, and looking at me with it he said, "I know very well how your grandmother tells stories, and she wouldn't miss any single detail, ever."

I swallowed the knot in my throat. He was a gentle, social and nice man, but he was huge, like a bear. Sometimes I would get intimidated by his size, appearance and scars.

"I know you want more information, Sigurd. It's just natural. I think you're becoming a man in front of our eyes. So, tell me plainly, what's bothering you?" he said, breaking the uncomfortable silence that had been created by his previous statement.

"Uncle Harald was also part of The Twelve, right?" I asked, now knowing that I could be blunt in my approach and, to be honest, that was exactly how I felt more comfortable.

"Yes, but there weren't only twelve, they operated in groups of twelve. There were more of these groups scattered all over Scandinavia," he answered.

"Then, why are they known as The Twelve?" I continued.

"People like to put nicknames, Sigurd. But the ones that were known as The Twelve were the last ones to operate as a unit. All the other groups were disbanded long ago." He now opened his eyes and turned his head towards me.

47

"This is more complicated than it looks like, Sigurd. Your grandmother probably did a great job explaining to you the origin of these warriors, but most probably she didn't explain that within these mighty warriors, commonly known as berserkers, there were two types: Berserkers and Ulfhednar. As you know, 'berserker' is the term that we use to describe Odin's warriors who are identified with the bear. They wear bear hides in battle, and they usually identify themselves with that animal.

"Ulfhednar, on the other hand, were very rare. Stories have little information about them. They were considered among the closest warriors to Odin. Their connection with the All-father was absolute. They also fought with wolf pelts as only armour, and they also invoked the spirit of their animal, the wolf, when going into battle."

Things started to make sense now. But, it all seemed too extraordinary to be true. I had to dig deeper.

"So, by the looks of it, if I can dare... You would be a berserker. And Uncle Harald and Father are Ulfhednar? Wolf-warriors?" I hoped that I didn't push it too far. But I really was desperate for answers at this point.

"I used to be a berserker. I then felt that I didn't have the same connection to Odin that I used to. So I came here, built me a humble house, and now live near The Great Temple, trying to regain Odin's trust," he replied as he lowered his head. Shame could be read on his face. "Your father and uncle had the strongest connection with the gods that I've ever seen. At times, I thought that your father was Odin himself. But, you'll have to ask him if you want answers about him or your uncle."

"I understand," I replied, "Thank you, Olaf."

He placed his enormous arm around my neck, brought his head back again and closed his eyes. I rested my head against his arm and also closed my eyes. We spent a lot of time like this, or at least that was my impression.

It was a moment of peace. All the pieces of the story were starting to fall into place. It was very strange to think that a few days before that moment, I didn't know about any of this.

While resting against the wall of the house, I was wondering how someone knows when their 'connection' with Odin weakens. And so, seeing that Olaf was in a sharing mood, I decided to follow his advice and ask plainly.

"Olaf?" I whispered, not wanting to wake him up in case he had fallen asleep.

"Yes, boy," he replied with his characteristic deep voice.

"How did you notice that your connection with Odin was weakened?"

He exhaled deeply, like remembering some shameful or painful event, "Well... I noticed in battle. My berserker rage didn't last the entire battle. In the middle of it, I found myself out of the trance. A simple big man, in the middle of mud, blood, spilt guts, screams and iron. I felt lost. Abandoned. The image of my mother going away with her Swedish husband and bidding me farewell was the only thing that I could see."

I didn't know what to answer. I wasn't expecting this from this fearsome man.

"I froze. There I was, shirtless, foam at my mouth, blood over my body, either mine or the enemy's. I had lost my bear hide. I could feel the cuts in my body that I couldn't feel before and could hear the battle cries that I couldn't hear before. The stench of blood, wet earth, urine and faeces invaded my senses." He exhaled again.

"I looked upwards, hoping that Odin would help me, as he always did. And I didn't feel him. I asked Thor and Tyr too. But I felt nothing. I looked downwards again, and a man came swinging his axe at me. I couldn't react. Before hitting me, his arm was amputated by a brother of mine. I turned to him and almost couldn't recognise him. He looked like a beast from Hel or Niflheim." He now put his hands over his face in shame.

"I used to crave battle. I dreamt of it with eagerness. But, at that moment, I didn't belong there. Everything looked foreign..." he now rested his elbows on his knees, still with his face covered by his hands, panting, as if he was reliving the memory.

I put my arm on his vast back, not knowing if he would even notice it.

"What did you do then? How did you survive?"

He turned his head and looked at me while sitting straight again.

"Well, I was lucky that your uncle saw me. He immediately noticed that I wasn't in the state that I should've been in anymore. He was incredible, despite him being totally into it, in battle mode, he could still sense me. He sensed that I wasn't close to Odin anymore.

"He came near me and slew anybody that ran at us. He then looked at me, and believe me Sigurd, I was scared. I was terrified when I saw his eyes. The Helm of Awe in his forehead was one of the few parts of his body that weren't covered in blood or battle paint, he was growling, killing enemies with his bare hands, biting them in the throat, slaying them with his axes. He was fast Sigurd. He wielded one axe in each hand but it looked like he had four arms, the speed..." he started staring at the nothingness, like visualising and reliving his memories.

"Your uncle grabbed me by the throat. You know Sigurd, your uncle was very similar to your father, they were twins after all, shorter than me and also of a smaller build. But the strength with which he grabbed me... I never felt something like that. I was terrified. He then looked me straight in the eyes, piercing me with those ice-cold eyes, and said, 'You may not feel him, but he's watching you. If you die like this, you will not join him. And when I die, I'll look for you, and I'll spend eternity killing you until you become a bear again. Worthy of Valhöll.'"

He now smiled while moving his head from side to side, "Your uncle was able to make me smile even in that situation..."

"What happened next, Olaf?" I asked, intrigued. I really needed to know more.

"I grabbed your uncle's arm, then one that was holding my throat. I grabbed it strongly, very strongly, and started to get enraged.

50

The more I looked him in the eyes, the more enraged I became. I then started focusing The Helm of Awe on his forehead and started feeling rage again. I then told him: 'There are only two men in this field that can send me to Valhöll, and they're my brothers'. Then he released my throat at the same time that I released his arm. I grabbed my battle-axe from the ground and the carnage continued."

"So, you recovered. Why did you leave them then?"

"Sigurd, the moment you doubt Odin once, it can happen any other time."

"I understand. You're afraid that if you go into battle and the same thing happens, there won't be anybody to bring you back, and you'll die."

"Die? I'm not afraid of death Sigurd, I seek it. I'm afraid of an unworthy death. Your uncle will make my afterlife miserable if I die an unworthy death!" We burst out laughing.

Father woke me up by putting his hand on my shoulder. I had fallen asleep sitting on that tree stump. Olaf was standing near me too.

"Let's go Sigurd," said Father.

"We're going to the *Thing*," said Olaf.

"Why?" I asked, still struggling to open both my eyes after the nap.

"We're celebrating the beginning of the *blót*," said Father.

"Wasn't that what happened yesterday?" I asked again.

"No Sigurd. Yesterday we asked the gods for permission. We cleared our debts with them. We asked them what we wanted. Made our promises and vows to them. Today we'll celebrate. And tomorrow... It'll start," said Olaf.

"But, I thought we already did it yesterday. Do we need to start again?" I insisted.

Father then looked me straight in the eyes and squeezed my shoulder, "Too many questions can turn you from a smart person into a goat in a moment. Come if you want."

He then turned around and started walking towards the town hall.

51

"Let's all grab some mead!" said Olaf with a smile as he started walking while signalling me with his head to walk alongside him.

We entered the *Thing*. All kinds of people were there, mostly adults. Many long tables with long benches were following the direction of the building. In the middle, meat and fish were being roasted over the fire pits; there were barrels of mead, wine and beer everywhere.

At the very end of the long hall, there was an elevated platform where the most prominent would feast. Several slaves would serve the wealthiest men. People were singing, yelling, dancing… There was much confusion overall. The air was charged with smoke, sweat, mead and food smell. I loved it.

We sat at the end of one of the long tables. We had some mead and some food. Olaf already started singing some songs and shouting. Father was drinking with a serious face. From time to time, he would smile a little when Olaf did something hilarious. I laughed all the time, watching Olaf hugging people, singing and teasing Father for not being 'happy'.

This was supposed to be a celebration that we officially had started the *blót*. The sacrifice made the evening before was an opening ceremony, apparently. I was still trying to put all the pieces of the puzzle together since nobody ever told me what we were supposed to do once we would arrive here. I was supposed to figure this out on my own, for a change. "Who knows how the *blót* would be the next day," I thought to myself.

We spent most of the evening in the town hall. Father allowed me three cups of light mead, "You're becoming a man, but you're not quite there yet" he said regarding my wanting to drink more.

During the evening, the Dane that I saw at the tent camp and in the temple joined us. He hugged Olaf and Father.

"Hello boy, I'm Knut. I've heard a lot about you," he said.

"Hello sir, I'm Sigurd," I respectfully replied.

"I know who you are very well!"

His spirit was very similar to Olaf's. He would sing and joke all the time. His beard braid would fall into the mead cup from time to time and he would suck the mead out of the beard while winking at me jokingly, "Not a single drop can be wasted!" he would yell.

He was shorter than Father but had such a developed muscular body covered with scars and inscriptions that made him almost as scary as Father, even though his eyes weren't as intense.

I had a great time with them. Knut picked me up and put me on his shoulders, and we would jump and sing with Olaf.

At a given moment, I headed towards the entrance. I needed to go out to pee. Three cups of mead was a lot of mead, at least for me. Before reaching the door, a man stood in front of me. He was visibly drunk. He was an enormous man, almost the size of Olaf, and had placed his hand on the door, not allowing me to open it.

"Let me open the door, sir," I said, trying to be as polite as possible.

"'Let me open the door, sir'," he mocked me, "Are you a slave, boy?"

"No. I'm not a slave. Are you blind?" I said to him, feeling the rage growing in me.

"Perhaps you're the blind one, little rat. I could take your head if I wanted to. Do you want me to try?" he said while stumbling closer to me.

I froze. This man looked very violent, and I didn't have my axe with me, even though it wouldn't have made much of a difference. Right when he was about to grab me, a man stood right between us. He entered from the side, hitting the man's arms with the side of his body. It was Father.

The man immediately reacted violently. He took his axe and prepared to strike. Father stood there, looking upwards due to the height difference. His relaxed arms dangled on the side of his body. He was simply staring at this man.

As soon as the man looked at Father before striking, he froze, and I noticed how at that moment the chanting, shouting and dancing in the hall had halted. You could hear everybody breathing in that great hall. The man looked as if he just had seen Jörmungandr, the great Midgard serpent, he was shocked. So shocked that he stood there for a moment with his axe raised, not knowing what to do.

"I believe you were going to take my son's head if I'm not mistaken," said Father, calmly.

"I... I... I..." babbled the man, "I would... I would never dare, Eirik. Never."

The man finally realising he still had his axe risen, dropped it and took a couple of steps back.

The tension in the room could be cut with a knife. At that moment, a deep voice came from behind me.

"Well, let's keep the celebration a celebration and let's not make it a funeral," said Olaf, "Leif, could you be kind enough to let us through? I think it's time for us to go home."

The man, Leif, I suppose, quickly grabbed the door handle and opened it for us.

"Sure Olaf, sure thing. Eirik, I would never dare. You know that, right? I was kidding, it was the mead, I'm a bit drunk..."

"It's fine, Leif. You're a good man. Mead can be like Loki sometimes. It can make good men do stupid things. Rest well, friend, tomorrow is going to be a great day," said Father while putting his hand on my back and gently escorting me out of the hall.

Olaf followed us and patted Leif's shoulder, almost as if he were congratulating a person who survived a close encounter with death. The door closed behind us, and as soon as it closed, I could hear the entire hall murmuring.

While walking back home, I was thinking, how could a huge strong man like that be so terrified of Father? I mean, I knew Father was strong and skilled in battle, but that man looked younger and stronger. I also wondered what would have happened if Olaf hadn't cut the tension, or if the man hadn't lowered his axe.

I was immersed in my thoughts when I passed by the young man that I saw talking to the old man on the bench a few days ago. He was talking to other men like him, probably also traders. The moment we passed by, he looked at Father and then signalled the other men. Then they started talking and murmuring. I didn't have a good feeling about it, but I didn't want to bother Father also with this. I already caused enough trouble for one day.

As soon as we got home, I asked Olaf if I could speak to him outside for a moment. He agreed.

"Olaf, what would have happened if the man would have swung his axe against Father? He didn't look prepared, and he was also unarmed..."

"Bad things, Sigurd. Bad things would have happened..." he replied.

I didn't want to ask any further about this matter, but I wanted to tell him about the trader. Maybe not the entire story, though.

"When we were returning home, I saw a man that I had seen a few days ago. A trader. I overheard a conversation, and he really hated Father and everything that he stands for."

"Well, that doesn't surprise me. As you may already know, most people think badly of your father and his kind. I myself had issues when I arrived here, but with time, locals accepted me, especially thanks to my bonds with The Temple people and the fact they only had suspicions about me."

"I understand. You had issues because you were once a berserker too..." I added, thinking out loud.

"Indeed," he said. And entered back into the house. I followed him.

Father was resting in the backroom. Mother and Grandmother were sewing and preparing our white gowns and dresses for tomorrow's ceremony.

"Go rest Sigurd. Tomorrow's going to be an intense day, especially for you," said Olaf, and so I did.

Chapter 9

The Great Blót

Mother woke me up gently, whispering something into my ear that I couldn't recall.

It was still dark outside. Mother and Grandmother were already dressed. My sister was still sleeping. She had her belly uncovered, arms and legs extended, and was snoring. Olaf was occupied with the fireplace, maybe cleaning it or refuelling it.

As I stood up and went to wash myself, I saw Father from the door gap. He was outside, sitting on a tree stump with his eyes closed. He looked asleep. I stood by the door looking at him, and the moment I did so, he opened his eyes, gazed at me, stood up and walked away.

"Father took off," I announced in the house.

"He's already going to The Temple," said Olaf with a very serious expression as he stared at Mother.

"Yes, I know…" said Mother, visibly concerned.

We finally got ready and started heading towards The Great Temple. The sunlight was dim, and fog covered the town. We could recognise The Great Temple because of the number of torches placed all over the place.

Before I could make anything out of Olaf's and Mother's behaviour, we found ourselves in the big circle formed by the temples' compound. The buildings had their door open, but all the attention was on Odin's temple. Everybody headed there.

Once inside the temple, we started positioning ourselves around the big stone in the middle. I felt goosebumps the moment I got close to it. Then I passed in front of Odin's statue, immediately remembering my previous experience in that place. I greeted the All-father, with respect and admiration, like I would greet a Grandfather.

There wasn't much light in the temple, only the one entering from the big open door and the torches. This time, there weren't any fire bowls on the floor.

We stood there for a while, waiting for everybody to join us. I heard horses neighing and dogs barking outside the temple, but I gave little thought to that.

Once most of the people joined us, Odin's *völva* entered the room and all the murmuring inside the temple ceased. At that moment, I wondered where Father was.

The *völva* was dressed similarly to the opening ceremony. She had her entire head painted in black and gold, with some white runes. She arrived at the big rock and started caressing it while circling around it.

Then she went towards the end, towards Odin's statue. She bowed respectfully and started talking loudly so that everybody could hear.

"All-father, eternal wisdom. Today, we start the first of our nine *blót* days with your permission. Today, we'll pay with blood for your knowledge, your help and your protection. May our prayers be heard. May we be blessed with Kvasir's blood. May your knowledge be spelt on us. May your grace fall upon us."

She now moved towards the enormous stone. Everybody had to stay in a semicircle, looking towards the stone and Odin. Only she was giving her back to the god, standing near the massive rock.

The silence was total. And now the sound of the dogs and horses was louder than ever, impossible to ignore.

"Bring the first one!" she ordered. One of the temple assistants who was near the door went outside in a hurry. I heard the dogs barking louder, agitated, then they went back to barking as previously.

The helper came into the temple with a dog. The dog seemed more relaxed than usual as if it had drunk a relaxing herb drink. They walked through the long corridor that went from the door towards the boulder. Once they got there, they stopped, waiting for instructions.

This whole time I was thinking about my dog back at home. My neighbours were taking care of him right now. I loved him; I used to play with him and when we were tired from playing, I would sleep resting my head on his body. He wouldn't move until I would wake up. I hoped nothing would happen to him.

While I had that thought, the temple assistant took the dog in his arms. The *völva* signalled him and he placed it on the big stone. They made the dog lay on its side, and secure it gently with their hands.

Now I was scared. I think I was panicking. I didn't want that dog to suffer!

"Be strong," said Grandmother as she grabbed my hand firmly.

While Grandmother's words were still resonating in my ears, I could see the scene playing in slow motion. The *völva*, holding a dagger in her hand, was pronouncing some words as the assistant secured the dog with his arms and, without further ado, she slew the dog. It almost didn't make any sounds.

I broke inside. I couldn't help but feel a tear running down my cheeks. I wanted to clean it but I couldn't. I was frozen. Grandmother caressed my face gently, cleaning it from any tears.

The blood was flowing from the stone's groove and falling into the floor's groove. It started circling through these canals until it fell into Odin's small pool of water.

The *völva* was serious and focused. She seemed like she wasn't even there with us. She looked absent. "Blood for knowledge," she said in a clear and loud voice. And all the people repeated the same. After this, the assistant took the dog's dead body and left.

I didn't know what to think. I felt horrible, but I knew that indeed if you want the gods' favour you need to give something in return. Odin sacrificed himself to himself. He essentially killed himself in order to receive the knowledge of the runes. I guess, the harder the sacrifice is for you to make, the more it'll be worth for the gods. I didn't look for anybody's reaction to what had just happened. I just was hypnotised by that enormous stone full of inscriptions now dripping blood.

I turned, eager to know how my sister had reacted, after all, she was a small child. The moment I looked at her, I couldn't believe it. She was serious and silent, staring at the blood-dripping boulder without even blinking. It almost looked like this wasn't her first time assisting such a spectacle.

Suddenly, I heard a big splash. I turned and saw that an assistant filled a bucket with water and threw it on the sacrificial altar. The water was taken from Odin's well.

"Bring the first one!" said the *völva* right after the splash.

Wait, what? Wasn't the dog the first one? I understood nothing. But again, an assistant took off and went towards where the horses and dogs were being held. A few moments later, the helper entered the temple, pulling a horse effortlessly.

At that point, you could better see the inside of the temple, considering some time had passed and there was more sunlight coming in from the open door. This place was massive. Finally, I could see it clearly. The ceilings were very high, the entrance door was very wide and tall. The horse entered the room, and it didn't feel claustrophobic at all.

They stood in front of the stone again, the same as with the dog. The *völva* signalled, and the helper held firmly the rope. The other two assistants stood to the sides, securing the horse.

The *völva* then pronounced some words that I didn't understand. They sounded similar to some of Father's prayers or *völvas'* murmurs during the opening ceremony. I wondered what language it was.

The *völva* strongly hit the horse in its throat, similar to what she did with the cow a couple of days before that. A big splash of blood hit the ground. She must have known perfectly where to hit. The horse neighed while the helpers pulled it down strongly falling on top of the stone.

The amount of blood was such that it was overflowing the grooves in the stone and wetting our feet. The red stream soon reached Odin's well and got mixed with the water and the blood from the previous sacrifice.

The *völva*, gasping from the effort, said in a loud voice "Blood for knowledge," and I repeated the same alongside the rest of the people.

Then two men came with some sort of carriage. It looked more like two wheels with a big wooden plank on top. They lifted the horse, tied it to the carriage, and took it away. Around five strong men were needed for this task.

I had never seen anything like this. In our town, we also make sacrifices, especially to Freyr for better crops. But we usually sacrificed chickens and, sometimes, goats. On rare occasions, we would sacrifice cows.

I looked back and Mother and my sister had the same facial expression, serious and focused. Grandmother too. I looked at her and she looked back at me.

"How is it going so far?" she asked with a gentle voice.

"So far?" I asked, "Aren't we done?"

Grandmother's reaction worried me. She would usually smile at me, but this time she looked even more serious than before.

"No Sigurd. The most important part is yet to come," she said with a deep voice and a severe expression.

I was concerned. What was yet to come? I didn't know what to expect.

"Just be strong, Sigurd. Do it for Odin. For the gods. Do it for your father..." she finally said.

Father! Where was he? How could he not participate as devoted as he was?

Splash! The assistant cleaned up the stone again. He was pouring water mixed with blood in order to clean blood. It looked counterintuitive to me but it worked. The stone was mostly getting cleaned, even though many blood marks remained.

"Bring the first one!" ordered the *völva* again.

"Again?! Now what?" I thought to myself while one of the assistants took off. No barking was heard, no neighing, nothing. A few moments later, he came in accompanied by a man. A tall man, he was only wearing his pants and his body had been painted with several symbols and runes. He didn't have any visible inscriptions inked, but he had some scars. He looked relaxed, very focused, almost in a trance. They stood in front of the stone.

"Where is the animal?" I wondered. At that moment, a succession of events occurred. The *völva* gave her signal, and the moment that she did, Grandmother squeezed my hand strongly. The man then laid on the stone, looked at the *völva*, and nodded. Then two assistants held the man, one held him by his arms and chest. The other one, by the legs. The *völva* then pronounced the words while holding the dagger again and cut the man's throat.

I couldn't believe it. They just killed the man in front of all of us. This time I wanted to see the reactions of the people, maybe just to see if I was dreaming or if this was really happening.

Many of the women were visibly shaken, and some men had teary eyes that glowed. I then turned my head and saw Mother with watery eyes. But my sister was calm, as she had been with the previous sacrifices. She was observing respectfully, focused, and willingly. I was fascinated by her. She looked like she was a hundred winters old trapped in the body of a four-winter-old child.

While I was in the middle of these thoughts, the bubbling and suffocating of the man caught my attention again. He was still dying.

I was surprised by my inner feelings. I didn't feel that bad when the horse was sacrificed. And I wasn't feeling much pain when this man was suffocating in his own blood in front of me. As a matter of fact, it sparked my curiosity. But the dog sacrifice killed something inside me. I could sense that part of me that died with that dog. This wasn't right, something must've been wrong with me.

The man finally died. His blood joined the other blood from the previous victims mixing in the well. I stared at that well in the distance. I couldn't take my eyes off it, how the three different animals got their blood mixed with the purity of water.

"Blood for knowledge," the *völva* yelled, interrupting my thoughts. We all repeated. Then the corpse was taken away by two assistants.

"Enough blood has been spelt for today," said the *völva*, "may it suffice the gods. Odin, All-father, may these sacrifices be enough to grant us your knowledge and your favour."

I then started hearing Grandmother murmuring her own prayers, in that other language that I didn't understand. She was begging Odin for something. That was the only word I could understand: Odin.

The *völva* continued, "Once every nine winters we gather for this," she was now talking directly to all of us, "Focus on what you want from the gods. Be wise and be truthful." She then started walking towards the entrance of the temple while an assistant splashed some more water from the well on the sacrificial boulder.

Once the *völva* left the temple, the silence and the tension broke. A tremendous noise of multiple murmurings and some people crying invaded the temple. We all started walking outside behind the *völva*, following her to the grove near the compound.

The fog was still quite dense even though it was getting slowly dispersed. When I arrived at the grove, I saw it. The gigantic trees with huge branches could be seen above the fog that covered the ground. From those branches, I could identify the shape of a dog, a horse and a man, all three hanging upside down over the fog.

It almost looked like bodies that were falling into Niflheim's fog. The *völva* started singing, and then some of the temple people joined with harps, drums, bells and other instruments. One of the temple's older assistants started throat singing.

The words in this unknown language sounded as old as Midgard itself. The fog, the mist, the blood, the fire of the torches, the shadow of the trees… I felt it. I felt the reason for this.

Once every nine winters, we would remove the gap that had been created between men and gods. We would need to pay with blood for their presence, and after what Grandmother had told me, it made sense that we paid with blood. We had refused them, thus they wouldn't want to come otherwise.

I felt transported to another time, to a time when gods and men would mingle together, would fight together and would even breed together. How could we have been so naïve and arrogant as to refuse the gods? To cast them aside so that we could have more control over everything? Making pity excuses for the berserkers, ignoring the gods' requests, taking their visions as simple dreams, and some even renouncing them. I was feeling surprised that we didn't sacrifice more blood. We owed them so much.

I felt a hand on my shoulder that interrupted all these thoughts. I didn't realise it, but I was almost alone in front of the enormous tree. There was no more music, no more singing, and no more people. Most of the people either went back to the town or were mingling around the temples. It was Grandmother's hand.

"You remind me of your father," she said, "He would understand things in ways that nobody would. That's why Odin chose him."

"I think I'm starting to understand many things, Grandmother. I feel stupid if I think that two moons ago I just wanted to play with sticks."

"Stupid? You're a child, Sigurd. You should want to simply play with sticks. Don't feel guilty about it. *The Great Blót* can change people, forever. Let's just hope that the change is not for the worse."

"Where is Father?" I asked as soon as she finished talking. She leaned over a side, revealing behind her a group of men. They all had their shirts removed and were fully painted, exactly like the man who had been sacrificed. Amongst them, I could see Father.

I immediately looked back at Grandmother, waiting for answers. A mixture of rage and sadness invaded my body, I didn't want to say what I was thinking or suspecting. Grandmother put on a severe face. She looked downwards, turned around and started walking back towards the temples and the town.

Near Father and the rest of the men, there was a small barn-like building with dogs and horses. I counted them. Eight of each kind. Eight men, including Father, eight dogs and eight horses.

I understood it. They were there to be sacrificed. The assistants didn't pick them in any specific order; they were being picked randomly by the will of the gods. And Father was amongst them. He could have been sacrificed that very day in front of me. He could be sacrificed the day after.

I was so enraged I wanted to kill him myself. I ran towards him, feeling tears of rage coming out of my eyes. I could feel the rage going from my lower stomach to my upper stomach, my belly, my chest, and my head. I was in a total frenzy. If he wanted to die, I would kill him.

I launched at him, kicking, punching, head-butting, biting... He subdued me pretty quickly, not without making him bleed, though. He blocked my hands and hugged me from behind, blocking my legs with his legs. He put his head sideways so I could not headbutt him and he also put his arm under my chin so I could not bite him.

Rage blinded me and even impaired my ability to speak. I was foaming from my mouth, tears running down my cheeks, growling, fighting...

"You knew, little one, you knew it all this time. You know where I belong..." he started whispering in my ear.

I couldn't talk or think straight. I could only growl, fight and think that if he wanted to leave us to die on a piece of stone, I would help him do it. I would do it myself with my own hands. But I wouldn't wait for the gods to decide. I would do it right now, right there.

"Control it, Sigurd. Channel it. Channel this rage. Remember Odin's statue? Fixate your thoughts and mind into Geri and Freki. Visualise them, look at them, and what do you see? Tell me Sigurd, what do you see?" he kept whispering.

I didn't want to listen to him, but his words entered my mind and poisoned it. Suddenly, I could only see the statues of Odin's wolves, Geri and Freki. I could see them and their amulets. Freki with The Helm of Awe and Geri with the intertwined triangles. I then saw Father in Geri's place, and my Uncle Harald, or how I imagined him, in Freki's place. Sitting there, fearsome but relaxed, at Odin's feet.

I started to relax, even though I didn't want to. Finally, I could barely start speaking again.

"Why would you abandon us, Father? Am I that bad of a son? Is Mother that bad of a wife? And Thrúd? Can't the gods wait?" I said while gasping.

"Why do you think you exist, Sigurd?" said Father.

I didn't have an answer. I didn't understand the question. He released me. I turned and sat in front of him. We stared at each other.

"Why do you think you're here, Sigurd?" he insisted.

"I don't understand, Father," I honestly replied.

He looked at me as he always did, with those ice-cold piercing eyes. But today they had some warmth in them. There was silence. We were still at the grove near The Great Temple. Everybody had left. The only people in the area were some people minding their own business and praying. I could hear the ropes' noise when the hanging bodies dangled with the wind. I could hear the blood drops.

"Your mother and I wanted a child for a long time. We tried, but the gods denied us. Nine winters ago, during the last *Great Blót*, I made a pact with the All-father. If he blessed me with a child, I would offer myself in sacrifice during the next *blót*," said Father. I didn't know how to react or what to reply.

"You're a blessing of the gods, Sigurd. You're the gift that Odin gave to me for all my time of service to him. And this, my child, is a promise of blood that I made to him. I'll rejoin my brothers through means of blood. I couldn't be killed in battle, but I will be sacrificed for Odin. It's a great honour, and will earn me a seat in Valhöll near your uncle."

I was speechless. I had so much information that needed to be taken in that I couldn't come up with any further questions, surprisingly enough.

"Don't be sad, Sigurd. This is one of the highest honours of my life. Almost as high as marrying your mother or having you and your sister," he continued.

My jaw must have dropped at that point. He was displaying feelings by recognising Mother, my sister and even me.

"I regret nothing, Sigurd. And I'll leave knowing that your mother and sister are being taken care of by Sigurd Eiriksson, a man who makes me very proud," he said in a deep voice while grabbing my shoulder.

A tear ran down my face. I was feeling a mixture of emotions, not knowing how to react to them. I mustered all the courage I could summon and asked, "When will it happen?"

"When the gods will it, Sigurd. The *völva* can either decide the order or let the picking be random, guided by the gods. She usually chooses the latter."

"I understand... And Thrúd? Did you think what would happen when Thrúd sees this?"

"Sigurd, Thrúd is not a normal child. Her connection with the gods is the strongest that I've seen in some time. She'll be fine. She'll know."

After that, questions were popping all over my head at once.

"Do Mother and Grandm-"

"They know, Sigurd. They've known about it for a long time. Olaf also knows if you were going to ask next."

"Fine..." I replied in resignation, not knowing exactly what to do with all this information.

"Let's go, Sigurd," he said while standing up and slapping his legs and bottom, getting rid of the attached leaves, "Let's just go."

I stood up, got rid of the leaves and some dirt all over me, and started walking. Father had put his shirt on again, but people seemed to know. They nodded when he passed by them, especially the more devoted to the gods. Some of them came and shook hands with him, as a sign of respect.

I wanted to tell him about the people that hated him, all those people that thought that he was a filthy criminal, a monster. But this wasn't the time, and besides, soon enough, all of that would not matter anymore.

Chapter 10

Lessons

Our walk towards Olaf's place was silent. We were immersed in our thoughts. The whole town seemed to be in the same mood as us, a more introspective mood. There was less noise and chatter. Even traders weren't trading or talking business in the middle of the street anymore.

I was starting to understand why during the entire trip to get here Father had been so serious and absent. He knew what he would need to do to keep his promise. He knew it since the day Mother found out to be with child.

We passed in front of the bench where I saw the old man and the trader talk and overheard those horrible things about Father and Uncle Harald. To my surprise, there was the trader, surrounded by young and strong men. They all glared at Father. They despised him and everything he stood for. A few days prior, I didn't quite understand why, but after what Grandmother and Olaf had told me, I understood it. All the stories made about the Berserkers and Ulfhednar poisoned people's minds. What could be done to undo this? How could I explain that these were just stories? That these men were amongst the most honourable men alive!

"I hate them," I murmured.

I didn't want Father to hear it. I just needed to say it out loud, or I felt I would explode.

"Why is that, Sigurd?" asked Father calmly while walking past them and greeting them with a nod.

"They hate you, Father. They hate Uncle Harald too. I overheard that trader the other day. They hate everything that you stand for..." I replied while feeling frustrated with Father's attitude towards his detractors.

"And?" he replied without even changing his calm and deep tone as if none of this matter had anything to do with him, "And what do you care about what they think or say? What do you think Odin is going to care more about? What is said about you or what you do here in Midgard?"

I shrugged. I didn't quite know the answer to that. It was just bothering me.

"Sigurd, if I wanted to be popular, I would have tried being a trader, a poet or a musician. Let them talk as much as they want. Your mother, my mother, and Olaf know the truth. You seem to know it now too, even though there is much that you still need to learn. Many of these stories that people tell, Sigurd, they're true. One bad story can make all the rest of great stories meaningless."

"But, Uncle Harald died serving Odin. You have your body covered in scars, your face... Your missing finger... All of that is without recognition because of some powerful men that used men like you and uncle and then threw you away like dogs!"

I couldn't stand Father's passiveness. How could he always be so calm?

"I know the story, Sigurd. Better than you ever will. I don't need history lessons. We made a vow many generations ago. Whoever was chosen by Odin to fight on his behalf would do it, no matter the fight," he said as we approached Olaf's house.

He then stopped, placed his hand on my shoulder and looked me in the eye, "Remember this when I'm gone, Sigurd, not all battles are fought with iron. The hardest battles you fight with your head and your tongue."

He then tapped his temple with his finger and then continued walking.

When we arrived at Olaf's, Grandmother was resting with my sister. They were exhausted even though it wasn't even noon. Mother was preparing bread and Olaf was sitting by the fireplace, staring at the flames. The silence was total in that house, except for my sister's snoring. We sat near Olaf. No words needed to be spoken, everybody knew without the need to outer the painful words.

Looking at the dancing flames, a thought popped into my head. I visualised Father and the drunk man in the *Thing*; I visualised the respect with which many men looked at Father. The image of Father's scarred body popped into my head. How could such a peaceful and calm man survive so many incredible deeds? Olaf himself admitted Father was the only man that he feared. How would he, hypothetically, be able to beat giant Olaf?

During lunch, only the noise of plates and chewing could be heard.

"I'm very proud of you, Sigurd. Thora, your children are incredible," said Grandmother. Mother nodded proudly.

"Odin blessed us with them. Not without cost though…" said Mother while staring at Father.

He glared back at her. Grandmother put her hand on his arm making him immediately focus back on eating the food on his plate.

"Well…" said big Olaf, "Today went well. It was a special day, just as I remembered it. And Odin blessed us with one more day of Eirik's charm!" and started laughing. Everybody laughed. Even Father laughed a little. Well, at least he smiled. "Only Olaf could make us laugh in a moment like this," I thought to myself.

Once we had finished our meal, Mother and Grandmother worked on the house chores. I helped by going outside to cut some wood. Father also went outside. I saw him talking to Knut, the Dane who was also a remnant of The Twelve. They started walking together until I lost them in the distance.

After some time of cutting wood, a boy came by. I recognised him. He was Knut's son. He was a little older than me, no more than twelve winters old. He had blue eyes, dark blond short hair and was slightly taller than me. Mother would later say that we looked alike. It always bothered me because it wasn't true. I'm light blond with a bob cut and my eyes are green, not blue.

"Hi, there!" He greeted me with his thick Danish accent.

"Hi," I replied. I didn't like him. He had this way of carrying himself around as if he were an adult when he was clearly around my age.

"What are you doing, boy?" he said, quite arrogantly.

"I'm finishing my chores. And I'm not more of a boy than you."

"I see... I'm sorry that I couldn't join you at the town hall yesterday. I had some business to attend to at the temple," he said while playing with his knife.

I ignored him and focused on finishing my task, unleashing my rage onto the wood chunks.

"I guess you don't have many friends around here, right?" he insisted.

I didn't want to dignify that obvious question with an answer. He kept playing with his knife, making small holes in the wood in one of the house's walls.

"So..." he started saying, breaking the awkward silence, "We're going to be brothers-in-law. What do you think about that?"

What? Brothers-in-law? I would kill this boy before he even got close to my sister!

"Measure your words, 'boy'", I quickly replied, "If you ever get too close to my sister, you might end up with your own knife inside your skull," I added while standing up and staring at him.

He laughed, then he put his knife away and also stood in front of me. "Don't worry Sigurd, I'll take good care of Thrúd."

I launched myself towards him, ready to end him. How did he dare! While I was in mid-air, an enormous arm grabbed me. It was Olaf's arm. He was eating some oat bread that Mother had made with one hand and with the other he was restraining me and laughing. I was furious. The boy stood there. He didn't even move. He wasn't afraid nor surprised, as if he was expecting my reaction and that Olaf would block me somehow.

"I'll kill you if you ever come near her!" I said. The boy smiled.

"It was a pleasure finally meeting you, Sigurd Eiriksson. I'm Björn, son of Knut. We'll be family one day and, believe it or not, we'll even be friends."

He then turned and went back towards his camp. Olaf was still grabbing me and laughing.

"You sure are a handful, Sigurd," he said while biting his piece of bread. "You know, boy," said with his mouth full, "You should try to control that temper of yours. It may get you killed one day," and laughed even louder.

"Do you find this funny, Olaf? That boy threatened my sister and your reaction was laughter?" I was still fuming.

"Threatened? Boy, your sister is spoken for. Their marriage has been arranged by Knut and Eirik. They're probably celebrating this union at this very moment..."

Was this true? Did Father negotiate with Knut to marry his son to my sister? Why? What would the benefit of that transaction be?

"Father wouldn't dare. Thrúd can have better men than that arrogant prick," I said, while strongly squishing my fists together.

"Sigurd, relax. If your father made this deal, I'm sure he has his reasons. He doesn't do things without thinking, your old man."

"Yes, well, that's what I thought. He won't be around to find that out, will he?" and with that, I left. I needed some time to be alone.

I started walking aimlessly, looking down at my feet, while reliving all the events that happened during the last few days over and over in my head. Spinning like a wheel.

Father's speech on the top of the mound when we arrived here, the dog sacrificed, finally meeting Olaf, the opening ceremony, the man killed for sacrifice, the sound of that man suffocating and drowning in his own blood, the vision in Odin's temple, the old man on the bench and the trader, the arrogant Danish boy...

Suddenly, I found myself in the middle of a fog. I had left the town without realising it. When I raised my eyes, I saw the dog, the horse and the man hanging in front of me. Dangling with the breeze. There was total silence there. I could only hear the breeze through the leaves, the sound of the tight ropes moving from side to side, and some owls and ravens.

The ravens were mostly on the trees from which the sacrificed were hanging, but they didn't devour them, at least not totally. The

71

most preserved of them was the man, for some reason they seemed to respect him, or maybe they didn't like his taste very much.

"What do they tell you, Young Sigurd?" a recognisable voice in the fog asked.

I turned, looking for the owner of that voice. On the side, sitting on a tree stump at the main tree's feet, I saw the old man from the bench. He had a long staff, still had half the face covered from his white hair, and had some ravens pecking the end of his cloak.

"Hello sir, I didn't see you there. When did you-" I started babbling but quickly got interrupted "What do they tell you?"

I cleared my throat, looked at the hanging bodies, and took a moment to think. He didn't move during that time. He was sitting there looking at me with the uncovered eye, staring at me with that ice-cold eye while the ravens kept pecking playfully the edge of his cloak.

"The first sacrificed, the dog, is the one that caused me the most grief," I started saying, and right when I finished saying these words he smirked.

"Go on," he said in a deep, calm, and low voice.

"The second one, the horse, intrigued me. It didn't bother me much though, it was just the thought of it being such a useful and big animal."

At this point, he slightly changed his posture, changing from being sideways and facing downwards to sitting straight and facing towards me. He was looking forward to my next words.

"The third sacrificed, the man, was… Strange. I didn't expect it. It was the first time that I saw a man being slaughtered in front of me like that. He walked in there by his own will and, and… He never looked afraid. On the contrary. He looked happy, glad to be there. Proud."

His smirk turned into a smile. Not a mocking smile nor a cheerful one, more like a paternal proud smile. "And why do you think he felt that way?"

"Well… He believed in what he was doing. He believed in Odin and in the fact that his sacrifice would have helped all of us. He completely let go of himself and only thought of the common good. Or at least that's what I think. It may not be that way, I might be wrong..."

He lowered his head slowly while exhaling. "Ay... Young Sigurd... Don't doubt yourself, son, for you have great wisdom despite your young age."

Then he raised his head again, looking at me with that uncovered eye of his, and with a very serious expression asked me, "And now tell me, boy, why was the dog the one that caused you the most grief?"

I felt intimidated by that look. It would pierce you and you would have a feeling of being naked in front of him as if he could read your mind.

"The horse is a magnificent animal. I like horses very much, and their use is priceless. The man... He's like me, a man. But I know men can be evil, they can do terrible things. I didn't know the man, I didn't know to what extent he deserved to die or not, to what extent he was sacrificing himself for the rest of us, for Odin's grace, or if it was to escape from himself, from his past. Maybe he was just trying to die honourably after living an unhonoured life."

The man kept staring at me. He slightly changed his posture, looking more interested in me and what I was about to say. Almost asking me with his body language to answer his initial answer.

"The dog... I always felt a special connection with dogs. I felt their loyalty, their rage, their strength, their sense of duty and their survival instinct. When I was smaller, I would howl whenever I heard dogs or wolves howl. I felt I was communicating with them."

Again, another smirk on his face appeared. He looked satisfied with what he was hearing as if he had heard exactly what he had hoped.

"When I saw that dog being sacrificed, I felt like a piece of me was being sacrificed. I felt Father, I felt Uncle Harald. I felt their pain and sacrifice. They spent their whole life sacrificing themselves for Odin. Like that dog was doing in front of me, unwillingly."

I don't even know why I was telling all these things to a total stranger. We only had a brief and casual conversation in the past, but I felt he knew me better than I knew myself. I felt I could trust him with my life, and I couldn't understand why. The old man smiled and leaned back against the tree trunk.

"Incredible…" he said in a very low voice, almost like thinking out loud. "You're exactly like your father and your uncle. I don't remember a family like that…" he said while caressing his beard with a thinking expression.

"What do you mean, sir? And how do you know my family?" I suspected that this man was probably some old friend of Father's that I didn't know about.

"I'm old, Young Sigurd, older than you imagine," he murmured.

I could hardly hear him. I waited for an actual answer, but he said nothing else. So I decided not to bother the man even further.

My attention went back towards the hanging bodies and I started thinking of Father. He was ready to be sacrificed. Any day I could see him have his throat cut in front of me, see how he drowns in his own blood. See those ice-cold eyes closed forever. And he didn't even warn me. I had to find that out by myself like I always had to do…

"Don't worry, Young Sigurd," the old man said. "Don't worry son…"

"What do you mean, sir?" Was he really able to read my mind? Or was I showing too much of my worry through my face?

"Your father won't be sacrificed. Not during this *blót* at least," he calmly said while staring at the nothingness.

It almost looked like during these last moments he discovered something special as if he had solved a great mystery. I froze. How could he possibly know? I looked at him without being able to speak. I could hardly breathe. He turned his attention to me and smirked.

"He was amongst the men that were meant to be sacrificed, boy. And he's a very well-known man. Wasn't that hard to figure out," and winked his eye at me.

That made sense. Nevertheless, how could he know I was thinking about him? Well, maybe my face and me staring at the sacrificed bodies. But again, what he said… How could he be so sure of himself saying that Father "won't be sacrificed"? Suddenly, a firm hand grabbed my shoulder, "Here you are!"

I jumped like a scared cat and turned in the air while screaming. Father was standing there. Near him stood Knut and his son, Björn. Father looked very concerned, as a matter of fact, they all did.

"We've been looking for you the whole day!" said Björn.

"The whole day...?" I replied, confused.

"Well, we found him now. Problem solved," said Knut with his deep and strong voice, and an even thicker Danish accent than his son.

"I was just talking to-" I started saying while turning around and pointing towards the tree stump when, amazingly enough, the stump was empty.

"To whom, Sigurd?" said Father.

"To the old man…" I babbled, still in shock.

Father glanced at the empty tree stump, then looked at me and finally pensively gazed at Knut who smiled in return.

"Well, it must have been a pretty fast old man then," said Knut as he laughed while turning and heading home.

Father didn't laugh. He looked at me and simply said "Let's go home, boy. Your mother is worried."

Chapter 11
Cornered

There was a mystical atmosphere in the town. These sacrifices were very important and powerful. People were taking them seriously, at least most of them.

Some went to the fields or to the woods to meditate. Others went to the town hall, got drunk and celebrated the presence of the gods, others stayed in their homes or camps.

The following day was very similar to the previous one. We woke up; went to The Great Temple, and dedicated ourselves to the gods again. The second dog was sacrificed and hung in the same tree as the first one. The second horse was sacrificed too but was hanged in an adjacent tree. Then came the turn of the second man.

Father wasn't with us. We all knew he was with the other men to be sacrificed. I didn't accept this, but I couldn't do anything to avoid it either. I was hearing in my head the voice of the old man. "Your father won't be sacrificed," I kept hearing repeatedly.

I was praying to Odin, asking him to spare Father, to allow me to know him better, and to allow him to teach me how to be a man. I didn't know him that well. He was away for long periods of time, either raiding or in some battles. I never actually knew where he went or who he fought against.

The *völva* announced the next man to be sacrificed. I closed my eyes and prayed as strongly as I could. "Please Odin, spare him." Still, with my eyes closed, I heard the steps of a man entering the building with the temple's assistant. I couldn't look. I didn't want to.

"Be brave, Sigurd," I heard near my ear. It was Grandmother. She was grabbing my hand and whispering encouraging words to me. I finally opened my eyes. It wasn't Father.

This time, it was a short man, quite old, I would say. He wasn't in great shape but had some huge scars on his back and he was limping. He must have fought many battles when he was young and now wanted to depart with honour.

The sacrifice took place, and we all went outside to the grove and said our prayers, sang the songs and paid our respects.

I noticed a common pattern these days. An old dialect that I couldn't understand was being spoken sometimes, especially when praying or addressing the gods in any other way.

On the way back from the grove, I asked. "Grandmother, what's that dialect or language that you, Father, Olaf and the *völvas* speak when addressing the gods?"

"It's the old language. It's a common language between gods and men that we used to speak in ancient times when the gods mingled among us. Now they rarely appear..." she replied with an aura of nostalgia.

"Understood. But then, how come you know it? Aren't those ancient times many winters before you were even born?"

"Yes, Sigurd, it was a very long time ago. But it has been passed down for generations. The most devoted and connected to the gods passed it to younger generations."

"Why didn't I learn it then? Am I not worthy?"

"Well, child, that's exactly why you're here. During this *blót*, much can be unveiled. We can discern between the worthy and the less worthy. We can see who's brave and who's not. Who cares about the gods and is really connected to them, and who isn't..."

I nodded and didn't want to keep asking more questions. After all, this was a time for thinking and meditating, for feeling the gods and speaking with them.

On our way home, I passed again in front of the trader. This time I wanted to pay special attention. I didn't like him and I knew I would cross paths with him again. He was camped near a caravan with plenty of boxes, scales, bundles of clothes and textiles and some trunks. His tent was big and looked expensive. He was surrounded by other men who also had their tents there. These tents were smaller than the young chief's but also of good quality.

They looked at me while I passed in front of them as if they knew me. One of them tipped the chief trader, the young one, and pointed in my direction with his head. The trader nodded and stared at me.

At that moment, I exhaled strongly. I really didn't like these men. Grandmother looked at me and then at them, "Something wrong Sigurd? Did those men ever bother you?"

"No, Grandmother. Everything is fine…"

That day the town felt more alive, more festive. I could hear more people singing, instruments playing, laughing and dancing. We were approaching the middle of the most important *blót* in Scandinavia. People were rejoicing amongst the gods, and the initial tension of the first sacrifices was disappearing. Grandmother explained to me that Uppsala and that entire area were known for being one of the principal places that the gods would visit in ancient times, and that's why The Great Temple was there. Their presence was way stronger there than in any other place.

The day went on, and I decided to go for a walk. Passing by the Danes, I saw Knut teaching Björn how to properly sharpen swords and axes. I passed by several camps and houses and wondered what was all that camping space used for when there was no *blót*.

Suddenly, I saw Father. He was talking in the distance with the other man that survived The Twelve; I guess a former berserker. He was a wealthy man. His thick golden arm ring could be seen from a distance. It greatly contrasted with Father's iron arm ring.

I sat on a pile of cut wood to observe them. They were talking respectfully to each other. The wealthy man was huge, not as big as Olaf, but close enough. He was treating Father with the utmost respect and affection. Once they finished talking, they hugged and Father started walking back in my direction.

He passed by the entrance of a big tent. It wasn't a tent for sleeping but rather an armoury and, in part, a warehouse. Probably the traders were using it to store weapons, armour and other valuables to trade. Two men were standing at the entrance. They were armed and wearing chain mail, which I thought was strange since nobody was armed or ready for combat.

The moment Father passed in front of them, they stopped him by placing their hands on his shoulders. Father stopped and looked at them with a face that was a mixture of surprise and anger. But before he could react, they grabbed him dragged him inside the tent and closed the leather door.

I ran towards the tent and peeked through one of the small holes that I found in a corner. There he was, the trader, the young trader surrounded by those men that I had been seeing these days. They were all wearing armour under their clothes and were armed to their teeth.

I could count seven of them. Father stood in front of the trader, surrounded.

Father looked extremely relaxed. I was panicking, gasping. I could feel my heart in my mouth. He was looking all around him, like counting the men, looking at what that tent was containing, the entrance… It seemed to me that he was trying to figure out a way out of that situation.

"Go guard the door," commanded the chief trader. Two of his men, the ones who had grabbed Father, left the tent, closed the leather door behind them, and stood in front of it.

The moment the two men left the tent, Father looked back at the trader while raising his eyebrows in surprise, almost feeling insulted that the trader reduced the number of men that were surrounding him.

"Enough…" said the trader, "enough to allow such scum amongst us."

I couldn't believe what was happening. I could feel the rage invading my whole body and, at the same time, the panic overwhelming me. After all that Father went through, he would not die in battle, he would not die at Odin's home… He would die in a tent, surrounded by cowards, like a dog.

Father didn't react to the trader's words. He simply stood there, staring at him. He had a very serious face, a menacing face, and one of the deepest and most piercing looks that I have ever seen.

The trader started looking at Father in the eyes, but after a moment, he looked down and laughed, "Ah! Yes! The Mighty Eirik, they say! 'His ice-cold eyes' they say…" and right when he finished saying these words, he launched an unexpected punch at Father. He didn't dodge it, nor did he block it. It hit right in the mouth's side.

The other men laughed. Father had his head turned sideways from the impact and the trader had placed his hands on his waist, holding his buckle and laughing.

Father turned his head slowly back towards the trader. He didn't even flinch at that punch. The men stopped laughing. A single drip of blood ran from the mouth to the edge of Father's chin. He stared back at the trader without changing his expression in the slightest.

"I know, I know Eirik… I know this is but a caress to you. Probably that whore that you call a wife hurts you more while humping than I just did, right?" and kept laughing. This time Father pressed his jaws together, starting to get enraged.

"There he is… There he is! You know, men, this man here has killed more men than all of us combined. According to legend, at least. Of course, he kills for gold and women and then comes here pretending to be a pure man; a man most devoted to the gods. What would we understand, eh? We're nothing like him, just simple traders that decided to earn silver honestly instead of slaughtering innocent people for it."

After saying this, he launched another punch, a stronger punch right to Father's side of the face. His eyebrow cut and a considerable amount of blood ran down his face. He recovered again from this punch, very slowly, as if he was thinking about every single movement he had to make in order to stand straight again.

This time, he looked directly into the eyes of the trader and started smiling. I could hardly remember Father smiling, but in this situation, he was smiling widely. He then said with his calm and deep voice, "Young man, you know nothing. I've seen death and pain. I've seen it so much that I became death and pain." He now started slowly taking his hands to his face, almost covering it, then brought them towards the back of his head, spreading the blood all over his face and hair, and tied his hair that got loosened with the punches.

He continued talking while transforming his smile into a sinister low-volume laugh, "Young man, you would be wise calling those two men inside again, for you have these men on your side. I have Odin himself on mine." The moment he said this, he started breathing very fast and strangely, like a dog when it gets mad and wants to fight another dog.

His eyes, somehow, didn't have the same colour anymore. I couldn't see it from where I was standing at least, and he had his jaws strongly clenched together. He only looked at the trader's eyes, all the time his eyes, he never looked at anything else. Blood started dripping from his beard. It looked like he wasn't the same. He looked like an enraged animal. His breathing got faster and deeper, his whole body was in the utmost tension, and all his powerful muscles looked stronger and bigger. His scars somehow became more visible.

The men surrounding him started taking a couple of steps back, not knowing very well what was happening. I very much wanted to know what was going on, what was going to happen, but I couldn't risk Father's life for my curiosity. After all, he was surrounded by five men, seven counting the two guarding outside. He was unarmed and without armour. I had to call for help immediately. Father was about to be murdered.

I ran home as fast as I had ever run before in my life, passing the Danes' camp so fast that I couldn't even identify if they were still there or not. I wonder if they even saw me.

I opened the door of the house with a kick, "Olaf! Father! They'll kill him!" I yelled with the last air left in my chest. Olaf jumped out of the chair. I never thought he could move that fast, being so big.

"How many?" he asked me with his deep voice and with an unusually serious expression.

"Five now. They'll be seven. The traders from down the road, the caravan camp!"

As soon as I said these words, Olaf's expression completely relaxed. He exhaled deeply as if he had been relieved from a heavy burden.

"Fine, Sigurd. Relax then. We'll head over there," he said while calmly grabbing his battle-axe. He had his huge battle-axe lying on long nails, hanging on top of the door. It was larger and probably heavier than me!

After he grabbed it, he stood in front of me and said, "Just breathe. Relax, Sigurd. We're heading there."

"Let's go! Father will die!"

I couldn't believe how he could be so relaxed when his best friend was about to get slaughtered.

"Yes, yes, boy. Relax. If you don't start breathing, perhaps we should be worried that you won't survive the day!" he said while walking towards the big tent. I walked near him, urging him with my jumping and small runs to go faster. He seemed more annoyed than worried. Maybe Olaf didn't really want to help Father for some reason. After all, there were many things that I didn't know and discovered during this voyage.

While we were getting closer to the tent, we heard men screaming for help and people commanding the masses not to get near the tent.

Once outside of the tent, I could see huge splats of blood throughout the white tent cloth. A man was crawling out of the tent covered in blood and begging for help, and I could hear horrible growls and noises of butchering.

At that point, Olaf changed his attitude and went from strolling to running towards the tent. He was alert and grabbed the axe, ready for combat. He ran past me like an arrow and went straight towards the entrance of the tent, jumping over the crawling man.

I was right behind Olaf; had my axe in my right hand and my knife in my left. I probably couldn't do much, but at least I could help. Olaf opened the leather door and what I saw I could hardly describe.

The boxes, chests and all the other valuables that were stored in that tent were broken and spread all over the floor. There were pieces of men all over the place: arms, hands, a head, entrails... Some men were still alive, trying to look for help, others were clearly dead.

At the opposite side of the entrance, I saw him. I saw the back of this figure that reminded me of Father. He was butchering with two axes an already dead body. That body had already the chest and stomach completely open. All the entrails were scattered near the sinister figure, one arm missing and one leg chopped multiple times. The figure was covered in blood, shirtless, and completely bent over, focused on butchering and dismembering that dead body.

It looked like it didn't matter that we entered the tent. The figure kept hitting with his axes the dead body while growling. "Eirik!" yelled Olaf while putting himself between me and this beast, protecting me. "Eirik!"

The figure turned around slowly. It was Father, or something similar to him. He had his face entirely covered in blood, especially the area around the mouth as if he had been eating a raw animal. His chest, arms and legs had some visible cuts, but they didn't look too deep at first glance. His eyes were as white as ice. I couldn't see any blue in them. He looked at us and didn't seem to quite recognise us. He was still growling and breathing exceedingly fast. Olaf took a tiny step forward. I was terrorised. That couldn't possibly be Father!

Suddenly, this mad animal swapped his attention from Olaf to me, and I felt like a thousand arrows pierced me. I've never felt more afraid in my life, ever. I felt like there was absolutely nothing that I could do, nothing that I could hide from this creature. It was inside me. It could see right through me.

His beard and arms were dripping copious amounts of blood. He was moving extremely slowly, studying me while repositioning himself for an attack. It didn't look like he quite knew what he was about to do. He was deciding if we were friends or foes.

Olaf started speaking in that ancient dialect to him. At that moment, he turned his attention back to the redhead giant. By Olaf's body language, voice tone and some random words that I could understand, I understood he was calming him like a man would calm his enraged and uncontrolled dog.

After that, the savage creature started moving to the side. I could finally see the dead body it was butchering. It was the trader. He had a vast hole in his throat as if it had been bitten off. The rest of the face and body was a complete mess.

I turned my attention back to the figure and looked at it in its eyes. It was impossible to recognise any humanity in them, nor did I perceive evil. I just sensed instinct, pure wild and untamed survival instinct. I could understand it. The rage, the feeling of having that rage take over you and let it dominate you. I had hurt many of my friends during my life because of my rage, but of course, I never did nor saw anything like what I was witnessing in that tent.

The more Olaf spoke to it, the more he kept taking steps forward, and the more the figure started to look like Father. Suddenly, he dropped the axes and sat on the floor, almost collapsing. When that happened, Olaf ran to him, grabbed his head and put it against his own. "Welcome back, brother. Welcome back, old friend..." he murmured.

I stood there without knowing what to do. The place was a mess. There was blood everywhere, rivers and puddles of it. People started helping the wounded men who managed to crawl outside the tent. Only two of them, I recall.

A man stomped inside the tent, accompanied by two other men. They were armed and wearing armour, but I don't think they had anything to do with the traders.

"Move Olaf, let me slay that animal," the man said.

"Leave," said Olaf without even separating his head from Father's.

"Olaf, move or you'll fall with him!" said the man. I could hear more and more people gathering outside the tent.

Olaf stood up, huge as he was, truly a bear. He grabbed his axe and faced the man whose head was at Olaf's beard height.

With the most serious and menacing tone that I ever could imagine, Olaf calmly said, "Bjarni, you either leave by your own feet, or you leave in pieces. Either way, you'll leave this tent right now."

The man, Bjarni, I suppose, turned around and left the tent. His men followed.

"Olaf, you know this can't go unpunished!" yelled Bjarni once he was outside.

"Just leave, and take all the people with you," said Olaf.

He then looked back at me, "Sigurd, listen to me carefully. Go to Odin's temple, look for Odin's *völva* and tell her that your father needs shelter, tell her this: 'Geri was hungry'. She'll understand."

I didn't question, I just ran. I ran towards Odin's temple and right near the entrance the *völva* was standing there, almost as if she was waiting for me.

"Hello young cub," she greeted me, "What brings you to Odin's house in such a hurry?"

"Hello, I'm very sorry for not greeting you properly and for stomping in here like this. But Father needs shelter. He needs your help."

She almost interrupted me, "Calm down, boy. Breathe and calm down. Do you want some water? I'll ask an assistant to bring you some wat-"

"Geri was hungry! Geri was hungry!" I yelled without even knowing what this meant.

She immediately changed her expression. She launched over me and grabbed me strongly by my shirt, lifting me from the ground. "How many? How many did he slay?"

"I don't quite know… Maybe four? Five?" I babbled terrorised.

"Bring him here right now. They cannot take him to the *Thing*. Hurry, boy! Bring him here now!" she yelled while releasing me in such a violent way that I fell on the floor.

I stood up and ran as fast as I could. When I arrived at the tent, it was surrounded by guards. Many guards, from different chieftains, earls and perhaps even a king. The men who survived were taken away to have their wounds tended. Olaf was standing outside, arguing with a dozen guards. Grandmother and Mother were also outside, arguing and shouting.

"Olaf! Olaf! We need to bring him to the temple!" I yelled while getting closer to him.

"Agh…!" he exclaimed while pushing three guards at the same time and turning around towards me. "It's too late, Sigurd. They took him. He'll be judged tonight at the *Thing*," he said while kicking a rock from the floor and grabbing his axe.

"What does this mean, Olaf?"

"Means that the people at the *Thing* will judge him for this, and we all know what people think," he replied while walking away, infuriated. He wasn't going back home, he was going towards the river and the woods near the town.

Mother and Grandmother ran to me and hugged me. We hugged for a long time, and then Grandmother said, "Come on. I left the little one alone in the house. Let's eat something and recover our strengths. Maybe they'll let us see him before the *Thing* meeting starts."

We left the horror scene and went home. Many people were already cleaning up the tent, picking up body pieces and entrails and putting them in baskets while pouring water on the blood.

Chapter 12

The Thing

We arrived at Olaf's home and started looking for my sister. We found her standing on a barrel placed on the bed, looking out the window.

"Finally, you're back," she said, like a mother grounding her children. "Where have you been?"

"There was a problem with your father, Thrúd, but everything will be fine," said Mother while sitting on the bed near her, trying to appear calm.

"I know, Mother. I'm not worried. Nothing will happen to him," Thrúd said as if she had some information that we didn't have.

She would often surprise us with her behaviour like that. She reminded me of Mother because of the resemblance, even though she had Father's dark blond hair and ice-blue eyes.

We started preparing the food, tidying up the house and nervously doing chores to keep ourselves occupied until the *Thing* trial. I went to cut wood outside for the fireplace. I couldn't get out of my mind the image of Father in that state. He looked like a wild creature, totally transformed. It was such an impact to see him that way; I was used to seeing him so calm and patient.

"Hey Sigurd!" said an irritating voice. It was Björn, he was the last person I wanted to see at that moment.

"Go away," I said while chopping a log with my axe.

"I'm sorry for what happened to your father, Sigurd. But I'm also glad."

Well, now he was asking for it. "You're glad? Glad of what, exactly?" I replied while holding my axe and staring at him.

"Glad that he destroyed those men. The only pity is that I couldn't see any of it."

"Trust me, Björn, you wouldn't have liked the view. But why do you care about those rats?"

"Sigurd, do you think they were plotting only against your father? Remember who my father is," he said in a very serious and mature tone. It made me think that indeed Father may not have been the only person those men were after.

"Well, they won't bother your father anymore, that's for sure," I said while returning to my wood-chopping task.

"He'll be fine, Sigurd. I know he will," Björn added while walking away.

I could only think of the bloodbath that the tent had turned into. Moments before, when I was there, watching how the man was punching Father, surrounded by armed men, I was convinced that he would be murdered. How was it possible that not only did he not die, but he slew most of them? What kind of powers did he possess?

"Sigurd!" called Mother.

"What now?!" I annoyingly replied.

"Wash yourself and get ready. We'll be heading towards the *Thing* as soon as you're ready."

I don't remember ever getting washed and ready faster than that day. We were finally heading towards the *Thing*.

Guards were at the door. When they saw us, they let us through. Many wealthy and powerful men were talking nervously and simultaneously. They all looked angry and concerned about what had happened.

"Where is Father?" I asked a guard.

"He's out in the back. I can take you to him, but you need to be quick, or I'll get in trouble," he said.

"Thank you, sir," I replied, surprised.

We started moving through the people that gathered in the great hall, arriving at a side door near the higher stand where the chieftains used to sit at a large table. The door led to a side chamber, and from that chamber, another door led outside.

"Why are you helping me, sir?" I couldn't help but ask while he took me to see Father.

"I wouldn't be here if it wasn't for him," he replied, with a smile.

I wasn't expecting that; this man was a Swede, and we were Norwegian. And I never remember Father talking about fighting alongside Swedes. Thinking about it, I don't remember Father divulging many details about his life at all.

We finally were outside, and near the door, attached to the wall of the town hall, there was an iron cell. Father was lying there, covered in dry blood, shirtless. He still had all his cuts and wounds unattended. "Why did nobody tend to his wounds!? He'll die if he's left in this condition!"

He had an arm hanging out of the cell. I fell to my knees, grabbed his hand, and started crying. I couldn't help it. Moments earlier I saw this wild beast that had butchered seven men, but now I saw a wounded and vulnerable man thrown into a cage, like a dog.

"Don't." He whispered, "Don't you dare." He said while turning his head towards me. Struggling to breathe, he could barely speak.

"Father, you need help…" I said while trying to stop crying.

"This is a scratch, Sigurd. I'll be fine. Go back to the *Thing*, don't get yourself into trouble," he said with a thread of air.

The guard then gently grabbed my shoulder and signalled with his head that we had to go. I didn't want to leave Father in that condition. The guard started dragging me slowly and finally, despite my biggest effort, our hands released and I left Father behind.

The number of people in the town hall had doubled. I looked for Mother and Grandmother, and found them in a corner, close to Knut and his son Björn. After struggling to pass through the crowd, I reached them and hugged them. They saw the tears still on my face. I explained to them I had seen Father. I also told them the condition in which I found him.

The *Thing* was a long great hall. On one side there was the entrance, on the other, an elevated sort of platform with a big table. It wasn't very elevated though, just a couple of steps, enough for everybody to see the most important among the men sitting at that table.

A man, standing on the platform, started asking for order and silence. Everybody sat down, ready for the big meeting where Father would be judged. While people's heads were disappearing while sitting down, I could see more clearly who was sitting at the table on the platform. Many wealthy men and women were sitting there. They all looked very important, but not all looked like Swedes.

Three men, in particular, caught my attention. The first one was sitting in the middle of the long table. He didn't look more wealthy or more important than the other men, but probably he was the chieftain of Uppsala.

Another man looked like a king. He had a golden oval brooch holding his expensive clothes. He had a thick golden arm ring, several rings and pendants. I could also see the mark of a bear's paw on his clothes and some of his jewellery. It was the same symbol that I saw on the shields of some of the best-geared guards.

The third man that caught my eye was Father's friend, the wealthy man who, apparently, was also a remnant of The Twelve. I saw him talking to Father right before the attack took place.

Once everybody was silent, or as silent as a packed *Thing* could ever be, the man that was yelling for order started talking loudly.

"Welcome everybody! Welcome to the *Thing* of this incredible place that we all have the honour of visiting every nine winters. A place known for its devotion to the gods, its ancient history with the gods and, above all, its respect for the laws of both gods and men."

Everybody seemed to agree with these statements.

"As you all may know, every nine winters, the most devoted and lucky people from Scandinavia gather here for their encounter with the gods. From farmers to kings, from earls to poets..." he now pointed towards the long table where all the wealthy and important men were sitting, "Amongst the most honourable, we're lucky to count on the presence of our Earl Svein Urolfsson..." and he pointed towards the man sitting in the middle of the table. "With King Harald, from Norway," and he pointed towards the man who looked the most wealthy and prominent among them.

He continued to announce the most important people sitting at that table. And he finally arrived at Father's friend.

"And with our dear Gudrod, who needs no further presentation..." and, at this point, the man that he was pointing to stood up and greeted everyone with a slight hand gesture. The crowd cheered. It looked like he was highly favoured amongst the people.

"As you all know, today a horrible crime has been committed by a horrible man, and I struggle with calling him that." When he said these last words, Gudrod seemed very annoyed. The king, King Harald, didn't show any emotions.

"That animal slew innocent traders in an attempt to steal their valuables. The valiant men defended themselves the best that they could but weren't expecting an act of such violence. Bring in the man that goes by the name of Eirik 'The Berserker'! Bring in that animal!"

The guards brought in Father. He had a chain across his neck that was connected to the chains on his arms and legs. He was covered in dry blood. Even from a distance, we could see his wounds. Some of them were still open. After all, the event had happened that very day.

The guard threw him on a chair that was placed on the side beside the announcer. Everybody started murmuring the moment Father was brought in. Mother couldn't help herself and started crying, even though she was trying her best to resist it. Grandmother clutched my hand.

The chieftain that was sitting at the table stood up.

"We all know what happened today. There is no need to relive these horrible events. We open our house to any person who comes here seeking close contact with the gods. The only thing we ask in exchange for our hospitality is that you all leave your feuds at the doors of this honourable town," he said while pointing at the crowd.

"Today, an act of extreme violence happened. Six men died at the hands of the man sitting in that chair in front of you. The seventh man is fighting for his life as we speak."

The moment he said this, I immediately looked at Grandmother. She whispered, "One of the two survivors died from his wounds and, probably, the other man will die too..."

91

Earl Svein continued, "It is our duty to judge this man in the *Thing*. Not as an earl nor as a King," he said while respectfully pointing with his arm at King Harald. "Our duty is to judge this man as a community. A community that has been devoted to the gods and to obeying their laws since ancient times."

After this last statement, he sat down again and signalled the announcer to continue where he had left.

"Thank you for your words, Earl Svein. Now that we are all gathered, know what happened and why we're here. Who thinks this man is guilty and should pay with his life?" said the announcer, raising both his arms towards the crowd.

The entire crowd started shouting. Mostly I could hear "Guilty!", "Assassin!", "Animal!", "Beast!", "Criminal!", and other types of insults. Knut had his arms crossed, was very focused and serious, and didn't pronounce a word. He looked ready to jump with his axe and slay the announcer.

A few people yelled "He was attacked!", "He defended himself!", "Ask the gods!". But the announcer was ignoring those claims and focusing on the majority. He then asked for silence and started speaking again.

"The People, The Community, have spoken. This man will die before the sun sets today. And we'll do it by-"

"Why so much haste?!" yelled Gudrod while standing up violently and almost flipping the long table, "Why such a quick and unfair trial?"

The silence in that Great Hall was total. Apparently, he was an important man in that community, and by the looks of it, he was either feared or respected, perhaps both.

"Since I joined this community a long time ago, I've never witnessed such a one-sided and predetermined trial in this *Thing*." The moment the announcer heard these words, he started articulating his immediate response, but before he could emit any sound, Gudrod kept talking.

"I've served this community the best that I could. I joined for the same reason that Olaf 'The Bear' did. We came here for its ancestral history and connection to the gods. We serve both the people, The Great Temple and the gods. My riches are your riches, my wealth is your wealth and my axe is your axe," he said while staring at the announcer.

Gudrod was a big and strong man. He was well dressed and wealthy, but you could see in his arms and neck multiple scars and inked inscriptions. You knew that this man could be dangerous if he wanted to, and you also knew that he went through many battles and performed many deeds.

The announcer stayed still and silent. Gudrod continued with his speech after a brief pause.

"We are lucky enough to count on the presence of a great Norwegian king, King Harald." He pointed towards the king. "I believe Eirik served under you and helped you conquer many lands, regain other lost lands, and defend your people from foreign attacks. Is that correct?"

The king nodded, and then Gudrod continued. "I fought alongside Eirik." When the crowd heard this, there was a great noise of murmuring across the hall. "We were part of a group known as The Twelve. I fought with Knut 'The Dane', Olaf 'The Bear', Eirik and Harald. Both brothers were known as Odin's Wolves-", at this point, he was interrupted by a higher level of murmuring and some people even started shouting in disapproval. Gudrod resumed with a high, deep and threatening voice, "And they were the two most honourable and skilled warriors that I ever met in my life!"

The crowd stood in silence again. They probably never saw this man behaving in such an aggressive and menacing way.

"You appreciate me and respect me," he continued, "otherwise I wouldn't be sitting at this table. And I was one of them! Yes, I was a berserker too. I stole nothing in my life. I never killed for pleasure. I dedicated my life to Odin and came here to live peacefully, away from the violence, the butchering, the death..." Nobody dared to move or speak.

"Now you know the truth about me. Some people knew but were kind enough to keep it a secret. Now you know where I got my scars and why my body is inked with inscriptions. Now you understand my devotion to the gods. By condemning Eirik, you're condemning me. We were brothers for a long time and will always be in the eye of the All-father."

The mob now started to talk to each other, asking themselves what to do. The men at the table were also arguing. Gudrod sat down again, his head high and proud, his eyes still on fire. He looked ready for war.

While this moment of general commotion was taking place, a guard whispered something to the announcer. He asked for silence again. The moment the crowd went silent, some sporadic shouts could be heard, "Free him!", "He was defending himself!", "Free him for Gudrod!". The announcer started talking.

"I see that Gudrod's impressive speech has already made you lose your senses. It was an excellent speech, I'll give him that. I'm surprised at how we let one of these criminals penetrate our community without even knowing it!"

Chief Svein stood up violently and visibly angry. He was about to say something while pointing towards the announcer, but the announcer was faster, "Another man died!". Svein's surprise didn't allow him to continue with his intentions of reprimanding the announcer.

"Now it's official," continued the announcer, "the animal killed seven men in the worst possible way. Seven innocent traders that were taken by surprise and butchered by this criminal. Who will come to this town to trade now? How will we guarantee safety for our next *blót*? Who is going to pay compensation to these men's families?" he said while challenging Chief Svein.

Now the confusion was even bigger than before. People were still recovering from Gudrod's revelations in his speech and now the news of the seventh death made things worse.

"We will butcher him the same way he butchered these innocent men! We will prove that we obey the laws of men in this community! 'Aye' if you're with me!" praised the announcer.

Some people yelled "Aye!", others simply yelled "Kill that man!", "Animal!", and many other insults and threats. Another part of the crowd, this time I would say was half of it, yelled in favour of Father, "Free him!", "He's one of Odin's Wolves!", "They deserved it!"

"How do you dare challenge me in public like that? How dare you put that sentence on people's lips!" yelled Chief Svein.

"This is a sacred community! Older than men! We need to decide as such! No chief can give a sentence! Only the gods and the people can!" said the announcer while pulling strongly Father's chains, the ones closer to his neck, making him fall from the chair.

Suddenly, a huge redheaded man jumped onto the elevated platform. He was shirtless; his body covered with inscriptions and huge scars. He was only wearing part of an old bear's hide and was wielding a massive battle-axe. His face was painted with blood and his hair was covered in dried mud. He stood in the middle of the platform, in front of the long table, and stared at the announcer, ready to pounce.

He was Olaf, completely transformed. I could never have imagined him like that. He looked almost as fearsome as Father when he was butchering those traders. The announcer was an average-height man, a wealthy one by the looks of it. He had a bit of a belly and you could see he worked little outside by the colour of his pale skin. He had very blond, almost white, hair tied in a ponytail and a short and very well-cured beard.

He was terrified. Olaf was breathing faster and faster, his eyes were transformed. You could see he only had one thing on his mind: Kill the announcer.

With the last air that the frightened man had in his chest, he commanded, "Take this man!". Not a single guard moved. But who did move were Gudrod and Knut.

Gudrod stood up with a jump, violently kicking the table and flipping it. He raised his battle-axe and shouted an incredibly loud battle cry. All the men sitting at the table stood up and jumped backwards, except for King Harald, who remained on his chair, as if this whole situation had nothing to do with him.

Knut jumped on the platform behind Olaf, also menacingly pointing towards the announcer. He had removed his shirt and had all his scars and inscriptions exposed. He was wielding one axe in each hand and started growling. You could see the veins in his bald head getting bigger and bigger.

More blood would be shed in that hall. There was no way that Olaf, Gudrod and Knut would allow Father to be killed. More and more guards surrounded the platform. Mother and I hugged Grandmother. The crowd panicked, but nobody moved.

Right when it looked like the tragedy was about to happen, a deep authoritarian feminine voice was heard from the back of the *Thing*, from the entrance. It was the *völva*; she appeared with some of the temple assistants. She commanded and talked in that ancient dialect that some used to address the gods. Olaf started relaxing and changing his body posture. The same happened to Knut and Gudrod.

She didn't walk forward; she stayed at the entrance, almost like someone who didn't want to enter too deep into men's world but simply peek. Olaf, Gudrod and Knut finally adopted a more neutral stance. Then, the *völva* talked in the common tongue.

"How dare you imprison Geri? One of Odin's fiercest and mightiest wolves? How dare you judge one of Odin's warriors?" Right after she said these words, the announcer wanted to reply something, but she lifted her arm towards him in a menacing way. "How dear you, worm, to even think of responding?" The announcer lowered his head in silence.

"You're all here because 'We' are here. You're all here because of the gods, and I represent the gods. Seven men were slaughtered and seven men needed to be slaughtered to appease the gods, who better than Geri 'The Hungry', one of Odin's Wolves to devour the flesh of the sacrificed in an offering to the Knowledgeable one?" she said with authority.

Nobody dared to even breathe after her intervention. She never entered the *Thing* before. She barely ever left The Great Temple. But one man was brave enough to talk. It was King Harald.

"The day the *völvas* feel the need to step into the *Thing* and solve the problems of men is the day that men have failed at solving their own problems. Not only that, they failed at respecting the gods' will."

He now stood up from the chair and moved forward over the flipped table. Each of his steps was followed by noises of cracking of all the food, cups and plates that were on the floor after Gudrod's act of rage.

"I am King, but I am king in Norway. This land has no King but a Queen. A Queen that serves the kings of Asgard, rulers of Midgard," he said while bowing slightly to the *völva*.

After that, he turned towards Father, still on the floor. And while helping him get up, he said, "You helped me stand up against my enemies. Fierce as they were, they weren't a good enough match for you and your brothers. These blessed warriors slew more foes than my entire troops combined. But now, loyal friend, it is I that helps you stand up," and finally lifted Father.

"Are you feeling well?" asked the king. "It's a scratch," said Father, barely with any voice left. He couldn't even stand properly.

"If the *völva* agrees," King Harald continued, "I would say that all the men that needed to be sacrificed in this *blót*, have been sacrificed. And by an expert and honourable hand, I would add." He stared at the spiritual woman. She nodded with a sigh of relief.

"Then, unless Earl Svein has any objections, I think we should conclude this meeting before any other man dies," said the king while handing Father to Olaf, Knut and Gudrod and giving an intense look to Svein. The chief nodded, and Father was carried away to be tended.

Then the king turned again towards the crowd, "For whoever thinks that justice didn't prevail today, let me add this. I never saw men being 'surprised and killed' while wearing armour and being armed," and gave a look full of hate and contempt at the announcer.

"When I arrived at the scene and heard the testimonies. I saw a closed tent with five armed and armoured men surrounding an unarmed man, wearing simple cloth. Two men were guarding the entrance," he said while looking at everybody's faces, one by one.

"This wasn't an 'animal unexpectedly killing some innocent traders'. This was an execution. And, as you all know, the only blood spilt in this place should be in The Great Temple, by the *völvas*. Odin condemned those men for their actions, for they intended to slay one of his warriors. We're lucky. You're lucky! That no more blood has been spilt," and he looked again at the announcer.

He then jumped from the platform and left. At that moment, all the guards that surrounded the stage also started moving. I didn't realise it earlier, but these were all his guards. They had the bear's claw on their shields. The crowd started moving around, some leaving the hall, others crossing it, looking for friends and family. Nobody was talking, just some murmuring here and there.

I tried to find the *völva*, but she wasn't there anymore. The announcer sat on the same chair where Father had been sitting for most of the trial. He looked defeated and overwhelmed by the whole situation.

Mother and Grandmother hugged me. We couldn't believe what had happened. Now, the only thing that we wanted to do was go see how Father was and stay with him. Tend to his wounds and hopefully try to make sense of all that happened that day.

Chapter 13

Healing

We took Father to Olaf's house. He was weak and tired and had many wounds that had not been tended to properly.

Grandmother prepared some sort of liquid medicine in a bowl containing water, herbs, leaves and smashed roots. She put some bandages inside the bowl, soaked them and then cleaned Father's wounds with them. After that, she covered the wounds with the soaked bandages and wrapped them with a dry and tight cloth. Father didn't complain. His eyes were fixated on the ceiling the whole time. He looked absent. After his wounds had been treated, Grandmother asked us to let him rest.

I was waiting for a chance to talk to Olaf to make sense of what had happened that day and understand the consequences of it.

The following day, after finishing my chores, Olaf was sitting on the tree stumps outside his house, with his back and head leaning against the wall. "Olaf, are you sleeping?" I whispered.

"Not anymore, boy," he said with a smile while patting the free tree stump near him. By now I felt he already knew me inside out. He knew that a battery of questions was coming his way.

I sat near him, deeply exhaled, preparing myself to ask him all the things that I wanted to know. "Shoot," he said.

"Why wasn't Father condemned? Why was he set free? He killed seven men after all…" I tried being as direct as possible.

"As you saw, the *völva* intervened, and she represents the gods. She said that those seven deaths could be taken as part of the nine that needed to happen. So, the men that assaulted your father, without knowing it, volunteered to be sacrificed by and for Odin," he calmly responded. I could feel that he was treating me more and more like a trusted friend, like a man, and less like his friend's son.

"I understand," I said while trying to make sense of all of this, "But then, why did King Harald get involved?"

"Well Sigurd, your father served King Harald. Your father served plenty of powerful people, the same as I did. But King Harald was the most important of them all, not only because he became king, but because he understood the gods, and he understood us. Things will change Sigurd. Things already have." He said while grabbing his enormous axe and starting to sharpen it with a whetstone.

"Is there going to be more bloodshed? What will happen with the *blót*?" I asked in a scared voice.

"Ah… Sigurd… This should be an event of rejoicing and happiness. This happens once every nine winters. We're never as close to the gods as we are now, here. But, what happened with your father never happened before. At least I never heard of anything like it. During a *blót*, the only blood comes from the sacrifices," he said while sharpening his axe. "Perhaps there will be more violence, perhaps there won't. In any case, I'm ready, and I'm not the only one," he added while lifting his head and, with a slight head motion, signalling the arrival of Knut and his son Björn.

Knut was shirtless. His kind face looked serious and ready for business. He had his two axes sharpened and hanging from his waist strap. Björn also had two sharpened axes. He was normally dressed but had a wound on his arm.

As they approached us and got closer, I noticed that Björn's wound wasn't a normal wound, his father had inscriptions inked into his skin. I could read them clearly. They were an invocation to Odin.

"Good day, Olaf, my brother. Good day Sigurd, young cub," said Knut. Björn looked at me and nodded.

"Good morning, brother," said Olaf. "Are we expecting trouble anytime soon?"

"I don't know about that, but if we were, plenty of blood would taint this sacred place," said the bald man.

"Well, let's hope it doesn't come to that," said Olaf while placing his axe near him and putting the whetstone back in his leather pouch.

He then looked at Björn's arm, smiled and asked, "Following your father's steps, Björn?"

"Aye, sir. Aren't we all?" said Björn, while looking at me.

"Did your father explain to you the significance of that ink on your arm?" said Olaf, while staring at Knut.

"Yes, he did Olaf. I embrace it."

Olaf then looked at Knut with a serious expression. "Are you sure about this?"

Knut nodded. The redheaded giant wasn't satisfied. "Knut, brother, you know times are changing fast. And you know how peopl-"

"I know the gods, Olaf. I don't care about people. My son has it. He really does. And Odin chose him. It happened in The Great Temple. He can be one of us, if he survives, of course."

Olaf then exhaled in resignation, then he smiled back at Björn, "I'm sure you'll do fine young one, Odin is wise."

"Thank you, Olaf," said Björn, smiling back at him.

"How's the old wolf?" said Knut, interrupting the moment between Olaf and Björn.

"Holding on. He'll do fine, he just needs time. There isn't a better person to heal wounds than his mother. You know it well, eh?" Olaf replied while giggling and pointing to one of Knut's biggest scars on his chest.

"That woman has magic hands, Olaf!" replied Knut, laughing.

They stayed with us for a while; we talked a little and then they went back to their camp. After they left, Olaf and I embraced the silence. Meditating. Thinking.

"Why didn't we go to The Great Temple today, Olaf?" I asked the giant after some time of reflection.

"The *völva* didn't want drama in there. She wouldn't tolerate it. It should be a time to dedicate to the gods, not to men's affairs. The whole killing and trial were too fresh. I guess tomorrow the *blót* will resume."

"Well, it makes sense. If you say that things changed, it's better to leave some time for things to settle down, I guess," I replied.

"Indeed, Sigurd, indeed," said Olaf while patting my back.

"What's going to happen to the slaughtered men? If they're treated as a sacrifice, will they be hanging too? Or are they going to be buried?" I asked. I was really curious about this. Not that I cared, but it was something that I didn't know how it was going to be addressed.

"If I'm honest with you, Sigurd, I don't know. For all that I care, they could feed those 'men' to the ravens," said Olaf with decisiveness.

I went back into the house. Grandmother and my sister were near Father, tending to his wounds. Mother was preparing food. I asked her if she needed help and, since she didn't need it, I sat near the fireplace.

"She's a natural, Thora," said Grandmother, "Your kid is a natural."

"Is she now?" said Mother in surprise.

"Yes, she knows exactly where to apply pressure, where and when to clean, how to prepare the bandages, everything!" yelled Grandmother, almost forgetting that her son was lying asleep near her.

"I'm not dead," murmured Father.

Grandmother rejoiced when she heard Father talking again, "Of course, you are not dea-"

"I'm not dead because in the afterlife my mother wouldn't scream in my ear..." said Father while slightly smiling.

We all laughed. I couldn't believe how Father, always so serious, could joke in a moment like this. Mother rushed to him. "You're finally back. How are you feeling?"

"Well tended by the looks of it," said Father, looking at my sister.

"She's a natural," said Grandmother, full of excitement and pride.

"So I heard," said Father ironically, still joking about how loud Grandmother had been.

"Grumpy's back!" we suddenly heard. It was the deep and loud voice of Olaf from the door. He had just entered the house and witnessed the entire scene.

"I will never be able to sleep again..." said Father, while staring at Olaf.

Olaf laughed so loud that I thought the house would crumble on top of us. He then came near Father and patted him so hard that he bounced up and down the bed.

"Careful, you big brute!" yelled Grandmother.

"Agh... He's fine!" yelled Olaf. "He'll survive this one too! Hard to kill your boy, you know?!"

"Not if you keep beating him up!" replied Grandmother jokingly.

Immediately, Father returned to being the serious and intense person he usually was. "Olaf, how bad is it?" he asked.

"I don't know yet, brother. But, whatever happens, we'll deal with it. Knut is ready too," said Olaf.

"Hmmm..." Father didn't quite like what he just heard.

"He inked his son, Björn, you know?"

Father's eyes got bigger, full of surprise and concern. He then looked at me. "Knut..." he murmured.

"What's wrong?" I asked. Tired of the secrecy with this inking thing.

I always noticed that few men had inscriptions on their skin. Scars were pretty common for every man has had to fight at least once in their life. But inscriptions weren't that common, and even less the amount and size that Father, Knut, Gudrod and Olaf had.

"It's not a life one would want for her children," said Mother.

"Well, if Odin chooses your son..." said Grandmother.

"Helga, you know as well as I do that this is not a life of peace and happiness. You spent most of your life wondering if you would ever see your sons returning home," said Mother, visibly emotional.

"If Odin chooses you and you pass the trials. Then it's your path. No men nor women can do anything about it," categorically said Father.

Mother exhaled in resignation and kept working on preparing the meal.

"So? What's wrong?" I insisted.

They all exhaled, it seemed that the topic was a delicate matter to them.

103

"That ink, Sigurd, that inscription is the first step. An initiation, if you will," said Olaf, "Apparently, Odin chose Björn to follow his father's steps."

"I see," I replied. I must admit, I felt jealous.

"You see Sigurd, we ink our skin before facing our biggest challenges and trials. We summon all the might of the gods and fill our bodies with their protection and strength. We need all the help that we can get," continued explaining Olaf while looking at some of his inscriptions with nostalgia.

"This is not a simple task that the gods have put on Björn's shoulders. From now on, his path will be of suffering. He won't be bound to men anymore, only the gods. And, as you have noticed, men don't accept that," said Father.

"But, if men treat spiritual warriors, berserkers, this way... What's the point in even being one?" I asked bluntly. It made little sense to me.

"How do you think we were never conquered, Sigurd?" asked Father. "How do you think Scandinavia is still owned by its own people? Sure, we kill each other in different feuds and power plays. But it's our land. Many other lands have been invaded and conquered all over Midgard. But our land is still our own.

"You see, Sigurd, Odin's warriors were created in ancient times. Times without politics, without mundane interests. Times when gods and men walked Midgard one next to the other."

"I see..." I replied, "And how is it decided who controls the berserkers? I mean, how do you choose where to fight? On which side of the conflict do you stand?"

"The answer to that question may be too complex to explain, Sigurd," Olaf quickly replied.

Suddenly, a very strong knock on the door interrupted the conversation and made Mother and Grandmother jump in the air, startled. Olaf headed towards the door, he grabbed his enormous axe and signalled us to take cover. He then opened the door quickly and prepared himself to combat. As soon as the door opened, Olaf relaxed. It was Gudrod.

"Can I come in, brother? Or you'll chop my head off?" said Gudrod while smiling. "The axe would break if I tried..." replied jokingly Olaf while hugging his friend and inviting him to come inside.

Having these two gigantic men in the house made it look even smaller than it already was. Gudrod walked inside the house as if he owned it. He came near Grandmother, who was still sitting near Father, kissed her on the head and looked at Mother, nodding his head and greeting her, "Thora..."

He then placed his hand over my sister's head. She also was still sitting near Father. "Hello pretty one! You'll be something special, won't you?". My sister smiled, stood up and went to her bed. It looked like she knew she had to let the two men have their space. Grandmother did the same. She went near the fireplace and sat on a chair.

Gudrod now sat on the bed in front of Father. "How are you holding up, old friend?"

"Just a scratch, brother," said Father, proudly.

"Yes, a bear's scratch!" said Gudrod, while inspecting some of the wounds. "This one was way too close, Eirik. Too close."

"It wouldn't have made a difference," replied Father seriously while looking at me.

I knew he was referring to the fact that he volunteered to be sacrificed. It still hurt me that he would do something like that without even talking to me about it, but, on the other hand, he never talked to anybody about his plans.

"Well, you know him. He changes his mind very often, depending on what he sees. I believe this is for the best," said Gudrod while pointing towards Father's triple triangle symbol inked in his chest.

"Is it?" said Father, looking Gudrod in the eyes. "Is it, Gudrod?"

"You worry about me now, Eirik?" asked Gudrod jokingly.

Father didn't reply, nor did he move a bit. He kept his serious, and concerned look in Gudrod's eyes.

"Things have changed. I won't lie to you," said Gudrod, "But I can deal with this. Let's wait and see where the leaves fall."

"Will you have to leave? Is your life threatened?" said Olaf while playing with his axe in the middle of the house. He was trying to hold the axe vertically with one finger while listening to the conversation.

"I don't know yet, Olaf," said Gudrod, "I really don't know."

He now paused and exhaled. "I must admit that the situation isn't looking bright. Most of the people in this community didn't know what I was or what I did before coming here. I didn't arrive here like you, Olaf. I came here through my father's wealth and contacts. People never would have guessed it."

"Well, you don't look like an earl to me... Wasn't that hard to guess," replied Olaf.

Gudrod shrugged and then continued explaining while looking at Olaf and constantly looking back at Father. "I just needed to be close to the gods, you know that feeling, right Olaf?"

Olaf stopped playing with the axe. He leaned on the wall and nodded while deeply exhaling. "It all fell apart. After what happened when Harald and the others died, it all fell apart. I couldn't keep going..." added Gudrod with a trembling voice.

"It was never up to us, Gudrod," said Father.

"I know Eirik, I know. But even Olaf had his moment of weakness. Not everybody can be like you and your brother. For Odin's sake! I even wonder if you belong in Midgard at all!" replied Gudrod. He looked visibly worried, but also ashamed.

"You were chosen the same as I was. You passed the trials the same as Olaf, my brother, and I did. Odin saw something in you and chose you. That's the end of it. To question that is to question Odin himself, Gudrod," said Father with a stone-cold voice accompanied by a judging and deep look.

"I would never question the All-father, Eirik. You know that," said Gudrod in a calming voice while laying his hand on Father's chest. Father relaxed again. "I just wish that we could do something meaningful. I just wish that we could be recognised by people for the things that we did. We've been through things that people couldn't even imagine. We've done things that would be worthy of countless sagas and songs. But we're still forced to hide, or to live in shame..." said Gudrod while looking downwards.

Olaf deeply exhaled again and also looked downwards. Father kept staring at Gudrod. He held his look even when Gudrod lowered his own.

"Many of our brothers had to endure such discrimination that were basically forced to steal and kill for survival..." said Gudrod with a thread of voice so low that it was almost a whisper while still holding his head low. Father extended his arm, visibly in pain, and gently placed his hand on Gudrod's head.

"The gods... It's hard to distinguish when they're blessing us and when they're cursing us. Sometimes both at the same time. But one thing is for sure, Gudrod, we shape our own destiny through our actions. Never feel pity for those who weren't strong enough, for you are encouraging weakness by doing that," said Father with a serious and deep but paternal tone.

Gudrod raised his head, looked Father straight in the eyes and whispered, "You speak like your brother...". Father half smiled and quickly responded, "Or maybe he spoke like me."

Everybody laughed at that. It wasn't a cheerful laugh but more of a nostalgic one. A laugh that one has when remembering something beautiful that will never happen again. Gudrod laid back against the wall and everybody remained silent for a while.

"What will you do now, then?" asked Olaf, breaking the silence.

"I think I'll have to leave. But what about you? You managed to stay here all this time by not entering into social and political affairs. After your display at the *Thing*, I think you pretty much blew that up, right?"

"To be honest, I haven't thought about this. For now, I just want Eirik to recover his strength. I want to keep dedicating the remaining days of the *blót* to the gods, as it should be. And after that,

I'll see how things are going. As you said, 'let's see where leaves fall'," said the red-headed giant.

"You could return to Norway with us, Olaf," I immediately said.

I didn't want to interrupt the conversation, but after all, if they wanted a private conversation, they should have said it.

Olaf laughed out loud, as he always did. He then turned and messed up my hair playfully. "Agh... Sigurd! That sure sounds like fun, eh! I could go walrus hunting again!". He then patted my back and neck. I almost felt my eyes popping out. He turned and, facing Gudrod and Eirik, said with a more serious tone, "Ah... Home. What does that word even mean? So many unresolved things in Norway... Who knows..."

After this, Gudrod stood up, ready to leave. He greeted Father, kissed Grandmother on the head, and stopped in front of my sister. He kneeled and took off his silver Mjölnir pendant and put it around Thrúd's neck. "May the blessed hammer of Thor give strength and guidance to a blessed child."

She grabbed it with her small fist and looked at it, then she looked back at Gudrod with her ice-blue eyes and smiled while nodding respectfully. He stood up and switched his attention to Olaf.

"Hope for the best, prepare for the worst. Nothing might happen, but the worst could still occur. There are a high number of people that hate everything that we stood and stand for and, especially, hate Eirik," said Gudrod, visibly concerned.

"Let them come, Gudrod. Let them come..." said Olaf while gripping strongly to his axe.

The giant blond man then gently patted my sister's head, nodded at Mother, waved at me, and finally left. We had our meal and spent the rest of the day doing chores. Olaf taught me how to properly sharpen a battle-axe and some key moves for defending myself from a blade by using just body movement.

The following day started like any other day before Father's incident: We did our chores, ate something, got dressed and went towards The

Great Temple. Father also came with us. He could hardly walk, but he still wanted to come.

The walk towards the temples' compound was incredibly weird. Some people would nod when we passed near them, others would avoid eye contact. Some would stare and perhaps even say some mean things to us, and a couple of men even spat on us.

We ignored all the negative lashing out against us, deciding to honour our commitment to the gods. We journeyed for almost a moon across mountains, woods, snow and mud to come here and be in close contact with them and didn't want the incident to further interrupt our spiritual journey.

Once arrived at the temples, Father wanted to go inside every single temple before entering Odin's house for the sacrifices. We slowly dragged him to each one of them so that he could murmur some prayers in the ancient dialect to each God and Goddess represented in these temples and then, finally, we found ourselves in front of Odin's house.

The *völva* was at the steps of the building. Her face was painted, and she was wearing her ritual garments. She looked like she was there for quite some time. The moment we got close enough, she looked at Olaf and with a slight head motion signalled him to bring Father inside. The temple was still empty. Everybody waited outside.

We entered with the priestess. She placed us where the temple assistants usually stand and then sent the assistants outside to tell the folk to come in.

People's reactions were much lighter in the temple. The *völva*'s presence was intimidating. Once everybody was gathered there, or at least most of the crowd, she started talking loudly.

"A few days ago, Odin chose a different path for this *blót*. Perhaps an unprecedented path, but nonetheless was Odin's will, and as such must be respected." Everybody looked at her in total silence. Nobody dared to emit a sound.

"We're in The Great Temple. This place has existed since ancient times when the gods walked amongst us. Here, traditionally, we always respected their will." She said while looking at each one of the attendants, even though there wasn't much light except the one that came from the torches.

"This place exists because of people like me, *völvas* from the past who served the gods and built this place with their help and guidance. You all come here from nearby towns and communities, but also from distant countries and places. You come here once every nine winters because you know about this place's history, about its sacred foundations."

Most of the crowd was nodding at all that the *völva* was saying. They all seemed to strongly agree with her.

"You know or should know that in those ancient times, while *völvas* like myself were serving the gods in the temples, warriors like them served the gods on the battlefield!" she said while pointing at us.

Every single person in that place stared at us. I could sense the admiration, the hate, the indifference, the jealousy... I would rather have been in any other place than there, exposed in front of that crowd.

Near me, Grandmother was holding my hand. Mother had my sister between her legs and had her arm around me. Father was leaning over Olaf, trying his best to stand up. I didn't realise it at first, but near Olaf, I saw Knut, Björn and Gudrod. They were standing strong, proud and challenging, even Björn.

The tension was abruptly cut by the *völva's* loud voice again.

"Who defended these grounds? Who fought alongside Tyr and Thor against the Giants that escaped Jotunheim? Who fought against foreigners keeping this land safe for us to live in? They did!" said the *völva*, visibly angry.

"I never had to enter the world of men all the time that I've been here, and I was born in these very temples... It seems that Loki played one of his twisted games during this *blót*, poisoning your minds with rage and mischief. The gods will take care of him. But rest assured, we'll take care of his accomplices here," she threatened.

Her anger, her icy eyes piercing every single person in that room, the dancing light of the torches reflecting on her body paint, Odin's statue in the background watching over us... We were petrified. Everybody was.

She then turned to one of her assistants and after a while, she performed the sacrificial ceremony normally.

After the ceremony had finished — I still couldn't get used to dogs being sacrificed — we headed outside towards the grove. Three days of sacrifice we had so far, three dogs and horses were hanging from the branches of several trees. Two sacrificed men were hanging, too. But no sign of the men that Father slaughtered.

Once we got close enough, I could see several baskets on the floor, surrounding the trunk of the tree where the sacrificed men were hanging. With a closer look, I identified what it was. The baskets were filled with the body parts chopped off during Father's incident, and near them, several bodies piled up. Those were Odin's sacrifices, by courtesy of Father.

Some people were disgusted at that sight, not because of the visceral aspect of it, but because of how it happened and because of the hand that did it. Everyone started to leave, returning towards the town to have the feast that usually followed the sacrifices. I stayed there. I got so distracted by all that had happened that I completely missed the whole point of us coming to this place: The gods.

I looked at the trees with the sacrifices and asked myself what would Odin think about all of this. Was he pleased? Did he really plan it this way?

"I missed you, young Sigurd," I suddenly heard.

There he was, the old man with the rugged cloak sitting down on a tree stump under one of the trees that held sacrificed bodies. How didn't I notice him earlier?

"Hello sir," I replied while still confused about how I didn't spot him earlier.

"What a strange *blót*, and trust me, I've seen plenty of them. But this one is the messier one that I recall," he grinned. I shrugged, not knowing what to say to that.

"Why do you think all of this happened?" he asked with as much curiosity as a man his age could ever have.

"I guess that, as the *völva* said, Loki is behind this…" I replied.

"Yes, he probably is. But don't get it wrong, this is men's doing. Maybe guided by The Sly One, but still, it's the hand of men wielding the axes," he said with a less joking voice, almost a concerned voice.

"I think it's ignorant and evil people that have no other way of behaving than trying to ambush Father in a tent and assassinate him," I said.

"I sense much pride in you, boy," the old man said. I nodded strongly. "I also sense fear," he added.

That completely took me by surprise. It was a feeling so deep within me I didn't even fully recognise it myself, but this man could sense it from a distance. Since the incident happened, I had dreams of Father covered in blood, growling, breathing like an enraged animal, biting and mutilating those men with his axes.

"How...?" I murmured, almost whispering.

"Well, the town talks, boy. I'm an old man sitting here and there. I hear things," he promptly replied.

There was something that didn't convince me; his look wasn't the one of an innocent old man sitting around. He had a smart look, a piercing look that could see right through you, just like Father, but even stronger.

"Do you think your father would ever harm you?"

"No, sir. Never."

"Then, why the fear, Sigurd?"

"Well... I don't know, sir. I just felt it, and since then, I've always felt it in the most inner part of my being. I can't describe it, it's so deep within me I sometimes don't feel the fear itself, just the presence of it there. This makes no sense..." I started babbling.

The old man laughed, hitting the ground with his staff. "I knew it!" he yelled, "I knew it the moment I saw you!"

"You knew what, sir?" I asked while getting deeply annoyed at him laughing at me.

"I knew you had it in you, boy. It's been a while since I've seen it like this..."

"Seen what?" I asked.

"It doesn't matter. What matters is that you don't ignore or run away from that feeling inside you. Embrace it, own it. Ask your father about it during these days, before it gets worse."

"What gets worse, sir?" I asked while worrying.

"Sigurd... You'll have to go now, but promise me you'll do two things for me, will you?" he said while changing his mood into a more serious one.

"Yes... sir," I murmured.

"First, you'll go to Odin's temple. Alone. And you'll talk to him. Alone. Understood?" he ordered.

"Yes..." I replied. I would never take orders from anybody other than Father or Mother. But, this time, I felt like I had to do everything that this man asked me.

"Secondly, remember this: 'Not all evil things are done by evil people, and not all good things are done by good people.' Beware of falsehood and mischief. Be true to the gods. And always remember, the worse the situation gets, the stronger you'll have to be."

I nodded nervously. I felt like something horrible was about to happen, but didn't know what. It looked like he was preparing me for war, even though the worst had just passed. He interrupted my thoughts with a deep and authoritarian "Go!"

I left and immediately ran towards Olaf's house. I didn't feel like going to Odin's temple at that moment. The confusion and the fear were such that I couldn't do any other thing that wasn't run home towards Grandmother, Mother, Father, and Olaf. I needed to feel shielded and protected.

Chapter 14

Revelation

I arrived home; as I was about to open the door, it opened by itself. It was Olaf, getting out of the house.

"Sigurd! Where were you? Still at the grove?"

"Yes sir. I mean, Olaf. Yes! I was still there!" I nervously replied, still worried about what the old man had told me.

Olaf looked at me concerned, he took my arm and abruptly sat me in the tree stump against the house wall. "What happened, Sigurd?" he asked while bending towards me.

"Nothing, Olaf. Nothing..."

"Sigurd," he said with a deep, concerned, and serious voice. I hardly ever saw him this concerned, even less when talking to me. "What. Happened," he ordered.

I felt I had to explain to him what had happened. "Well... I saw the old man again, under the trees in the grove, and he told-"

"Old man? In the grove? Under the trees where the sacrificed are hanged?" he interrogated me.

"Yes..." I timidly replied.

"Is this the first time you see this man, Sigurd?"

"No, Olaf. It has already been several times that I've seen him and talked to him."

Olaf looked downwards, worried, pensive. "Did you ever talk to him before the sacrifices ever began?"

"Yes. I did. Actually, the very first day we arrived. It was also the day I heard the trader say those things about Father. This old man was the one who defended Father."

"Oh, dear..." Olaf started murmuring, "It can't be... "

"Olaf? What's happening? What's the matter?"

"What did he tell you today?" asked Olaf, ignoring my previous questions.

I told him the whole conversation. After that, he wanted to know about all the other interactions with this old man. Once I finished, he grabbed my wrist and dragged me inside. Mother was cleaning some plates and cups. She wanted to do it before going to the feast. Grandmother was playing with my sister and they were both being loud. Father was lying on his bed. Olaf dragged me across the house and sat me on the bed in front of Father.

"Eirik, it happened. It happened as it did with you and Harald. It happened again," said Olaf bending over Father.

The moment he said that everybody in the house froze. Even Thrúd stopped shouting.

"What did you just say?" asked Mother, concerned.

"It happened Thora, it just did," Olaf replied.

"How? When?" asked Grandmother.

Mother looked anxious and worried. Father exhaled deeply and looked at me as if I had just died as if he had lost me forever.

"Since the day you arrived here. He talked to him immediately and hasn't stopped ever since," replied Olaf.

"I knew it…" said Grandmother, proud.

"Helga! No!" yelled Mother.

"Are you sure about this, Olaf?" asked Father, very concerned.

"Yes, brother, it's exactly the same as… Well, you know."

Mother and Grandmother argued about how good or bad whatever was happening to me was. Father and Olaf started murmuring between them. My sister stared at me in silence, in awe.

"What's happening?!" I yelled. Everyone stopped again and sighed.

"Sigurd, this old man… What did he tell you to do?" asked Father.

"He told me to go to Odin's temple."

"Go," ordered Father in the most serious tone ever.

"But Eirik-" started protesting Mother.

"Go, Sigurd. There is nothing none of us can say about it," said Father, categorically.

I didn't want to continue arguing or make them argue more. I just left the house and headed towards The Great Temple. While walking, I looked at my feet, like I always used to do, thinking. Why would they argue? Why the concern? What's the big deal with this old man?

Soon enough, I found myself in front of Odin's temple. It still was full of blood from the *blót* running through the grooves on the floor and pouring into Odin's well.

I entered the building and found the *völva* near the entrance. She greeted me as soon as I stepped foot in the darker part of the building, where the light from outside couldn't reach. "You're late, Sigurd," she said.

"Late? For what?"

"You should have come much sooner. He was expecting you," she replied. After that, she signalled me with her arm to keep walking towards Odin's statue.

I walked between the grooves, straight towards the statue. Some temple assistants were cleaning the huge sacrificial stone. As soon as I got close to them, the *völva* commanded something in that ancient dialect. The assistants stopped cleaning and left the building. The *völva* followed and closed the doors behind her. I was now alone in the dark temple. The light coming from the open doors was no more. Only the torches on the walls and some fire bowls on the floor lit the room with a dim glow.

I stood in front of Odin. It had been quite some time since the first time that I stood in front of him. I had entered this temple several times for the sacrifices but never with the sole intention of talking to the All-Father.

I saw again the imposing figure of the One-Eyed god. Geri and Freki at his feet. Huginn and Muninn on his shoulders. What a sight!

His presence overwhelmed me. I felt the need to pet one of his wolves, Geri, the Hungry one. The moment I touched his head, all the torches and fires extinguished. It was pitch black. A small light came from the blood-filled well at Odin's feet. It looked like fish glittering. Looking downwards, I saw movement in the water, as if redfish were swimming and light was being reflected on them.

I then looked upwards and saw the eyes of Odin's wolves lighting up in the dark. They were blue, an icy glowing blue. I focused on those eyes. I wasn't feeling scared but rather felt safe, strong, hypnotised.

Suddenly, something hit my forehead. It wasn't a strong hit, but somewhat a gentle one. Somehow it knocked me down. Everything started spinning until I started seeing myself from above. I could see my body lying there, unconscious. I was in the air, high up, near the face of Odin's statue. An imperative need to turn towards him grew inside me. As I surrendered to that need, I couldn't believe what I saw next. The statue wasn't there anymore, but the God himself.

He was on his horse, Sleipnir, the eight-legged horse, and wielded his spear, Gungnir. His ravens were still on his shoulders, but the wolves weren't there anymore. He looked at me. He was ready for battle, dressed in his finest armour.

I forgot everything. I forgot what had happened, where I was and why I was there. My entire attention, my whole being, was sorely focused on him now. I could only see him, standing glorious and tall, in front of me.

"Are you afraid, Young Sigurd?" the All-father asked.

"No, Father," I replied without thinking.

"'Father'..." the God replied, pensive. After a while, he smirked and looked me straight in the eyes with his penetrating, ice-cold eye. "Does it hurt, boy?" he asked.

"Hurt?" I asked, very confused. He then pointed at my body with his spear. I looked towards my chest and saw a huge deep wound and several others in my arms, legs, stomach... A huge amount of pain started spiking all over my body. I couldn't bear it. But I couldn't show weakness in front of the All-father. If I did, and Father ever knew about this...

"No, it doesn't hurt. It's just a scratch," I instinctively replied while using all my strength to not faint from the pain. These words just came out of my mouth. He smiled. All the pain immediately went away. I could only feel a strong burning sensation in my chest, my left chest. I looked at the god, asking why I was feeling this burning in my chest.

He signalled my chest by looking at it, accompanied by a slight head motion. I looked at my body, all the wounds disappeared except for a wound in my left chest. It burnt. It was a symbol of three intertwined triangles, carved in my flesh. The same symbol Geri the wolf had in the statue, the same Father had inked in his chest.

I raised my head again, confused, begging for an explanation. He then pointed his spear down towards Sleipnir's legs. The wolves were standing there. Huge, proud and intimidating beasts. They both stared at me. I then saw Gungnir, Odin's spear, being raised again. I followed the tip of the spear until my eyes met with his ice-blue eye. He smiled. "You understand now?"

"Yes," I immediately replied, "I think I do…"

He laughed, loud and proud, then he pointed his spear at me and with a fast motion he moved it downwards as if he was slicing an enemy with it. The moment he did that, I fell with an immense force, right before hitting the ground I woke up on the floor of the temple.

The fire bowls and torches were lit again. I was sitting in front of the statue, feeling extremely overwhelmed, wondering if I understood correctly what had just happened. Looking around, I noticed I was still alone in the temple.

What just happened? Did Odin recruit me? Was I chosen? Was all of this a product of my imagination?

I had heard that this place was where we could feel the gods closer to us, but I never thought it could be this close. And the pain, I felt it so real. The burning in my chest… Yes! The burning! I checked my chest right away, and there it was. It was a burning mark, three triangles intertwined. But it was fading, disappearing right in front of my eyes. Then it was real. I was awake and could touch and feel the mark. The mark that Odin had given me.

"You keep your word, Young Sigurd…" I heard coming from the darkness. That voice! It was the old man. I went towards the voice.

He was sitting on a bench near Odin's statue, in the darkness, where the light of the torches couldn't touch him.

"Sir...?"

"Yes, Sigurd?"

"Father...?" I asked, not even knowing why.

"Yes, Sigurd."

I froze. The old man was... Him. All this time, it was him! I had heard of Odin disguising as men to mingle amongst us, but I never thought he would approach me.

"Why me? Why now?"

"You're special, Sigurd. Like your father and uncle were."

"Why didn't you tell me before? Why come here?". Again, I wasn't even thinking. I was just emitting sounds that formed these direct questions.

"Curiosity... Just like your uncle," he said while giggling.

"What am I to do now?"

"Be guided by my lone wolf. Be guided by my bears. Keep on this path, Sigurd, for this is going to be your only path," he replied with an authoritarian voice.

I needed more. Enough with the riddles! I grabbed a torch from the wall and rushed towards where he was seated. The need to have a more direct and honest conversation possessed me. I needed answers, not more questions. But the moment I got to where the old man was seated, I found an empty bench.

"Old man? Old man!? All-father?" I wondered and yelled, but nobody was there. "Odin!" I yelled in desperation, but only my echo replied. What did all of this mean? What were my next steps now? I felt lost and lonely. I desperately needed answers.

"You know that he's old but not deaf, right?" said a female voice from the entrance. It was the *völva*, she had opened the door and was waiting for me to get out.

"Yes, I know. But-"

"It is his will, and also his ways. You might not always agree, but this is how it is. You probably have many questions now. Go to your father and Olaf. They'll be able to provide some answers, but not all of them. You'll have to find them by yourself."

"Understood. Thank you. And sorry for any inconvenience that I may have caused," I respectfully said to her.

"Go now, young cub," she said while gently pushing me towards the steps of the temple.

I had many questions to ask Olaf and Father, and I was afraid that I might disappoint Mother. I just hoped that I could handle whatever was coming my way, whatever fate had in store for me. Running through the town towards Olaf's house, thousands of questions invaded my mind. I couldn't wait any longer.

While I was approaching the house, I saw two figures outside of it, but I couldn't properly see who they were. I felt my heart in my mouth. Who could it be? Maybe someone wanted to finish the job and kill Father? I ran as fast as I could.

Once I stood in front of the house, I recognised the bear's paws in the shields of the two men outside Olaf's house. They were King Harald's guards, but what were they doing there?

They let me get in the house without even paying much attention to me. As soon as I got inside, I saw Mother, Grandmother, and my sister sitting near the fireplace; Father was sitting on the bed with his back leaning on the wall; Olaf was standing up near him and on the bed right in front of Father's a man was sitting down. It was King Harald.

The king was a strong man, a little taller than Father, but definitely shorter than Olaf. He had long black hair tied in a ponytail, and a dark thick beard carefully brushed, shaped and oiled.

The moment I entered the house, everybody stopped doing whatever they were doing and stared at me. I felt as if I had just interrupted an important conversation. The king immediately stood up and greeted me.

"You must be Sigurd then! I've heard many things about you, boy!" said the king while opening his arms to welcome me.

"Hello sir, it's an honour to meet you," I timidly replied. I have to admit, I was pretty nervous. I had never talked to a king before that occasion.

"Polite like your mother and probably strong like your father?" he said with a wide smile.

"I don't know about the last part..." I murmured.

"Stronger!" yelled Olaf.

We all looked at Father, waiting for confirmation from him. "Soon," he said.

"Well, anyway, why don't you sit with us Sigurd?" said the king pointing towards the backroom where the beds were. "Sure, sir."

There were four beds in this backroom. One for Olaf, one for Mother and Father, one for Grandmother, and one for my sister and me. I sat on the bed near the one where the king was sitting.

"So, Eirik, have you taught your son how to fight?" asked the king.

"Something I've taught. But he still has much to learn," said Father. I noticed how Father was very respectful to the king, but he didn't treat him like the others did. He treated him like a friend.

"That's a start!" said the king.

"He'll be alright! It's in his blood, after all!" yelled Olaf. I often thought he was incapable of talking without yelling.

"Well..." said Harald, "let's see what the boy wants, no?" He then turned towards me and placed his hand over my shoulder. "What do you want to do in life?"

I lowered my head and put my hand on my chest. It still burnt, I could still feel it. After a deep exhale, I looked the king in the eyes and said, "Well sir, I believe I don't have a choice."

It must have been the way I said it, the voice, or maybe my look. But the moment I pronounced those words, Father sat up straight and leaned forward. He then stared at me and with a serious and almost menacing voice he ordered, "Remove your shirt, Sigurd."

I still had my hand on my chest, where I felt the burning. I didn't want to show the sign to them. I was afraid of what their reaction might be, but, on the other hand, I really needed answers and perhaps some guidance. I removed my shirt. The scar was still visible, even though not as clear as before.

Several reactions happened simultaneously. Olaf yelled, "Odin, be praised!" while he brought his hands to his head. Mother screamed. I didn't notice that when Father asked me to remove my shirt, Mother and Grandmother stood up near the entrance of the backroom. Grandmother covered her mouth. She was visibly shocked. The king stood up with a jump and stared at me as if I was some creature from Niflheim.

Father froze. His eyes got bigger, and he clenched his fists strongly then slowly laid back again against the wall. "You can put your shirt on again now, Sigurd," he said.

I didn't dare ask why they reacted this way. I guess they knew what this meant.

"Did it just happen?" asked Father.

"Yes, I came running as soon as it happened."

I was trying to focus as much as possible on Father and our conversation. I wanted to ignore Mother crying in the other room, Grandmother comforting her, and Olaf and King Harald murmuring amongst them while looking at me in awe.

"Do you know what this means?" asked Father. He was extremely focused on me, on my eyes. You could see that nothing else mattered to him in the world except me at that moment. I felt the same. The only thing that existed in the entire world was Father, his ice-blue eyes, his scarred and wounded body, my burning chest and, finally, our conversation.

"I think I do. But Father, I don't know what to do. I'm scared," I honestly replied.

"If you weren't scared, you would be a madman. Because from now on, Sigurd, you're a man," he replied.

I finally started paying attention to what was happening outside of our conversation. Olaf and the king stopped murmuring and were completely focused on my conversation with Father. The king sat down again, Olaf dragged his back on the wall downwards until he sat on the floor. Grandmother and Mother were leaning on the wall at the entrance of the backroom, hugging each other.

"I understand. I'm not afraid of being a man. But I don't know what I have to do with Odin's curse or gift. I still don't know what it is..." I said while caressing my almost faded-away mark.

"It's none of these things, and both at the same time. It's a path, Sigurd. A purpose. It's what you'll be from now on if you survive. Whether it becomes a gift or a curse... That depends solely on you," said Father.

"What do I have to do now? How do I prepare myself? Where do I have to go? How can I know what to do?" I was getting desperate at this point. The uncertainty and fear were rising the more I thought about it.

"Calm down. That's the first thing you'll have to do now. If Odin has given you such a task, such a path in life, means that you're not an ordinary man. You'll be able to handle it if I'm not mistaken about you," said Father.

"Slowly things will unveil, Sigurd. You're lucky, you have guidance. Your father and I had none," said Olaf, strangely enough, without yelling, but talking calmly.

"Midgard is lucky to have someone like you, Sigurd," said the king while patting me on the back.

King Harald then turned towards Father and said, "I want to be informed of anything that happens, Eirik. If you need my assistance, you have but to ask."

He then stood up, greeted everybody, and left the house. After that, he left, and an awkward silence prevailed in the house.

"First things first! Set that mark in ink!" yelled Olaf, breaking the silence.

"Ink?" I asked.

"With what's coming your way, you'll need all the protection and strength that you can possibly summon," said Father.

Mother finally stopped crying. But it wasn't Grandmother or Olaf who made her stop. Father didn't even try to. It was Thrúd who managed to make Mother stop her grief.

"It's the will of the gods, Mother. The same will that gave you Sigurd and me is the one dictating our fate. Not accepting that is the same as not accepting us being born in the first place."

The moment my sister pronounced those words, we all stayed in silence. Even Father's jaw dropped. We couldn't believe how sometimes my sister could be a kid playing with mud or ash or laughing at Grandmother's jokes hiding herself in plain sight, and other times she could say things like these.

After she said that, she came down from Grandmother's lap and ran towards me. She jumped over me, hugging me. We fell on the bed where I was sitting. We played for a while. I loved tickling her. But then she focused her attention on my chest. The mark wasn't there anymore.

"Carry it with pride," she said while placing her hand on my chest.

Then she returned to Grandmother and went back to being the small child that she usually was.

Chapter 15

Loki's doings

We had completed three days of sacrifices so far. After another six days, the great *blót* would be over.

The days passed with little difference between them. We would wake up, do some chores, and have something to eat. Then we would get dressed up, go to Odin's temple, attend the sacrifices, talk to the gods, roam the temples and return.

Usually, we would go back to the town hall to drink and celebrate, but after what happened with Father, we celebrated the gods at home, in private. Gudrod, Knut, and Björn would join us often.

I got to know Gudrod better. He was an honourable man. Born as the son of a wealthy man, but ran away from his home to fulfil his destiny as a warrior, Odin's warrior. He later inherited his father's fortune and settled here.

"Was it hard for you, Gudrod?" I once asked him.

"Leaving my family was hard. My mother died giving birth and my father never married again. Both my older brothers died from disease. It was hard for me to leave my father and uncles to pursue a life of battle, blood, and death. I was the only thing he had left..." he melancholically replied.

"I'm sorry to hear that..." I said.

"Don't be sorry for me, Sigurd. I found a new family. During our time of battles and wars, we lost many brothers, but a few of us always managed to survive. I would do anything for your family. I will do anything that I can to protect and help you on this journey."

"Thank you, Gudrod. That means a lot to me."

"Don't you worry, young one, you have two fierce bears at your side..." he said while pointing his head towards Olaf.

During our fireplace talks, I learnt that, in order to become a berserker or, in very rare and unique cases, an Ulfhednar, a warrior would have to venture into the wilderness during winter. But not in any place. The warrior would have to survive in the mountains, where bears and wolves abound. If that wasn't enough, the warrior had to return with a new hide, a hide either of a bear or a wolf. The killing of these animals didn't have to occur by looking for them, but it had to occur by chance, by destiny. One single bear or one single wolf would have to challenge you. Only that way the hide could be accepted. After they explained this to me, I understood why they kept repeating, "If he survives," referring to both Björn and me.

I still didn't trust Björn, I didn't like how he introduced himself to me and how he looked at my sister. Our parents arranging their wedding was irrelevant to me. I didn't fully accept him. But I tolerated him. I had no choice.

One day, Björn asked a question that I found particularly interesting. He asked how they managed to get enraged, how they got into that trance where they were able to forget everything, even ignore pain and focus only on battle.

"Many of us help ourselves with mushrooms. They help us feel the gods inside us. Ignore everything that is not the gods and the enemy. Channel all our rage into one single purpose," said Knut.

"How do I know which ones to eat?" said Björn.

"Fate will guide you, Björn," replied Father with his usual intense look and solemn voice.

"Red ones, with white dots, Björn," said Olaf.

"Fate will make him choose the correct ones, Olaf!" reprimanded Father.

"Yes, I know Eirik. Fate will make him choose the red ones with white dots. Trust me Björn, if you eat any other mushroom, your arse will burn for many moons..." We all burst laughing, even Father smiled.

The last day of the *blót* arrived. Until now, the reception that we had amongst the people had been mixed. Some hated us and others loved us for what Father did and represented. The announcer at the *Thing*, the one that was desperate to condemn Father to death, was always seen whispering and conspiring, pointing his finger at us, and talking to traders who were friends of the men who attacked Father. I hated him. I'm sure it was him and the leader of the traders who planned the whole attack. One was butchered, and the other one, sadly enough, was still allowed to breathe.

The last sacrifice was made. The ninth dog, the ninth horse. No more men. The *völva* sacrificed two whilst Father, unwillingly, sacrificed seven.

Sadness filled people's hearts at the realisation that the *blót* had finally ended. The time to walk amongst the gods had come to an end and now everybody would have to return to where they came from and only a few would stay in Uppsala.

The purpose of our trip was to get closer to the gods, ask them for their blessings, and help us in our daily lives. We did that; we had some disturbances, but we did that. I wasn't sure of many things, but I had no doubt that in that place I had lived through more experiences than in my entire life.

I headed towards the grove one last time. The rotten corpses of the first sacrifices were still hanging, even though there wasn't much flesh left. Ravens had grown fat these last few days.

I sat on the floor, closed my eyes and talked to the gods. I asked Thor to give me strength. Freyr, to help us with our fields back home, hopefully, we would have a good harvest. I talked to Freya, Tyr, Heimdall... All of them.

My attention then was directed towards Loki. I knew he was behind all that happened to Father. I knew he saw Father the same way he often sees Thor, as Odin's favourite. The strong and valiant warrior who fights for the All-father while he hides in the shadows, behind his treachery.

While I was having these thoughts, I heard a voice, a familiar voice. "Don't underestimate him, Young Sigurd."

I opened my eyes. Everyone had left. I could now hear in the distance the huge feast that the town was having. Being the last day, people were drinking, dancing, eating and celebrating more than any other day.

In front of me, sitting on a tree stump, I found him, the old man.

"All-father?" I asked, amazed that he would present to me once again.

"The pain will lessen in time, Young Sigurd. Rage will take its place," said the old man. He wasn't even looking at me, but rather towards the town. His eye was lost in the nothingness.

"Pain, sir?" I asked.

"Just remember, boy. You can steer a boat but you have no power over the wind," said the old man with a profound and maybe even sad tone.

I stood up, confused and afraid. What was he referring to?

"Run Sigurd, even if it's too late. Run home."

I didn't question his command. I ran as fast as my legs would allow me.

While I was sprinting through the town, I noticed how wild the celebrations were. Most of the people were either in the town hall, completely drunk, or lying on the ground somewhere along the way. The whole town was drunk. I must have lost the notion of time in the grove.

I passed in front of the town hall and saw Gudrod, Olaf, Father, Knut and his son near the entrance. They were drinking and talking.

Olaf caught me mid-air while I was sprinting past them.

"What's the rush, young one?" asked Olaf, yelling and laughing.

"Come join us, Sigurd!" yelled Knut while offering me a horn full of mead.

"I must go! Release me! I must go home! Now!" I said in desperation.

I must have yelled very loudly because other men who were standing by the entrance of the hall stopped doing what they were doing and started staring at me, wondering what was happening.

Father grabbed me from my chest with one hand, he lifted me from Olaf's arms and dropped me on the floor. He didn't say a word. He simply dropped me on the floor, got close to me and looked me in the eye. After a brief moment, his eyes opened wide, and he started running towards Olaf's house like a hound. He was still recovering from his wounds but somehow forgot about them and ran faster than lightning.

We followed Father even though we couldn't catch up to him. As we approached Olaf's house, we saw the door half open. Father dived into the house, throwing himself against the door with his shoulder to open it wider.

Silence upon his entrance. That's all that we heard. We finally reached the house. I was the first one to get there. Björn was right behind me, then Knut and finally the two heavyweights, Olaf and Gudrod.

I entered the house and saw Father standing in the middle of it. He was stiff, his hands were closed in fists. He was shivering. It looked like he couldn't move. The house was sacked. Chairs were broken and pieces of wood, plates and cloth were scattered all over the place. Everything was a mess.

I walked behind him very slowly. I could feel my heart in my mouth. My stomach was aching, and I felt cold sweat and goosebumps.

As soon as I got closer to him, he said with the deepest and most menacing voice I ever heard in my life, "Don't take another step, Sigurd."

I froze where I stood, but I had to find the courage. I heard how the others had arrived, but stood by the door. It took me all the courage that I had to take that next step. And I forever wish that I didn't.

Behind the table that was flipped and standing on its side, I could see the entrance to the backroom. A foot with a few streams of blood could be seen from where I was standing. A woman's foot.

I started crying without even knowing exactly what had happened. Tears dropped from my eyes, but I kept my posture high and took another step. Now I was exactly near Father, and I could perfectly see whose foot it was.

On the bed where Father had lain during his recovery, I saw a woman. She had her dress ripped off in many places, her belly was cut open, and she had streams of blood coming down her thighs. Her face had been beaten so hard that it was not recognisable anymore. But her hair was unique, easily recognisable. She had several flowers attached to her white and grey hair. It was Grandmother…

The world seemed to have crushed and crumbled over me. I felt the pain of a thousand spears piercing my body. But I had to keep walking. I still didn't know what happened to Mother and my sister.

I heard the others start to enter the house. From what I heard, Olaf grabbed and hugged Father. I could hear Olaf crying. I heard Björn entering the house and with a desperate whisper called for my sister and wanted to rush into the house, but Knut grabbed him.

I got near Grandmother's bloody foot. I could clearly see the entirety of the backroom. It was empty except for Grandmother's dead body. I could not bear to see her that way, so I grabbed a piece of fur and placed it over her.

The rage was such that tears would not stop running down my face. I didn't want to kill whoever did this. I wanted to destroy him. But my priority was Mother and my sister.

I rushed out and started yelling, calling for them. Soon after I started calling for them, I saw the announcer from the *Thing* and other traders nearby. They came drawn by curiosity. More people started gathering.

I went back inside. I needed help. Father was still stiff as a rock. He didn't pronounce a word, nor did he move. Olaf was hugging him still, but Father would not move his watery eyes from Grandmother. Gudrod was near Grandmother, fixing her with the utmost care and respect. He also was sniffing and crying, but doing his best to hide it.

Knut was in a corner with his son, still grabbing him. Björn pushed his father away, ran out of the house and started desperately to look for my sister.

I didn't know what to do. I went back outside, and I saw a circle of people surrounding the entrance of the house.

I was looking at everyone in their faces. Perhaps I could find Mother's face amongst the crowd. While turning and yelling, calling for Mother and my sister, I heard a voice elevating itself from the murmurs of the crowd.

"The gods' punishment was delayed, but just," said the voice.

I immediately focused my attention towards the source of the voice. It was the announcer, easily identifiable by his pale skin and lazy belly.

My rage was rising by the moment. I shivered when I heard what this weasel had said and started picturing in my head a thousand ways to torture him.

"Oh! Have a look at the pup! He has his father's menacing and insolent eyes. The entire family disrespects this town and the gods," said the announcer.

After saying this, I heard a voice that made me want to run, a dark, deep and menacing voice that sounded like it came from Hel.

"Where are they," said the voice. It wasn't a question, but a command.

It came from the entrance of Olaf's house. I turned towards that direction and there stood Father. Near him Gudrod, with his hands stained with Grandmother's blood, Olaf with his battle-axe and Knut too. They all had red, teary eyes.

"What is this? The parade of the crying warriors? Wolf-warrior, beast. If you can't control your wife, don't expect other men to know her whereabouts," said the announcer mockingly.

Suddenly, a strong hand pressed the announcer's arm with such strength that he screamed as if he had been pierced by a dagger. It was King Harald. He emerged from the crowd, holding the announcer by the arm and slightly lifting him from the ground. The announcer had to walk on his toes in order to keep in contact with the ground.

The king dragged the announcer into the middle of the circle formed in front of the entrance of Olaf's house and threw him on the ground.

"Talk now, pig, and I shall make it quick," said the king.

"What is this!" a voice from the crowd exclaimed. "What is this nonsense, king?!"

It was Earl Svein. "I demand an explanation right now. This man is my trusted man, and this is still my town, my land. You all have had our hospitality in exchange for what? Death? Disrespect?" claimed the chief.

The announcer was holding his arm and was gasping. He then implored his lord. "Please, lord. Help me, they're blaming me for what the gods have justly done!"

"Where. Are. They," repeated Father, with the same menacing and deadly tone.

"Silent!" yelled Chief Svein.

"His arm is bleeding, sir!" said someone from the crowd.

We turned towards the announcer, the chief's trusted man, and we saw that between the fingers that were holding his arm, blood started to pour.

The strong king grabbed the man from his shirt and ripped it open with three swift and aggressive movements.

"Mighty as I may be, I'm yet to pierce a man's flesh with just my hands!" said the king, stepping aside and revealing a fresh-cut wound in the announcer's arm.

"You!" yelled Olaf.

"It wasn't me!" screamed in a panic the wounded man, "It was Loki!"

The rage that had been rising since I entered Olaf's house, the image of Grandmother's body after she had been beaten, tortured and probably raped... I couldn't control it anymore.

When I realised what had happened, my small axe, the one that I always carried with me near my knife, was flying towards the pig's direction. I don't even recall grabbing and throwing it.

It hit directly at the man's throat. Blood started pouring out like a waterfall. He looked at me with a mixture of fear and surprise while fighting to breathe. I smiled. I still had Grandmother's image in my head.

The miserable man died in a puddle of blood, half-naked, in the mud. I stared at him for a while. I noticed that around me chaos had been unleashed, but I couldn't stop staring at this man's body with my axe planted in his throat.

From here, time almost stopped. Everything seemed to be transcurring at half the normal speed, like in a dream. The traders launched themselves towards me and were stopped by King Harald and his men. Olaf, Gudrod and Knut started cutting them to pieces. Some of the townspeople who hated us joined the brawl. Somehow, nobody managed to touch me. I was still in the centre of the improvised circle formed around Olaf's house, me and the dead man.

Suddenly, I felt a force lifting me from the ground and carrying me some feet away. It was Father. Strangely enough, he didn't join the battle. He looked distraught, sad, finished.

"Run Sigurd, run into the woods. Run far from here," he said.

"Father? But..." I mumbled.

"Sigurd. Have a look at what's happening," he insisted while turning my head towards the brawl.

In the middle of it, King Harald was being escorted out of the brawl by his guards, while slicing whoever tried to attack him. Olaf, Gudrod and Knut were fighting five men each. It was a matter of time before they would fall. Some men joined on our side, but most of the men were on the other side. The chief was shouting and commanding the town guards to slay all of us.

"I'm sorry Father, I'm... I just... I don't even know how... I-"

"Son, you did nothing wrong. What you did was the gods will. And it's done. But you killed the most trusted man of the chieftain of one of Sweden's most important towns. They won't let it go until they kill you."

Some men started disengaging the brawl and running towards us. As soon as they got close enough, Father, who was bending over talking to me, stood up and with an incredible speed killed four attackers with his axe. The other two attackers started running backwards and joined the brawl again, calling reinforcements.

"Don't worry about us, Sigurd. Save yourself. Run into the woods. Survive. Your path starts here!" he yelled to me while pushing me away and starting to fight off another group of men that came our way.

I ran towards the western gate, and then towards the river nearby where Olaf, Father, and I went fishing from time to time. Tears were running down my cheeks while the noise of battle faded behind me.

I crossed the river by jumping on some of the protruding rocks and kept running, following it. Turning around and looking at the town, I couldn't see what was happening behind the walls. Some noise of battle could still be heard fading in the distance. There was a big fire. It was probably Olaf's house.

I was desperate to go back, to help, to fight. I wanted to find Mother and my sister, to save Father, Olaf, Gudrod and Knut... But I couldn't. Father's command was clear and had to be obeyed. I had to survive.

Chapter 16

Survive

After circumambulating the hill that was in front of the eastern gate, from where we arrived in the town almost a moon ago, I figured that whoever was sent to capture me would look for me exactly where I was standing. I couldn't run in the exact opposite direction from where we came from. That would be too obvious and also would take me further south, far away from home. But I couldn't trace the exact steps that brought us here, because they would expect that too.

I had to head towards home by going north, following a parallel road from the one that we took. It would take double the time, but it would be safer, or so I hoped.

My priorities were clear: Don't get captured, don't die from animals, don't die from cold or hunger. In that order.

I headed towards a big hill that was further north. I would camp there for the night and then head northwest. Whenever I got to Norway, I would start heading towards Hladir, my hometown. That was the plan.

To get to that big hill, I had to cross a valley and then climb up the hill and make camp. The valley, luckily for me, had plenty of trees and high bushes. Perfect for hiding.

While I was crossing it, I heard men in the distance; they were circumambulating the hill from the opposite side I did and started crossing the valley towards the east. Our paths would cross in a matter of moments.

I threw myself to the ground and started walking like a snake would, avoiding at all costs being spotted. Reaching a big spruce at a safe distance from the men, I climbed the tree and waited there, hiding in the leaves.

The group of men passed right under the branches after a couple of moments. I recognised them easily. Two of them were with the group of traders and four of them were the chieftain's guard. They were talking about how much they wanted to land their hands on me and how they wished they could lay their hands on Mother and my sister. That was good news. It meant that they were still hidden somewhere, hopefully safe.

As soon as the men reached a considerable distance from my position, I left the camouflage of the leaves and started heading towards the big hill again.

I got to the feet of the hill a little before dusk. Finding shelter was now my priority. I started climbing and looking for someplace where I could hide and, hopefully, light a fire. It wasn't very cold but, nonetheless, nights were cold without proper clothes and furs.

Right when the last light was leaving the hill, I spotted a small cave a few feet from where I was standing. It was almost in the middle of the hill. The cave entrance was facing towards the town, but the other hill, the smaller one, was between the town and this hill, and being a cave, maybe a small fire would not be seen at night.

I approached the cave with care, for I knew caves were home to many creatures. While heading towards the dark entrance, I gathered some wood and sticks for lighting a fire. I dropped the wood and sticks on a small pile near the entrance, wielded my knife and started regretting not having recovered my axe from the announcer's throat.

I threw a couple of stones in the cave to measure the depth of it and, if it was the case, draw the owner of the cave to come out and face me. If I were to die, I would have preferred to be killed by an animal rather than Sven's men.

No response was heard. No growls nor movement. But, by the sound of it, the cave seemed deep enough. I decided to light a fire at the entrance, the smallest fire that I could light, and explore the cave with an improvised torch.

After I had my torch lit, I entered the cave with care, but with haste. I didn't want anybody to see that small light in the night's darkness. While entering the cave, I started thinking that it was truly strange that I wore my pouch, knife, and axe that day. It was a sacrifice day, the last one, and for some reason, I decided to wear all of this under the ceremonial robes.

Suddenly, I heard a crack. Looking downwards, I realised I had stepped on some bones. They weren't remains from naturally deceased animals, but rather of some illegal sacrifice. A ritual had taken place there and, by the looks of it, wasn't an accepted one. People usually went to the temples to make sacrifices and other spiritual rituals. Hiding in a cave was a bad sign. Only people with dark purposes would hide in a cave to perform dark magic.

This cave wasn't safe, if people made rituals in it meant that they knew of its existence, and it was too close to the town. But, at this point, I had no other choice than to stay there for the night.

The cave continued for several feet into the depth of the hill and, at a certain point, it turned left, continued for a few feet, and stopped. That was the perfect spot for a fire. Hopefully, nobody would discover me. I set a fire and surrounded it with big stones, then I went out into the darkness and fetched some tree branches to make myself a bed.

Before closing my eyes and giving myself to the fatigue, I thought about Grandmother, and how I saw her for the last time. I wondered where Mother and my sister were, and if they were safe. And, finally, I thought of Olaf, Gudrod, Knut and Father... Definitely dead. I was left alone now.

My goal was to survive, return to our town in Norway, and tell what had happened. I needed to save my strength for finding and saving Mother and Thrúd. I couldn't allow myself to fall into the trap of self-pity.

With these thoughts, I closed my eyes and did my best to sleep through the rage, sadness, and fear. Before falling asleep, I remember feeling my cheeks wet with tears. They never stopped pouring during the night.

At first light, I woke up. I slept little but at least I rested my body. Trying my best to hide my presence from the cave, I threw out the big stones, tree branches and any other thing that wasn't there the night before. I couldn't afford to be tracked down that easily.

I kept my course north, at least for a couple of days, until I felt I could start heading west towards Norway.

I ate what I found, mostly berries, bird eggs, some small animals that I could easily catch and any edible mushroom that I could recognise. In my pouch I had some string, with it I made myself a fishing spear by attaching my knife to a long rod. I managed to fish a couple of times like that, but it was too risky. I could lose my knife and then I wouldn't have anything to defend myself, hunt or survive.

Days passed, and I didn't see any big animals or people. I arrived at a place with dense bushes and trees. I decided to skirt it rather than cross it. Alongside the border, there was a strange rock formation, almost forming a terrace from which you could see the entire valley.

I was walking in the corridor formed between the edge of the heavy vegetation area and the steep rock wall, watching my feet and immersed in my thoughts, as I always do. Suddenly, I heard a deep, guttural growl coming from above me. I instantly froze. Some small stones rolled down the rock wall. The wall at this point of the way was a few feet taller than me.

When I raised my eyes, still without moving a single muscle of my body, I saw the face of a big wolf staring at me from the edge of the wall, prepared to pounce. I took a small step backwards and as soon as I made that minuscule movement, the wolf aggressively moved further towards the edge of the small cliff.

I could now see that it wasn't alone. It had three or four cubs with it and another five or six wolves near them. They were all standing alert, but none of them were adopting such an extreme attacking position as the wolf on the edge. Probably was the mother of the cubs.

I took another step backwards, towards the dense vegetation. The moment my foot touched the ground again, the mother wolf jumped down the rock wall and stood right near it, advancing extremely slowly while intensifying her growling. This time, another three wolves followed her and adopted the same attacking position as her. The other wolves stayed on top of the rock wall with the cubs.

The sight of these four animals showing me their teeth, their hair up and the growl growing louder and louder was terrifying. They were slowly advancing towards me. Eventually, they would pounce and tear me to pieces.

I was going to die. At this moment, Grandmother came to mind, lying on the bed in a puddle of blood. I also thought of Father, Olaf, Knut, Gudrod... They died fighting for me and now I would get killed by a pack of wolves. I was supposed to be one of Odin's warriors, to pass my test of defeating a wolf or a bear in some mystical way. None of that made any sense now. I grabbed my knife while tears ran down my cheeks. I didn't know if I was feeling more afraid of dying or sad thinking about how my family had been destroyed, how I was left alone to fend for myself.

While I was summoning all the strength inside me to face my end, I heard the sound of a big crack behind me. The wolves suddenly started taking steps backwards and their eyes and focus shifted towards something way higher than me. They felt very threatened.

I heard a strange sound, like a mixture between a very fatigued and a very excited breathing. I never heard something like that before. Slowly, I turned to see what generated such strange and intense noises and I almost fainted. A huge brown bear was right behind the bush that was at my back. It was a few feet away from me and was moving towards me nervously. Its breathing was intensifying at an incredible speed. Its mouth drooled.

As it got closer, I realised it was almost as tall as Father was, but it was still on four legs. It got right near me and I couldn't move. The sheer panic blocked my body. It was completely ignoring the wolves and focusing only on me. It made sense because I was closer. Once it got right in front of me, it stood on two feet and bellowed so loudly that the wolves scattered. I finally got control of my body again, even if it was just for an instant, and ran.

I still don't understand why, but I ran past the bear instead of in the opposite direction. Maybe because I knew that the rock wall was impossible for me to climb, or maybe because if I was about to get killed, at least it would be while heading towards home.

I ran as fast as I could. While running, I heard strong stomps behind me. I almost felt how the ground was shaking. I've always been fast. Nobody had ever outrun me in my life. Everybody always said that I was too fast for my age. The only time that I can remember myself being outran was a few days earlier when Father ran towards Olaf's house.

Despite my speed, I could feel the stomps getting closer and closer. At a given moment, I felt how the bear's paw almost hit my back. That miss gave me some feet of advantage in the race. But it wasn't enough. I saw a tall pine tree a few feet in front of me. It looked easy to climb. I continued running. The stomps were almost on top of me. I could almost feel the bear's breath on my nape.

I heard a change in the bear's noises. It meant he was about to attack. I jumped forward with all the strength that I had. The paw hit my pants but missed my flesh. I had reached the pine tree.

I had now very little time to try to put as much distance between the huge beast and me. I climbed the tree as fast as I could. This might have been the worst idea. Bears are exceptional climbers, but it was the only option that I had. I jumped from one branch to the next. My arms and legs were full of blood. The sound of branches and sticks breaking, my panicked gasping and the noise of cloth tearing was only interrupted by the bear's sounds while climbing the tree right below me. I had to make it to the tallest branch or the bear would be able to grab one of my legs and drag me down to my demise.

The paws were tearing the pine tree's bark half a foot from my own feet, almost reaching my toes, but I didn't have time to look downwards. I only had to climb as much as possible and hope that no branches would break and that, eventually, the bear would desist.

The beast didn't desist, but the branch where it was standing did. The bear fell and immediately tried climbing again. At that point, I was in the tallest part of the tree. Above me, branches that wouldn't hold my weight.

After several attempts, the bear stopped trying to climb the tree, instead, it would walk back and forth beneath the pine tree. The animal knew that I would have to climb down to drink or eat, eventually.

I stayed on that pine tree the whole day, getting hit by the sun, the rain and the wind. I was starving and extremely thirsty. The afternoon came, and the bear was still there. It would go to a nearby stream to drink water and then come back and guard the tree. During the later evening, the animal would sleep behind a bush near the pine tree's trunk.

It was a big territorial male bear, most probably, and I stepped into his domain. It was my fate to be killed or to make a run for it. But I couldn't climb down with it being there. I decided that whenever the bear would get far from the tree, I would climb down and attempt an escape.

I slept on the tree that night. Being afraid that the shivering from the cold would make me break a branch or fall, I tried curling into a ball and hugging the trunk of the tree, the least exposed part of it. Hopefully, the branches and the leaves would help me protect myself from the wind a little.

When morning came, the bear was still there. It tried climbing up several times during the night and also during the early morning, but it failed. The morning passed and so did the day. I didn't know if I was awake or sleeping. My eyes were closed most of the time, or at least half closed. I couldn't see properly. Everything was blurry. I got sunburned during the day, sometimes wet from sporadic rain and hit by the wind. During the evening and the night, I froze. My whole body was hurting. I felt cold and warm at the same time.

At one point during the afternoon, I was looking towards the rock formation while still hearing the bear beneath me trying to climb and making frustrated noises. To my surprise, I saw Grandmother walking on the rock cliff, that sort of terrace formation on top of the bushes and at the same height as the tree canopy. She stopped at the same spot where the wolf was ready to pounce on me the previous day. She was wearing a long white dress and was barefoot. Her hair was full of flowers and leaves, she had all her best jewellery on.

My vision was blurry, but I could see her clearly, even though she was quite far away. She smiled at me and put her hand on her left chest. She then closed her hand into a fist and patted her chest twice. Suddenly, the bear made a tremendous noise, and the tree shook so hard that I almost fell. I looked downwards, and the bear was standing on two legs pushing the trunk of the pine tree, shaking it in desperation. After a couple of attempts, the animal left in frustration. I looked back at the rock formation and Grandmother wasn't there anymore.

What did she mean by this? Was I losing my mind? Or did she mean something about the left chest where Odin's mark had appeared?

I decided to climb down. I was going to die from hunger, cold, or thirst. Eventually, I would have fallen from the tree and that would have been my end. If I was to die, at least it had to be while standing on my feet.

I climbed down as fast as I could, but I was sloppy. My legs and arms were weak, my body sore, and my strength wasn't there at all. I was almost dropping from one branch to the other. Somehow, I made it to the ground without falling. The moment my feet touched the ground, I felt panic rising in me. The bear was near. I knew it; it was somewhere behind the bushes.

I walked towards the north. My plan was still the same: get to the north of Sweden and then go west towards home. It was a huge detour but necessary, considering what had happened at Uppsala.

If I hadn't been that weak, I would have run, but my body could barely walk. After a few feet, I heard a vast noise behind me. The bear must have returned to the pine tree and didn't find its meal there. I heard it sniffing and getting closer and closer to me. It was the end.

There was a small stream of water in front of me, only a few feet deep. I crossed it as fast as I could and right when I did, the bushes behind me opened. I turned to look behind me, tripped, and fell. Strength had completely abandoned me and I couldn't stand up again. The big brown bear started walking towards me. I was finished.

Destiny would reunite me with my family. I just hoped that Mother and my sister had survived somehow, at least them.

I was ready to die. I was terrorised by the pain, but ready for the outcome of it. The animal started crossing the stream when it suddenly halted. Something caught his attention, something so much more important than his precious prize. I tried to drag myself away from him. I knew it would make no difference, but I couldn't help it.

The bear resumed his march towards his feast. I was terrorised when, suddenly, the image of Father came to mind. Father in the tent with the men who wanted to murder him. I remembered and felt inside me how he breathed, how he slowly changed into an enraged animal ready to rip his prey apart.

I took my knife, turned myself towards the bear and, while still dragging my body backwards, I tried to at least face him. I was Sigurd Eiriksson. My uncle and my father were the legendary Odin's Wolves. I would not die fleeing, attacked from behind. I would face my death.

The moment he put his paw on the other side of the stream, a few feet from where I was dragging myself, I growled and shouted at him. My breathing sped up. I didn't care about myself anymore. I didn't feel fear anymore. I just wanted to get it over with. The only feeling that I had inside me was rage. I could see Grandmother's body, my chest's mark, the announcer mocking us, Father enraged in the tent, the sacrificed bodies hanging… I started transforming into the animal that was about to kill me. I mumbled some words that I didn't even comprehend. They sounded like that ancient language that the *völva*, Father, Grandmother, and Olaf occasionally spoke.

The bear stopped again. This time it stood up on two legs and started sniffing the air. Its ears were moving in all directions. Its nose smelled every single thing that the breeze could bring to it. I must have shown him I was dangerous too, that I could be a threat, that the blood that ran through my veins was mighty. While the bear was still standing, I heard a horn being blown in the wind. The animal dropped on its four legs and ran in the opposite direction, disappearing through the bushes.

I couldn't believe it. I was in the middle of nowhere. There weren't many reasons to be in this place. Why would people venture there? Why would they be blowing a horn? Was it maybe the god Heimdall blowing his horn Gjallarhorn?

With this last thought, my eyes closed, and I lost my conscience.

Chapter 17

Gjallarhorn

I started hearing chatter at first. Some I understood, other words I didn't. I could hear a woman talking in two different languages and a man answering in both. One of them was his native tongue, my language. I occasionally heard a younger voice answering, but only with single words.

The sounds of conversation were distant as if they came from another world. Everything was still dark. I tried to open my eyes, to wake up, to stand up and resume my journey, but I couldn't.

I didn't even know if I was dead or alive if I was lying down or not. My mind seemed to float in the nothingness, in the dark. I couldn't feel my body. I just heard occasional chatter fading in the distance.

"You need to tend to his wounds or he'll die, Mielikki," the male voice said.

Then a very gentle female voice replied in an incredibly beautiful language, the most beautiful that I ever heard. It was so melodic, so relaxing that I fell deeper into my unconsciousness.

Seemed like an eternity had passed when I heard the male voice again. "We should wake him up, my love. Thorstein, go fetch more wood, we'll stay here the night," said the gentle male voice.

I felt a light pressure on my arm, like a feather. I started feeling my body again. Slowly, I was regaining consciousness. The more I gained it, the more the pain rose. My body was covered with wounds and scratches from running and climbing, trying to escape the bear. I also had nothing to eat or drink for days.

My senses were finally getting back to me. I heard a fire crackling, and a breeze blowing through tree leaves, but I felt sheltered. The noise was muffled by something. I smelled smoke, roasted meat and some extravagant herbs concoction. Slowly I realised I wasn't on the ground, but on some improvised bed. I had what appeared to be fur over me, but it was softer and warmer than usual. I was sweating but yet I was cold, my whole body hurt.

Finally, I started slowly opening my eyes, not by choice but because it was extremely difficult to do so. Once I succeeded, I saw a beautiful woman sitting next to me, her long hair was silver, and she was very short in stature, the shortest I'd ever seen in my life, but she had an incredibly wide smile and a loving look. But her eyes, I would never forget those eyes, for I had seen nothing like that in my life; she had such light and beautiful eyes, the colour of delicate pale silver but with the strength of a light grey storm sky. She was caressing my head and whispering something to me in that beautiful language that she spoke.

Confused, I struggled to understand what was happening, where I was and who she was. I was probably dead and this could be a Valkyrie welcoming me to Valhöll. But, why would she? I wasn't even a warrior yet. And my death… couldn't have been an honourable one. Surely not honourable enough to deserve to join Uncle Harald and Father in the Shield Hall.

"Welcome to our tent, boy," said a man with a strong Norwegian accent.

It felt like home, almost. It was a southern Norwegian accent, but nevertheless, it reminded me of home. I looked upwards, and a man was standing near this beautiful woman. He was of slightly above-average height, but very muscular and strong. He had very dark skin for a Scandinavian, and coal-black hair and eyes. His beard was long, thick, well-curated and black, very black. He had some inked inscriptions on his arm that I could see, some of them I recognised, some protection runes, for example; but others were unknown to me.

"Tent?" I struggled to say.

"Yes, boy. Our tent. You were lucky our son found you. You would have died," the man said.

"Am I not dead?" I asked, without even thinking about what I was saying.

"No, you are not dead, for now," said the beautiful woman with a very strong accent, an accent that I had never heard before.

"Let me tend your wounds or you won't survive the night, little one," she gently said while trying to grab my arm and rub a wet piece of cloth on some of my wounds.

I let her do that. I would let her do anything. Since I heard her voice, I was under a spell.

"Well, that's an improvement," said the man.

"An improvement sir?" I asked.

"You tried to stab us every time we tried to touch you. Once I took your knife, you started throwing punches," the man replied with a smirk.

"I did that?" I replied, astonished while trying to sit up.

"You have the heart of a fighter, boy. But the important thing is that-" he started saying when suddenly he interrupted his speech and stared at me.

At the same time, the woman stopped doing what she was doing and froze.

"What?" I asked, "What's the matter?"

They were staring at my chest, my left chest, to be precise. Oh, no! Maybe Odin's mark manifested again? Maybe they saw it? I could feel my chest burning the same way that I felt it when I got the mark at Odin's temple.

The woman extended her arm slowly and started moving my shirt, exposing my chest. I grabbed her hand as a reflex act.

"What are you doing?" I asked.

"Look," she said with a thread of voice and a worried face.

I looked downwards while releasing her arm. She slightly opened my torn shirt and a big wound filled with yellow liquid was revealed. I fainted.

I heard the woman nervously talking to her husband while I was fading deeper into the darkness of nothingness. "Come, Ragnar! Help me! It has a small piece of wood lodged inside it. It'll get worse..." I heard before everything went silent again.

I was in total darkness. Then I saw myself in a warship navigating through a black narrow river. Everything around me was covered in a dense fog. I headed towards the prow and leaned on the dragon's head of the warship. Staring at the shore, I suddenly saw my sister waving at me, crying. Then Mother also waved at me. I started crying heavily and turned my head towards the other shore, and there I saw Father standing proud and tall, with his two axes in his waist and his arms crossed, nodding at me as I passed in front of him.

After him, Grandmother was there, wearing a white dress, her hair full of flowers and leaves, waving at me too. I looked back at the other shore and I saw Olaf, followed by Gudrod. Then I turned my head and saw at the opposite shore Knut and Björn.

I started shouting and crying. Not only I couldn't save them, but they died saving my life, and I threw it away. I wasn't as strong as they had hoped. Not worthy at all of following Father's steps. Not worthy of being his son.

I then looked forward and in front of me, beyond the dragon's head, there was a huge waterfall. The waterfall fell into a lake of fire. An immense cloud of steam elevated from the base of the waterfall. I panicked and looked at the sides and saw all the people that I cared about on each side of the narrow black river. They had their arms extended pointing towards the waterfall, and their facial expressions were serious, menacing. The boat headed inevitably towards the precipice. I hugged the dragon's head and held on to it as strongly as I could before falling into the fire lake. While falling, I felt the heat of the fire getting closer to my face and right before impact; I woke up.

I was sitting on the bed, shouting my lungs out until my throat wouldn't emit any sounds. I was completely soaked and so was the bed, my clothes, and the weird fur I had on me. The beautiful woman and her husband were sitting next to me, worried, powerless.

A boy a few winters older than me was at the entrance of the tent. He had darker than usual skin colour, long dark hair with some light reflexes and light blue eyes. He was staring at me. Our eyes met. His look was intense and inquisitive.

My body couldn't shout any longer. A silent shout followed as if my body wanted or needed to continue, but my throat couldn't take it anymore. Tears came out of my eyes and I crumbled down again, losing my conscience.

I don't know how much time passed, it could have been days. But I started feeling some warm liquid passing through my mouth and throat. I slowly gained consciousness and found that I had been put in a sitting position. The beautiful woman was feeding me some warm soup and moving my mouth with her hand to help me swallow while unconscious. The moment I was aware of this, I swallowed by myself and slowly opened my eyes.

"He's awake!" she initially exclaimed, then continued shouting in her beautiful language.

She put the bowl of soup on the ground and jumped outside, shouting and calling for her husband. Immediately, her husband came into the tent with her and they both sat near me.

"How are you feeling, boy?" the man gently asked.

"He's back from Tuonela," said the woman.

"From where?" I asked, confused.

The woman replied something in her language, then added "It doesn't matter. What matters is that you made it. For how long didn't you eat or drink?"

"Drink… Not that long. Maybe a day or so before you found me. Eat… I don't remember. I was already starving when I encountered the wolves and… the bear," I replied while struggling to remember.

"Tonight you'll eat proper food. For now, soup," she said while picking up the soup bowl to feed me again.

"Thank you very much, but I think I can eat by myself. I don't want to be a nuisance," I said while gently grabbing the bowl from her hand and trying to sit up straight by myself.

I realised the boy was at the entrance of the tent and left as soon as I pronounced those words.

"Slow. Go slowly now," she said.

I noticed that most of the wounds in my arms and legs were almost healed; they weren't that serious, to begin with. As I started to sit up straight a tremendous pain came from my left chest. It hurt a lot, but not nearly as much as when I saw it the first time.

It took me a long time to finally sit up. I never realised how important my chest muscle was until that moment. Every little movement would make it hurt. I started eating by myself and the couple sat back on some small stools.

"So, now that you're feeling better and are out of danger. I'm Ragnar 'The Black', she's my beautiful wife, Mielikki. And you may have seen our elusive son, Thorstein. We're travelling north. And you boy, despite being the luckiest boy that I ever set my eyes on, who are you?" said the man.

"Luckiest?" I asked while having a look at my body full of bandages, wounds and torn clothes.

"You survived, didn't you?" added Ragnar.

"Yes, I guess so," I murmured while still contemplating my clothes and bandages.

"Indeed. What are the chances that you lost consciousness exactly on our path home? And, not only that, what are the chances that my son found you in the middle of that dense bushy area?" said Ragnar, smiling at me.

The man was right. The chances of them finding me were very slim, close to none. I lost consciousness in the middle of some bushes near the small stream of water. It was impossible to find me. And the horn? Why blow the horn exactly at that moment?

"Yes, sir. Thinking about it, I was extremely lucky," I replied while touching my left chest, trying to find Odin's mark. The moment my hand landed on my wound, I screamed.

"Easy boy! It's not healed yet!" reprimanded Mielikki.

"Yes, sorry. You're right..." I replied, almost talking to myself.

This was fate. Odin must have sent these people to save me from the bear's paws. Otherwise, there isn't any other explanation.

"So, who are you? Where do you come from? And what were you doing all alone in such a dangerous place? I'm surprised you didn't get killed by a wolf or a bear or even a boar..." said Ragnar.

"Well, sir… I didn't get killed by a bear only because someone blew a horn. I guess you did."

"Hmmmm… No. We didn't! We don't even own a horn. It must have been Heimdall blowing Gjallarhorn!" yelled Ragnar while widely smiling.

"Sir…" I staggered.

"Yes, boy?"

"I can see a horn hanging over there. As a matter of fact, I see three of them," I said while pointing at a pile of furs, hides, pouches, bags and horns hanging from a pole inside the tent.

Ragnar started laughing and shrugged, then Mielikki slapped him on the arm and, with her thick accent, reprimanded him, "Is this the time for jokes, Ragnar?"

"Well my love, the boy is out of danger, no?" replied the dark-skinned man while winking at me.

"We blow the horn while crossing these lands because we know that the population of wild animals is huge here, especially bears. And, in my culture, we respect the 'dweller of the land'. Our forefathers walk the land adopting the form of this creature. So we try to frighten them to avoid confrontation while crossing their territory," explained Mielikki with a sweet voice while ignoring her husband and smiling at me.

"Oh, I understand. In my culture, we kill them when they're too close to our towns and also for fur. Sometimes we might seek a confrontation with them to prove our strength and might. We respect this animal so much that defeating it means a lot," I proudly replied.

Mielikki murmured something in her native language while looking downwards when she heard this. Then she looked at me again and said while pointing towards Ragnar with a head motion "I know. I know your culture very well."

She then laughed and kissed her husband on the cheek.

"You haven't told us who you are and how come we found you in the conditions that we did…" said Mielikki.

"Yes, sorry. I'm Eirik Haraldsson," I convincingly said.

I don't even know why I lied but, although these people were very nice to me and even saved my life, I couldn't trust them. I didn't know where their allegiance fell or what they knew.

"My family was attacked, robbed, and murdered somewhere in Sweden. I don't know the exact place. We were travelling to visit family. I managed to escape, tried to survive and almost failed at it," I continued, completing my lie and hoping to make it convincing.

The couple looked at each other and smiled.

"But you're Norwegian, from the North, am I right?" asked Ragnar.

"Yes sir, how do you kno-? Ah! My accent..." I replied while feeling quite stupid and still nervous from lying.

"Yes, 'Eirik Haraldsson', your accent," he said while standing up and going outside, giggling.

"Why is he laughing?" I asked Mielikki, feeling offended.

"I don't know Eirik. But it's nice to see him joking and laughing. You don't want to see him angry, ever," she replied to me while gently placing her hand on my shoulder leading me towards the bed so that I could lie down again.

"Rest now, Eirik. You'll recover your strength today. Tomorrow we'll start travelling again," she said in her sweet voice.

With that beautiful sound, I closed my eyes and slowly fell into a comfortable and deep sleep.

Chapter 18

True love

I spent the day napping and drinking soup, feeling stronger after each sip.

Finally, while being left alone in the tent, I managed to completely sit on the bed. I stayed in that position for a long time, trying to remember everything that had happened and also trying to assess how my body was reacting.

Suddenly, the image of Father came into mind. When he was on the bed at Olaf's house after he massacred those men. My wounds were nothing compared to his, and still a little after that, he dragged himself to The Great Temple for the *blót*... I was weak.

I gathered all my strength and tried to stand up. My chest was hurting, but I had to resist the pain. My legs had no strength, but I helped myself with the rest of my body. Finally, I made it. I stood up again and, slowly, headed towards the entrance of the tent.

The moment I got out of the tent, a fresh breeze charged with the aroma of flowers and pine trees welcomed me. The light of the moon and stars would have lit an entire town. Near the tent, a carriage was parked with some wooden chests and barrels. Two horses were tied up on a pine tree near the carriage.

We were in a small clearing amongst the foliage of bushes and trees. In front of me, was a fire with two stools and a big oak tree trunk where two people could sit. Ragnar and Mielikki were sitting on the tree trunk, and Thorstein was sitting on one of the stools.

The couple was hugging. She was talking to them in her native language while pointing at the stars. Thorstein was creating a wooden figure with a knife and a piece of wood while carefully listening to every word his mother was saying.

I slowly got near the empty stool. Mielikki stopped talking the moment she saw me and, with a very pleasant smile, she invited me with a hand gesture to sit on the stool. Ragnar bent over the fire and took a plate that was near the big stones that surrounded the flames and gave it to me. It contained some roasted meat, roots, mushrooms and berries, amongst other things. It seemed like they were waiting for me.

"I see you've recovered your strength, boy," said Ragnar with a very calm voice.

"Yes, Ragnar, I have. Thank you," I said while accepting the plate from his hand.

I then looked at Mielikki and thanked her for everything that she did. She nodded and smiled.

"Hello Thorstein," I said now looking at the boy, "I'm Eirik. We haven't met."

Thorstein nodded but didn't pronounce a word.

I ate what Ragnar had offered me. It was delicious. The way they used the plants and spices was just incredible. I had never eaten something that good since... Well, since the last time that I ate anything cooked by Mother.

Once I started eating, Mielikki resumed her explanation of the stars, the moon and the sky. This time, she spoke in my language so that I could understand.

She explained how, in her culture, the sky was the upper cover of a broken eggshell. Ilmarinen, one of their gods, forged the stars. Ukko, on the other hand, was considered the god of the sky. He even had a hammer!

"That's Thor!" I yelled as soon as she described her god Ukko.

"Well Eirik, there are some differences. You see, Ukko is an old man married to an old woman. He is indeed the god of the sky; has a hammer, even though some people say it's an axe. He creates lighting with his weapon. But he is not the son, he is the father," replied Mielikki calmly.

"What do you think about this, Ragnar?" I asked. I was curious to know what somebody from my culture thought about what Mielikki was saying.

"I think that the same way that we discovered our gods, her people may have discovered theirs. Each person has their own stories, their gods and traditions. And we all should respect that," he replied while still hugging his tiny but beautiful wife.

"How did you two meet?" I bluntly asked. I don't even know why I asked that. Those words simply came out of my mouth.

Ragnar looked his wife in the eyes, kissed her, looked back at me, and started explaining.

"The earl of my town had dealings with the Finns, Mielikki's people. One time, one of these dealings went wrong, and he felt insulted, so he decided to raid them and get what was his."

The moment he pronounced these last words he hugged even stronger his wife and kissed her on the head again.

"I was sent as part of a raiding party. I was a warrior and a fisherman whenever I wasn't fighting. We arrived in her town and a huge fight broke out. Her people are all half the size of us, but they're cunning, smart, and resourceful. We were ambushed. We lost many men in the fight, but we still prevailed."

He now lowered his head in shame. Thorstein, at this point, stopped carving his piece of wood. He was staring at the flames with a sad look. I noticed a tear running through Mielikki's face.

"We slaughtered many of them during the fight. Many fathers, brothers and sons. They intercepted us while we were getting to their town, and instead of running, they faced us and fought valiantly… But it wasn't enough."

Ragnar now exhaled and caressed his wife's head. He still had his head lowered.

"The better warriors won, then. They had a warrior's death. You gave them the best death!" I said, trying to help the mood.

Thorstein gripped his piece of wood strongly and raised his eyes at me with rage.

"Thorstein, no. It's not fair, and you know it!" said Ragnar to his son in a deep and authoritarian voice.

"I understand what you say, Eirik. And you may be right, warriors died of a warrior's death. Norsemen went to Valhöll, and Finns went to Tuonela. But that fight should never have happened in the first place," he said while raising his head again and looking at me.

"The pact between my earl and the Finns was that they had to bring goods in exchange for not being raided. If they ever failed to bring those goods, they would get raided and the chief's daughter would have to be married to my earl."

He now cleaned his wife's tears from her face by caressing her. After a long sigh, he continued with the story.

"We killed every person who dared to oppose us, Eirik. When we were finished, half of us were still alive. None of their men were. We were wounded, tired, and proud. I was commanded to go fetch the ultimate prize, the chief's daughter."

He now kissed Mielikki's head and lowered his head in shame again. This time, Mielikki continued the story.

"I was hiding with my sisters and other women from the town in a farmer's house. We heard the noise of battle outside, the cries for help, the slaughter... Suddenly, the door opened and this giant entered the room. A tall man covered in blood, wielding a sword and a shield. The man stopped in front of us and asked, 'Which one is Mielikki?'. I stood up. He stared at me and looked me right in the eyes. He had his face covered in mud and blood. But I could still see his spirit behind his dark and deep eyes," she said while caressing Ragnar's hand.

Her husband now resumed the story. "She placed her hands on the side of my arms, looked me in the eye and gently said, 'None of this is your fault. You're a good man. You're simply doing what you're told. Don't torment yourself'."

At this point, he needed to stop. He sighed and after a while; he continued. "Imagine Eirik. She was about to be handed forcibly to a man she didn't know after her whole town had been slaughtered. And she said those things to me..."

He couldn't continue the story anymore. But Mielikki picked up where Ragnar left.

"He looked at me with surprise and sadness. Then he said to me 'I'm sorry, but you have to come with me'. He didn't grab me nor force me as if he knew I would comply. We left the house, and he took me to his earl. Bodies were all over the place. I recognised my brother's corpse near them. Once I stood in front of the earl, he smiled at me. But then Ragnar asked him if he had tricked us and if he had manipulated the goods that we had sent them to justify such an assault.

156

The earl replied by saying that the men needed battle and that he wanted a new wife.

"Ragnar then asked to speak with the chief, my father. And one of the earl's men held up high a head, my father's head, and mockingly said 'Here he is, talk to him now'. But, the most unpredictable thing happened. Ragnar challenged his earl. He said that he was going to take me for himself and that whoever didn't agree with this decision would have to fight him. The earl reacted but was immediately killed by Ragnar. The same happened with three other men that followed. Another man approached Ragnar. He was a giant man, taller than Ragnar, a redhead with a thick red beard. He was shirtless, wearing only a bear hide. His body was full of inscriptions and scars. He also was covered in blood and mud. I remember being extremely afraid of him."

Mielikki smiled while remembering this redheaded savage giant. The memory of this man gave Ragnar the strength to continue the story.

"He told everyone that whoever tried to attack me would have to first defeat him. Nobody dared to get close..." said Ragnar while laughing.

"Nobody would ever dare get close to him, that's for sure! He then recommended that I run away and find a life for myself. Before leaving, I told him he should do the same. I often wonder what old Olaf is up to these days. That old bear, the craziest man I've ever known but still, the most honourable..."

I froze. They were talking about my Olaf! Everything came back at me like a wave in a stormy sea: Grandmother's death, Mother and my sister's disappearance, Father, Olaf, Knut, Gudrod... I couldn't help it and tears started pouring out of my eyes.

Ragnar, Thorstein and Mielikki noticed. Thorstein looked down and started focusing solely on his wood carving. Ragnar had the reaction of someone who regrets saying too much but doesn't know how to react. Mielikki got up and came to my side. She hugged me and while caressing my head she started murmuring, "It's fine, little

157

one. It's going to be fine. You're with us now. Nobody will harm you anymore. It's going to be fine."

"I guess this wasn't the best story to be telling..." added Ragnar.

"He's just a boy, Ragnar. He acts tough, but he's just a boy without his mother..." she said while hugging and caressing me.

The more she hugged, caressed and treated me like this, the more I cried. I couldn't stop it. I believe I never cried this way and for so long. All the memories that I tried my best to suppress were hitting me at once. I remembered fishing with Father and Olaf, sitting with Olaf on the tree stumps outside his house, talking to Grandmother in front of the fireplace, Mother's hugs, conversations with Gudrod, feasting with Knut in the town hall... I felt I couldn't take it anymore.

I don't know how much time passed, but I was so tired from crying that I fell asleep. Finally, a deep and restoring sleep.

Chapter 19

Voyage

The family was preparing to leave. They started intentionally making noise so that I would wake up.

Thorstein was preparing the carriage and the horses. Ragnar was taking down the tent where I was sleeping. Mielikki was packing boxes and barrels and running around carrying stuff.

I felt the obligation to help. For too long, I had been a useless guest. I stood up surprisingly fast, feeling my body recovered, stronger. And started carrying boxes and taking them to the carriage when Mielikki grabbed my arm.

"Where do you think you're going?" she asked.

"Helping. I'm helping you pack," I replied.

"No. First, you eat something. Then we'll see what you'll be doing," she said while taking me to the only stool that hadn't been put in the carriage. It had a plate of food on top of it. "Eat. Then bring me the plate and the stool," she said while gently patting me on the back.

I ate as fast as I could. I didn't want them doing all the work. As soon as I was done, I helped them pack everything. But, while I was packing, I realised I didn't quite know where they were going exactly. I only remembered that they were going North, that was good enough for now.

We mounted the carriage and started our journey. Ragnar and Mielikki were sitting at the front, and Thorstein and I were sitting at the back with the boxes, barrels, tent and other goods.

At the beginning of the trip, we were in total silence. Sometimes Mielikki would sing in her native tongue or would blow her horn to scare bears and wolves away.

Something from the story that they told me the night before made little sense. Ragnar had a southern accent, and yet his town's earl made dealings with the Finns. Olaf was from the same town that I was from, and that's in the north.

"Ragnar, can I ask you a question? You don't have to answer if you don't want to," I finally asked.

"Sure. Go ahead," he replied.

"If you're clearly from the south by your accent, how come your town's earl was dealing with the Finns?" I asked him, hoping not to be too intrusive.

"I moved north. I was exiled from my native land for manslaughter," he calmly replied.

"Oh, I understand. Manslaughter. Makes sense..." I timidly replied, still thinking about what to do with this new information.

"Before you ask. My brother and I had a dispute over property with a wealthy man. That property was ours by birthright. The man didn't agree. He sent a group of men to kill us. They all died. But at the *Thing*, they wouldn't go against such an important man, but they wouldn't want me dead either because it wasn't my fault. So I was cast away, in exile," replied Ragnar casually, like he was talking about going fishing.

"Was your brother also exil-".

"Died. My brother died in the fight," said Ragnar.

"I'm sorry. I don't know what to say..." I said, feeling that I may have asked too much.

"Don't worry young Eirik. I've been through worse. Curiosity is knowledge like Odin always says..." said Ragnar calmly.

After that, a few moments of silence followed. Until Ragnar proceeded to ask a more intimate question to me.

"Well, Eirik, now that we're in an introspective and intimate mood. Who were those names that you shouted until you couldn't shout anymore a couple of nights ago?"

"I shouted out names? Which ones?" I asked in surprise.

In the beginning, I was concerned that they might discover my true identity, but if I had to be truly honest with myself, deep down, I wanted them to discover it. I trusted them, and it didn't seem right for me to lie.

"Father, Mother, Grandmother, Thrúd, Olaf, Gudrod, Knut, Björn..." said Ragnar.

It looked like he memorised them perfectly, almost like he was waiting for the perfect moment to ask me about them.

Suddenly, my defences were back up. Why did he put so much effort into remembering exactly every name? Why was that so important to him? I already saw the mischief that Loki pulled out in Uppsala. I wouldn't allow him to play those games with me.

"Well, Father, Mother and Grandmother are obvious. Thrúd is my sister. The others are family friends," I replied.

Wasn't quite the answer that I had in mind, but for some reason I couldn't resist trusting this wonderful and loving couple that saved my life.

"It's a curious combination of names. Especially considering that you're 'Eirik Haraldsson', don't you think?" he replied while smiling and looking at me.

"Why is that, Ragnar?" I replied, a little scared. I started thinking that I might have lowered my guard too much.

"As you know, I once knew an 'Olaf'. A huge redheaded warrior, strong as a bear. Well, this Olaf had a friend, his best friend, I might add. His name was Eirik," he replied while smiling.

I didn't know what to think. He might have known who I was. Maybe he sent his son to Chief Svein with a message while I spent all those days unconscious. Maybe he was taking me to the men who wanted me dead. Probably the reward must have been high.

"That Eirik had a brother, Harald. Casually two of your names. You may be Haraldsson, but you may also be Eiriksson. Who knows, right?" he said, laughing, almost teasing me.

Even though I was sitting in the back, I could see him smile. Mielikki was smiling too. In front of me, Thorstein was serious. He was still carving his piece of wood but was very serious. I had the feeling that I might have been in trouble all this time and I didn't even notice it.

"Eirik? What do you think?" asked Ragnar.

"Well, I don't know about any of that. My father is Harald, a farmer. I'm Eirik. And that's pretty much all I know. We went to Uppsala for the *blót* and when returning we got assaulted by bandits," I replied.

"I see. You know, there is another curious thing that I remember. Olaf, Eirik and Harald were extremely talented warriors. They were shaman-warriors. Or at least that's what the legend says. And, if the legend is true, Eirik and Harald were the most savage but yet the most 'shamanistic' warriors of them all. Some say they could cross the worlds and visit Niflheim and, sometimes, even Hel. They had powers," said Ragnar.

"Those are just stories. I don't believe in those stories," I said, hoping for this conversation to end soon.

"I fought next to Olaf. And all the legends about him and his kind are true. He fought shirtless in the coldest of winters, in the middle of the snow, wielding his battle-axe and slaying three men at a time. You know who were also his companions?" asked Ragnar.

"No, sir..." I replied, thinking that I should try jumping from the carriage and running as fast as I could.

"Well, no other than Knut and Gudrod!" said Ragnar while laughing.

The blood in my veins froze. He knew exactly who I was. Not only that, he knew it for days now... I could be in grave danger. While I was immersed in my thoughts, I heard a gentle voice that snapped me out of it.

"Stop behaving like a child, Ragnar. Eirik, or however you want to be called, don't worry. We won't harm you. Look at the sun. We're going north, just as we said we would. And we will keep taking care of you, just as we've been doing all this time," said Mielikki in her sweet voice.

"Sorry, 'Eirik'. I'm just a big child. Don't you worry. Everything will be fine," said Ragnar confirming what his wife had just said.

It wasn't what Ragnar said, but more what Mielikki said that calmed me.

We stopped to rest the horses and ourselves. We ate sitting at the exposed roots of a huge beech tree. I was still wondering if I could completely trust these people. I decided to ask Odin for some guidance. After all, he supposedly chose me. I asked the All-father for a sign, some sort of sign that would help me understand I was going on the right path. But nothing happened.

After we had finished eating, preparing the horses and packing. I volunteered to check on the horses one last time when suddenly a huge raven flew right at me. I dodged it and it posed on top of the horse that I was checking. It stood there for a while, looking me straight in the eyes. I stared back at it. I felt I was doing the right thing travelling with this family. The moment that feeling reached my heart, the raven flew away.

"He speaks to you…" said a voice behind me.

I turned around and saw Ragnar with an axe, at a couple steps of distance. I felt afraid at first, but immediately I embraced the feeling that I had just discovered while looking into the bird's eyes.

"Yes, he does," I proudly replied.

Ragnar simpered. "Well, I would lie if I said it surprises me…" he finally said while heading towards the carriage and carefully placing his axe inside it.

We resumed our march north. Mielikki did most of the talking, she explained to me how they ran away deeper into Finnish territory at first, how Thorstein was born there but also how Ragnar stood out so much that they decided to come to Sweden, where they would live in the utmost northern part of it, in the middle of the woods. Close to both Finland and Norway.

She also explained more about her gods and her devotion to wild animals such as the elk or the bear. How they hunted bears, just like us, but they have them in such high esteem they need first to ask permission from a sacred bear spirit and only then they can go bear hunting.

Mielikki also told me that Thorstein was extremely strong for his age. He must have been around fourteen winters old. When they found me, he was the one who carried me. He didn't speak much. As a matter of fact, I didn't even recall ever hearing him speak at all.

We must have been travelling for almost a moon when we finally got to the top of a hill where the carriage stopped. Ragnar and

Mielikki hugged and exhaled while watching what was lying before them.

I stood up and saw a vast flat land full of lakes and trees. It was a beautiful place. Some lakes were connected by small canals and streams, others by bigger canals and rivers, but other lakes were completely surrounded by land.

"Home…" the couple sighed.

"This is where you live? Where's your town?" I asked. I knew they lived in a small place close to nature, but that place looked completely unexplored.

"Past those trees, after the sixth lake counting from the first one at the feet of the hill," replied Ragnar proudly.

"What's the name of the town?" I asked.

"Home," said Thorstein with an incredibly deep voice for someone his age.

"Indeed. Eirik, that's home. We eat what we find. We adapt to nature. Like our ancestors did," added Mielikki.

"I see…" I replied, not very convinced of the idea of living in the middle of nowhere, alone, with no defences nor help if needed.

We jumped down from the carriage and started walking our way down the hill. We needed to lower the weight of the carriage to a minimum, especially for descending on some of the steeper slopes.

As soon as we finished descending the hill, Thorstein started running towards the trees and vegetation and, soon enough, we lost sight of him.

"Where is he going?" I asked, somewhat concerned.

"He's going home. He loves running in the woods. Usually, he leaves home in the morning and returns at night. He must have missed this so much…" replied Mielikki calmly.

"Isn't it dangerous? Aren't there swamps? Animals?" I insisted.

"You see Eirik, Thorstein didn't grow up with us. We were always very close to him and we would visit him often. But the reality is that we came here without him. We left him with other people who took care of him as a foster child," said Ragnar.

"Oh… I see," I replied.

"The people that took care of him are a hunter tribe. They live from the land without altering it in the slightest. Incredible trackers, great survivors and formidable hunters. They taught Thorstein how to survive in the wild, how to read the stars, rivers, trees and animal prints," he said.

"Is that why he never speaks?"

"Maybe. He lives in his mind. But don't allow his silence to fool you. He's smart as a fox," replied the proud father.

"I see. And why did you…?"

"Because people were looking for both of us. They wanted to steal Mielikki from me and, of course, they wanted me dead. After all, I had killed an earl and several of his best men. My kin, Norwegians like us," replied while holding his wife's hand.

"You protected him," I concluded.

Ragnar nodded while sighing. I could see that it must have been hard for them to abandon their child, even though it had been probably necessary for his own sake.

We continued walking for half a day and I didn't see any signs of people, houses, bridges or even Thorstein. We crossed water bodies with natural bridges made of huge tree trunks. They looked like they fell perfectly into place to allow a carriage to pass through them. Later on, Ragnar explained to me those bridges had been built by simply dragging tree trunks and placing them in such a way that they would communicate both shores of canals, rivers and small lakes without making it obvious that it had been made by men.

This place was the ultimate hiding spot. Even if someone would discover this immense valley of lakes, canals, rivers and tiny islands; it would be impossible to find their house.

It was the most entertaining walk I remember. We walked through very dense forests that formed these small islands, then we would cross a canal, stream, river or lake and get to another heavily vegetated island and cross through it. We did this over and over, and it always seemed that Ragnar's carriage fitted just right.

After losing count of how many islands we had crossed, I completely lost my sense of orientation. We arrived at the end of one of the forest islands where we found a big rock near a very narrow piece of land that communicated that island with the next. Water was flowing under the land that communicated both islands. This was an actual natural bridge made of rocks and earth.

Ragnar stopped in front of the big boulder, grabbed some bones that were scattered at its base, and started counting them. When he finished, he deeply exhaled, relieved, and then hugged his wife.

"Thank Odin. All-father... Thank Thor, greatest protector of all... Thank Tyr..." started whispering Ragnar while strongly hugging his wife.

He continued for some moments, thanking many gods. He even started thanking gods I had never heard about. I was utterly confused.

"What... Happened?" I stuttered, trying to understand but without interrupting the whole hugging and god-thanking situation.

Suddenly, almost as if Ragnar remembered I was there, he stopped hugging his wife and turned around. He strongly grabbed my shirt and threw me towards the bridge connecting with the island in front of us.

"Run boy! Run!" he yelled at me while smiling.

Mielikki was crying with joy, and Ragnar started running near me. I understood nothing, but instinctively started running.

We crossed the bridge and entered the vegetation. After some time of running between bushes and trees, following Ragnar, we suddenly arrived at a clearing. At that clearing, there was a small house that had been built under the land level. It had some steps going downwards to access the door. Turf grew on the roof and the crossed beams forming the entrance had red inscriptions and decorations. It had small openings on the roof where smoke came out. Near the house I could see a small crop field, a tiny stable and a smaller pit house, probably a workshop or a tool shed.

I didn't pay attention to any more details because my eyes stopped at Thorstein. He was at the front of the door, on the steps, talking to someone who was inside the house.

As soon as Thorstein noticed our presence, he smiled like I had never seen him smile before and moved away from the steps and the doorway.

We could see a yellowish light coming out of the doorway, contrasting with the ever-growing darkness of the evening, when, suddenly, a gigantic figure stood at the door, blocking the light. The figure stopped for an instant when it saw us, almost trying to assess who we were, and suddenly yelled the loudest battle cry ever heard and started sprinting towards us.

I didn't know how to react. Ragnar and I stopped as soon as we arrived at the clearing earlier and now this figure was growing at every fast step it was taking. Soon enough I started identifying some key features from this figure: Colossal man, what seemed like a bear hide, redhead... Wait! Redhead?

I ran towards the man and jumped on him. He caught me mid-air and hugged me so strongly that I thought he would break all the bones in my body.

"Sigurd! My boy! My Sigurd! You're alive and well!" yelled the man, excited and overwhelmed with joy.

"Olaf! Olaf! Olaf! Olaf!" was the only thing that I could scream over and over again.

I couldn't believe it. He was alive. I could feel his powerful arms hugging me, his characteristic smell, his loud voice, and the tickling of his beard falling on my head and face.

We both survived, and we both found each other. I had so many unanswered questions. How did he survive? Did Father survive? Gudrod and Knut survived too? Did he find Mother and Thrúd? How did he find his way here? How did he know Thorstein?

So many questions invaded my mind while I tried my best to stop crying. In Olaf's arms, finally, I felt at home.

Chapter 20

Friendship

The crackling of the fire was the only noise breaking a silence that seemed to be caused by our exhaustion because of the long journey and the fear of asking what happened.

I had many questions but, for now, I simply wanted to savour the happiness of reuniting with Olaf.

The house was divided into two rooms. The first room was the living space. It had a long fireplace on the left, surrounded by stones and with a wooden structure that came down from the roof and guided the smoke from the fireplace to a complex ventilation system that would make it come out from different openings on the roof. I had never seen something like that before, but later Ragnar explained to me that this mechanism would make the smoke come out scattered without forming a big cloud that would be visible from a long distance.

At the centre of the room, there was a table with benches on both sides and, at the right, a working station for food preparation and sewing.

A doorway led to another room that had beds on the sides and a small fireplace at the centre. Small scattered openings on the roof would make the smoke escape discreetly. I was amazed by how much work had been put into building this hidden house.

I sat near Olaf and Ragnar at the table. Thorstein was sitting on a chair near the door, almost as if he was guarding the house. Mielikki was preparing some food. She was such a superb cook!

"So, old friend... What happened? Can you tell us?" asked Ragnar with a deep and concerned voice.

Olaf was a skilled storyteller. I was eager to hear from him what had happened, especially to know if my family was still alive. He looked at me, then looked downwards and after deeply exhaling, he started to recount.

"It was chaos. The guards were prepared for that fight, it wasn't improvised. They were well armed, and they had a very specific plan: Kill Eirik."

After saying these last words, Olaf looked at me. He was about to continue talking when Ragnar interrupted.

"That would be Sigurd's father," he said while looking at Thorstein and Mielikki and pointing at me. He then looked me in the eyes, smiled and winked.

He always knew who I was? Why didn't he tell me? Now I felt like a fool, having lied to him for such a long time.

"Please Olaf, continue," said Ragnar.

"When the battle began, Eirik fought off a group of guards to send Sigurd away. The moment he came back, the guards ignored us and surrounded him. They had a plan and knew how to execute it. But, there was one thing they didn't account for…" Olaf then paused and took a big sip of beer.

Mielikki stopped doing whatever she was doing and sat at the table near me. Thorstein also moved closer and sat at the table near his father.

"What was it?!" impatiently asked Mielikki.

"Well, you see…" started murmuring Olaf. Something was holding him back. He then looked at Ragnar as if he was waiting for approval. Ragnar looked at his wife and son, took a moment to think, and after exhaling, he looked at Olaf and nodded. Olaf then continued his story, this time without pausing.

"You see, beautiful Mielikki, what they didn't account for is that in front of them, they had three berserkers. One of them, Sigurd's father, is an Ulfhednar, one of Odin's Wolves."

"The twin brothers? The legendary twin brothers?" asked Thorstein, excited.

That was the first time that I heard that much sound come out of his mouth.

"Yes, Thorstein, precisely," replied Olaf, while standing up. It seemed that the memory started getting too intense for him to simply stay still. He resumed while moving back and forth in front of us.

169

"When Eirik returned and was surrounded, the guards knew what they had to do, but they also saw how he easily killed the other guards and they all knew what he had done several days before. During this time of doubt, Knut, Gudrod and I looked at each other and something happened. Something that hadn't happened since the days of The Twelve. We felt a connection as if we all knew what each one of us was thinking. I could feel Knut's and Gudrod's rage and they could feel mine.

"The image of Helga, how we found her, what they did to her, that good and loving woman. I loved her like a mother and I know she loved me like a son... What they did... How they did it..."

During these words, I felt a huge amount of sadness and rage that was unbearable. I felt I was going to explode. But, suddenly, I snapped out of my internal thoughts when I saw Ragnar jumping out of his chair.

While recalling this part of the story, Olaf didn't realise it, but he grabbed his battle-axe and started breathing very fast and intensely. He was losing control.

Ragnar got hold of him and made him return to his senses again. Olaf sat down and respectfully apologised to Mielikki. He then resumed his story.

"Well, needless to say, that we were unstoppable. Knut launched himself at the guards that, in theory, had to prevent us from helping Eirik. Knut alone killed all of them, not without his share of bloodshed. Gudrod and I charged towards the guards that were surrounding Eirik, but, just when we were about to get to them, we saw them fall, cut into pieces. Eirik was unleashed. His eyes were blank, his breathing was of an animal. He couldn't feel pain or compassion. He had given himself into rage."

Olaf paused and took another sip of beer.

"I started going left and Gudrod right. We started killing every single one of the guards that had surrounded Eirik. He slew every single man that he had in front of him. We then found each other with our backs together and a sea of corpses, blood, entrails, and body parts all around us. The whole town that initially had gathered there, scattered and was now watching from a distance.

"Rage and the might of the gods had possessed us like it used to happen back in the day. I felt alive again. Eirik was growling and howling. Knut was laughing and growling while challenging the remaining guards. Gudrod was also growling and taunting the guards, and so was I. But then something unexpected happened..."

Olaf now stopped talking and drank all the beer that was left in his cup. He was visibly affected by whatever happened next.

"Almost out of nowhere, a group of warriors arrived. There were so many. Heavily armed and prepared for war. This wasn't right. Where did they come from? I never saw them in all the time that I spent living there. But it didn't matter. We launched ourselves at them.

"Soon enough, we were overwhelmed. Our wounds were starting to be too many and too deep. We were covered in blood and we had cuts all over our body. We weren't going to make it..."

Olaf deeply exhaled, preparing himself for what looked like bad news.

"Gudrod turned around, and looked at the rest of us and we all knew what that meant. He wanted to sacrifice himself so that we could escape. Initially, we yelled at him. We told him we would die together, especially Eirik. But then Gudrod yelled back, 'For Sigurd, Eirik!'.

"When Eirik heard these words, he froze. He came back from his trance, from his rage. Knut, Eirik, and I looked at each other. This all happened in an instant, but it felt like an eternity. Then Knut launched himself towards the guards, joining Gudrod and yelling 'To Valhöll!'. Gudrod smiled at us and launched himself deeper into enemy lines, dragging as many men as possible with him.

"Eirik and I started running towards the temple and left the battle behind. The noise of the slaughter lasted little."

Olaf stopped talking, his eyes were fixed on the flames. He was sitting in the chair with his legs extended and half open, holding his empty horn and with the saddest expression that I ever saw on him. Nobody dared talk after hearing such news.

171

"Eirik and I ran as fast as we could, considering the wounds that we had. We were almost at The Great Temple when a group of guards attacked us from the side. There is where Eirik and I split. Most of them attacked Eirik. I tried helping him but he insisted I had to escape and find you, Sigurd," said the giant while reaching for my head and playfully messing up my hair.

"What happened to Father?" I asked, hoping for the best.

"I don't know Sigurd. I never saw him after that and I will never find peace for leaving your father behind," replied Olaf while looking downwards in shame.

"You did what was right, Olaf. You did what needed to be done," said Ragnar while patting Olaf on the back.

Silence followed. We all needed some time to digest what Olaf had revealed.

Mielikki finished preparing the food. Thorstein and I helped her bring it to the table, and we started eating. Midway through that delicious stew, I felt I couldn't hold it inside me anymore.

"Olaf, I guess that if you knew, you would have told me by now, but... Any news about Mother or Thrúd?" I asked, hoping that he had forgotten about them and that they were safe.

Olaf shook his head and exhaled. "I'm sorry Sigurd, but I know nothing about them. I really wish I did," he replied with the saddest voice that I remember of him.

We continued eating and not much was said during the meal. Thorstein and Mielikki cleaned the table and the food preparation station. I wanted to help, but Mielikki would not allow me to.

We then sat outside the house, on the steps that led downwards towards the door. I found it a fascinating design to build the house below the level of the ground. Ragnar explained to me it helped maintain the house temperature and also allowed for the house not to be easily seen.

It was a fine spring night, a fresh breeze ran through the trees and the constant sound of the water surrounding the tiny island where the house was built made for a perfect atmosphere for relaxation. If no other pressing issues bothered you, of course.

Chapter 21

The past unveiled

The following morning I helped Mielikki with house chores. The house had been abandoned for more than a moon, so there was much to do. Thorstein took care of the small crop field outside. He spent the entire morning tilling the soil and planting new seeds. The field was tiny but enough to sustain a family.

Olaf and Ragnar had gone to the closest town. It took half a day to get there by carriage, a little less if riding a horse.

They would go there for trading but, most importantly, it was a source of information. Several traders would stop there to resupply on their way to or from either Norway or Finland. We were so up north in Swedish territory that we were a short voyage away from either of the neighbouring countries. But Olaf and Ragnar were more interested in the news coming from the south, from Uppsala. They were hoping to hear news from Mother or Thrúd, and also if they were still looking for either me or Olaf.

I spent that day sharpening and oiling all the tools and weapons in the house. Thorstein disappeared after that we had lunch together and Mielikki spent her time sewing. Late in the evening, I sat at the table near the fireplace. As Mielikki prepared dinner, the door opened. It was Thorstein. He was dirty. He had several mud and green stains all over his clothes and had a few scratches on his arms. As soon as he entered the house, he went to the back to wash himself with a water bowl, leaving the door of the house open.

Right after Thorstein, Olaf and Ragnar entered, carrying bags filled with carrots, cabbage, cheese and some dried meat they had bought in the town. Ragnar and Mielikki hugged and Olaf came to me and messed up my hair playfully. After they had washed themselves, we sat and had dinner together.

"So, any news?" Mielikki immediately asked.

"No news of Thora nor little Thrúd. But they're still looking for Sigurd," replied Olaf, visibly concerned.

"What's the matter, Olaf?" I asked.

"Well, the trader that we spoke to explained to us the search party that was put in place. He also told us that warriors have been sent to every town in Sweden looking for you," replied with an ever more worried expression on his face.

"All that for me?" I questioned, astonished.

"Yes. Which indicates that either you killed a very powerful man, or there is something that escapes our knowledge or understanding in this whole situation," said Ragnar.

I was furious. How could this be possible? The whole town of Uppsala saw what this man had done.

"Why did all of this happen, Olaf? Why didn't the townspeople intervene? Everybody saw what they did to Father and later, what they did to Grandmother. And where did all those guards that attack you come from?" I asked in despair.

"Those are good questions Sigurd. I wish I had the answers you seek. But I don't. The townspeople are mostly simple people who want to avoid trouble, and there was much trouble that day. Many things need further explanations and investigation, we'll get our answers someday. For now, we need to stay alive," said the redhead giant.

I sighed and shrugged. It wasn't the answer that I was expecting, but I also knew that Olaf was as clueless as me.

We finished our dinner and then headed outside. The sky was covered with thousands of bright stars. The sound of the water and breeze running through the tree leaves made it such a special place.

We sat outside in silence for a while. But soon enough, I had to find answers to some questions I knew could be answered.

"Can I ask you a question?"

Ragnar and Olaf looked at me and nodded.

"How come you know each other? And, was I found by chance or were you looking for me?" I dared.

Ragnar and Olaf smiled. "Well Sigurd, I've known Olaf for a long time now. We're old friends from the good old times. And yes, we were looking for you," replied Ragnar.

"But how did you know which direction to look for me?" I insisted. I was quite intrigued.

"Your father and I know you better than you think. Your father taught you well. I knew you would run home but would never go in a straight line if being followed. You would take the long way," replied Olaf.

That was surprising. He predicted my thoughts and knew which path I was going to take.

"But the fire in the middle of the night wasn't a great idea..." added Olaf, with a grin on his face.

"You saw me? Why didn't you come to me then?" I immediately asked.

"I was wounded and being followed. I needed to get away from you in order to lead the men chasing us astray," said Olaf.

"I see. But I still don't understand how you and your family found me, and why you didn't tell me all of this right away instead of letting me lie to you?" I asked Ragnar.

"Thorstein tracked you down. And we didn't tell you anything because you're a boy. You were a tired, confused, scared and angry boy who had lost everything dear to him and had been running for his life for many days. We needed to let you know that you still had some control and that your shield was still working. Besides, I knew Mielikki would make you lower your shield in no time..." replied Ragnar, chuckling.

We all laughed at that. Mielikki was indeed a special person. She reminded me of the goddess Frigg.

More questions came to mind, but I was afraid to continue asking. I could spend the entire night interrogating them, but I didn't want to be bothersome. I figured I would ask a couple of questions from time to time. Perhaps by spreading them over several days, it wouldn't annoy them that much.

"Go ahead, boy. What's your next one?" asked Ragnar with a smile.

"How did you...? Nevermind. So, how did you meet?" I finally asked.

"I was a former member of The Twelve. I thought you would have figured it out by now," said Ragnar, looking at one of the inked inscriptions on his arm.

"So, you're also a berserker?"

"Yes, Sigurd. He's one of us," replied Olaf.

"I see," I replied, astonished.

"And yes, I knew your father and your uncle. I knew Gudrod and Knut too. Before you ask…" added Ragnar somewhat mockingly.

"And how come they call you 'The Black'?" I asked, ignoring his previous comment.

"Well, isn't it obvious, boy? Look at my skin and hair colour. My father went raiding south and took many slaves back home to Gula, in Norway. During the voyage back, he had laid eyes on a particular slave. She had coppery skin with black hair and eyes. He took her for himself. After some time, he freed her and they got married. She was my mother. He called her the 'jewel from the desert'," he explained in a deeply nostalgic tone.

"That's fascinating!" I yelled. I truly believed it to be a fascinating story. Also, it had some similarities to how he married Mielikki. "But Ragnar, what's 'desert'?" I had never heard that word before, or perhaps I didn't remember it.

"If you go south, very south. As south as your ship can take you, you'll find places that are unique. Different worlds. One of these places is called 'desert'. These deserts are seas of sand," explained Ragnar.

"Hmmm… Beaches?" I asked, stating the obvious.

"No, boy. Not beaches. Endless seas of sand. No water to be found and so much heat that would weaken Thor himself!" replied the dark-skin man.

"How can people live in such a place?" I asked, amazed by this new world.

"I don't know Sigurd; was never there. I never ventured so far south. On the other hand, I went north and discovered the world where Mielikki comes from," he replied while hugging and caressing his wife.

"I see. But, is Mielikki's land that different from Norway or even Sweden?"

I knew that there wasn't much distance between our current location and Finland, so how different could it be? It was worth asking them.

"My tribe comes from the northern forests, far from the sea. It's not very different from the north of Norway. It's a land of ice, snow, forests and wildlife. I'm guessing that you've never been that far north?" said Mielikki with a gentle voice.

"I used to think that I knew what the north was. But now I'm starting to have some doubts... Olaf?"

"You're from the mid-north Sigurd. The same as me. You're used to the sea and milder weather compared to the northernmost part of Norway and Finland," said the giant.

"I see..." I said while immersed in my thoughts.

I was trying to make sense of all this information. Still, I couldn't quite understand how Olaf knew Thorstein that well. Even though he was friends with Ragnar, Thorstein was raised in Finland by some tribe.

I spent some time thinking about Ragnar, his family, and his story. Are they still looking for him? Why live in such a remote and hidden place?

Then my mind went towards Father, Mother, and Thrúd. I wondered if Father's death had been painless, and if Mother and Thrúd had been caught or still on the run. Grandmother... The image of her stained body covered in blood still haunted me. In my mind, I was still desperately running from a hungry bear. I was still running from danger, even though I was safe there.

"Boy!" I heard a call that seemed coming from a vast distance.

"Sigurd!" this time it sounded very close.

I snapped out of my thoughts. Olaf was calling from the steps that led to the house door. I had walked to the edge of the clearing towards the trees in the darkness.

"I'm here, Olaf!" I replied.

Olaf came towards my position. There was a bit of light because of the bright stars and moon in the sky, but not enough to see at a distance. Once he joined me, he sat on the grass and then laid on it. I did the same. We stayed there for a while, in silence, observing the night bright sky.

The fresh breeze caressed my cheeks. The noise of all the water bodies surrounding the small island merged with the sound of the moving vegetation and the howling wolves in the distance.

"What's this place, Olaf?" I finally broke the silence.

He deeply exhaled, like people do when recovering certain memories from the past.

"This was a safe haven for us, for The Twelve. Your father, your uncle Harald, and I used to lie down and observe the stars and talk about the gods. Just like we're doing now. In this very place..." said the giant in a nostalgic tone.

After a slight pause and another deep exhale, he continued.

"I remember Knut would make fun of us. He was a very devout man, but perhaps a bit plain. A good man, but a straightforward one. His love for the axe was almost as big as his love for the gods. Ahhh... Knut... My Danish brother..." added Olaf while exhaling again and placing his hands behind his head, forming a cushion with them.

"Gudrod and Ragnar would always sit at the steps of the house, the same way we do each night after dinner, and they would talk until deep in the night. They were the biggest friends. They were like brothers. We were all brothers..."

We both stayed quiet for some time. I didn't want to interrupt this moment of mourning and nostalgia that Olaf was having. I was having my own thoughts about my family.

"This place, Sigurd, was a place of peace. We would come here whenever we were in danger or whenever we needed to meet. It was chosen and built not to be discovered nor seen. When Ragnar decided to leave everything and protect Mielikki, we understood and supported him. We decided that they should have this place as their home. There isn't a safer place in Scandinavia," said Olaf.

"But why were they looking so hard for Mielikki and Thorstein? And how did you meet him?" I asked.

"Sigurd, Mielikki is of royal blood. She is the daughter of one of the most important chieftains in Finland, a king amongst their tribes. They want her back in order to marry her and have her unify the tribes. And the men of the earl that Ragnar killed want her because they see her as a valuable stolen treasure. She's worth a lot if sold to the right people.

"Thorstein is very similar. He's a link between Finland and Norway. He could unify the North. Unified Finnish tribes fighting alongside northern Norwegian clans. What an unstoppable force..."

"I didn't have a clue about this. I knew Mielikki was the daughter of a chief, but I didn't know the extent of it," I replied, amazed and worried at the same time. "But why didn't the tribe that raised Thorstein deliver him to the Finnish that are looking for him?" I asked.

"Sigurd, that tribe is a very specific tribe. They live isolated from the rest; have little contact with other Finnish tribes and even less with Swedes or Norwegians. They live off what they find, they pray to the old Finnish gods and they stay out of politics. Mielikki's family has blood ties with them, and her father was also something similar to a seer or a spiritual man. He had power over them."

"I understand," I replied, "but how did you meet Thorstein then?" I insisted.

"The tribe would bring him here every winter. They would spend some time here with Ragnar and Mielikki and then go back. I was here some of those times, the same as your father was. That's how we knew of Thorstein."

"I see. But why take the risk?" I asked.

"Trust me Sigurd, these people cannot be tracked nor seen if they so wish it," replied the redhead.

We spent quite some time in silence again, reflecting on what had been spoken and on the memories that had surfaced as a consequence.

Feeling my chest slightly burning again, I remembered Odin's mark, The Great Temple, the *blót*... This all started as a spiritual pilgrimage and it all went south at some point. But the gods' presence had been felt. They must have a plan, I was certain of it.

"Olaf, why do you think Odin chose me? What's the plan?" I finally asked.

"That's a good question, Sigurd. I only wish I knew how to answer it. Sometimes I feel the gods are bored and play games with us, other times I clearly understand what their intentions are. Usually, I would ask these questions myself, and I would ask them to either your father or your uncle."

"I see," I replied while not being quite satisfied with the answer. "Why are The Twelve always being chased? Why did you need a place like this? Weren't you the most elite of the Norwegian forces? Didn't you help protect our lands?" I finally asked some questions that haunted me since I learnt about The Twelve.

Olaf sighed and then laughed a little. It was a bitter laugh.

"The Twelve started dying the moment your uncle passed away, Sigurd. But we were never bound to a country or a king. Yes, we fought with Norwegian armies, but we also fought with Danish armies. Yes, we fought for King Harald, but we also fought for King Horik from Denmark..."

After this, Olaf took a moment to think of a good way of explaining how The Twelve worked. He then deeply exhaled and prepared for a more accurate explanation that, after all this time, I could finally hear.

"We're Odin's warriors, Sigurd. Not a king's warriors, not a country's warriors. But Odin's. We fight when and where our lifestyle, our culture and our gods are in danger. We fight against invaders, enemies on our borders or, sometimes, other Scandinavians that pose a threat to the things that I mentioned before. Our only allegiance is to the gods. That's why many earls, kings and other powerful people end up wanting to kill us. Because they never know when they'll hear our battle cry at their doorsteps."

I needed some time to process what Olaf had just explained. I wanted to quickly reply, as I usually did, but I couldn't quite find the words. Luckily, I didn't need to think much because the giant resumed his explanation as if he knew that my head was confused but still eager to hear the whole truth, once and for all.

"You're probably wondering how we could be 'controlled' or how it was decided where and when our services were needed. That's where The Great Temple plays a crucial role, Sigurd.

"The *völva* has special powers. She really can communicate with the gods. You've experienced your fair share of encounters during your stay in Uppsala. It was through her we could know the will of the gods, the will of Odin. It was decided there where our services were needed.

"And don't forget that the members of The Twelve are also people that are very close to the gods themselves. So we could also sense when and where we needed to intervene."

This made sense to me, but my being a sceptic by nature couldn't help but immediately ask a daring question, "And what about politics, Olaf?"

He looked surprised. Perhaps he wasn't expecting such a question from a boy my age. But his surprise didn't last long, for he knew that I'd always paid special attention to everything that people said in front of me. A common thing I would do was sit in a corner, close my eyes and hear all the conversations that adults would have while they thought I was asleep, even though Father always knew that I wasn't sleeping.

"Well Sigurd, I would be lying if I said that politics didn't pollute this process. It sometimes happens that powerful people make important contributions to temples in order to gain the favour of the temple people and use The Twelve for wrong purposes."

"I thought so," I replied. "Was that what led you and Ragnar to go north, into Finland, and slaughter Mielikki's people?"

"No," said Olaf, "Ragnar and I going with his earl had nothing to do with The Twelve. Understand Sigurd that we spent a lifetime perfecting our combat skills. We're forged in battle and it's in battle where we thrive. There isn't much that we can do to earn a living that doesn't involve using our axe. That's why Ragnar and I were there, and that's why often your father and I would go raiding with our townspeople."

"I see…" I replied while thinking about my next questions when suddenly Olaf interrupted my thinking.

"Come on Sigurd. Enough for today. Let's go to sleep," said the giant while getting up and heading towards the house.

Indeed, it was late, and I already had asked plenty of questions. Now it was time to go to sleep and give all this new information some time to sink in.

Lying in bed, my head spun, and I couldn't stop thinking. I went from Ragnar, his family story, his love for Mielikki, her story, her son's story… Then I would go back thinking about The Twelve, my uncle Harald, Father, Knut and Gudrod. How many battles have they seen? Why were such honourable men constantly having to run from people wanting to kill them? Why the greed of politics? Why do people forget about the gods and their might? Would I ever see the old man again? Odin… What do you want from me? What's my destiny? Why all of this?

With such thoughts, I fell into a deep sleep.

Chapter 22

The Plan

A few days passed. Thorstein would take care of the crops, place animal traps in the woods around the house, and hunt. Mielikki spent most of her time fixing house tools and sewing. Ragnar would fix the roof, carriage, and other parts of the house. Olaf and I would go out fishing. Whenever we didn't have to fish, either Olaf taught me how to fight or I would help Mielikki with house chores, the same way I did with Mother.

Olaf and Ragnar had gone out to the trading town again. This was the third time.

It was a little over noon. I was helping Mielikki clean a couple of rabbits that Thorstein had caught while he cleaned the fireplace when suddenly; we heard the carriage arrive at full speed. Before we could even react and go outside to see what happened, the door of the house violently opened and Ragnar ran into the house.

"Knut is alive! He's alive!" he yelled.

We were all in shock. Alive? How could he be? Olaf entered the house after Ragnar and explained.

"Knut is alive. They didn't kill him, but they captured him instead. Maybe they're trying to interrogate him in order to know where Sigurd could be hiding. They think I'm dead and they know nothing about Ragnar or Mielikki!"

"Slow down, you two. Sit at the table, I'll bring you some beer and you'll calmly explain what's going on," said Mielikki, trying to bring order into the house.

The two strong and fearsome men did exactly as Mielikki instructed. We all stopped doing whatever we were doing and sat at the table. Except for Thorstein, he was still covered in ash, focused on cleaning the fireplace. He reminded me for a moment of Thrúd playing with the ashes.

After a calmer explanation, what had happened was that Olaf and Ragnar went to the trading town, and overheard a conversation between some traders saying that one of the "fanatic scum" had been captured and probably being tortured. They described him as a muscled, bald, Danish, scarred and heavily inked warrior captured during the disturbances that happened the day I ran away from Uppsala. There wasn't much room for doubt. It was Knut.

"So, how do you know they think that you're dead, Olaf?" Mielikki asked after this first calm and contextualised explanation from the two men.

"We asked to speak privately with the trader and asked him to give us some more information on the matter. He kindly told us that the word is that the redhead giant fled like a coward, mortally wounded and that it was a matter of time before Knut would reveal Sigurd's location, hiding spot, relatives or friends," explained Ragnar calmly.

"Ragnar, 'He kindly told us'?" asked Mielikki, with an inquisitive look.

Ragnar extended his arm and grabbed his wife's hand with care, and while caressing her hand, he slightly shook his head, whispering, "My love…"

She reacted with a concerned and surprised expression. She then kissed her husband's hand and whispered, "Ragnar, you didn't…?"

The delicate and romantic scene was abruptly interrupted by Olaf's brute and loud voice.

"We stuck a hoe's handle in his ass and told him that either words or the handle would come out of his mouth," said Olaf between burps while finishing his cup of beer.

I burst out laughing. I couldn't resist seeing how Olaf was the farthest thing from romance or delicacy.

Ragnar looked at his wife and shrugged. Thorstein also started laughing and Mielikki, at the end, smiled, shaking her head in resignation.

"Well then, what did he say about us?" she finally asked.

"He knows nothing. Nobody ever mentioned our name. We're clear," said Ragnar.

I then asked the feared question, "Any news about my family?"

"Sadly, nothing. But perhaps this is a good thing, Sigurd. Sometimes, no news is good news," said Olaf.

"Sometimes..." I murmured.

We kept drinking our beer in silence for a moment. But then the question that everybody had in their minds was finally uttered.

"What are we going to do? How can we help Knut?" Mielikki asked.

We all drank another sip.

"We'll do exactly what Knut would do in our position: Everything that is possible to save him. We just need to think of a plan. This needs to be properly thought through," said Ragnar.

After that, each one of us returned to doing what we were doing before the blazing news was delivered. Thorstein continued cleaning the fireplace and fixing it. Apparently, part of the smoke-guiding structure fell down during their absence. I helped Mielikki clean the rabbits. Ragnar and Olaf unloaded the carriage.

After dinner, we went outside, on the steps, where we usually sat in the evening, right before going to sleep. We stared at the stars in silence, thinking.

The first one to speak was Olaf.

"All right, this is what I suggest doing. I dress myself as a peasant, perhaps an old and sick one. I try to get close to where Knut is being held. Once I'm close, I get rid of the guards, grab Knut and escape in a straight line that, previously, Ragnar would have cleared for me using the same disguise. Thoughts?"

We all looked at each other, and then Ragnar replied.

"Olaf, I've always admired your heart, courage and skill in battle; but not your strategic thinking, my friend. You're as tall as a giant and as big as a bear. How can you possibly pass for an old and ill man? You've also lived there for several winters. You would be immediately recognised."

"Hmmm... Perhaps you're right," said Olaf, frustrated.

"Perhaps? We don't even know how many guards they have. We don't know if the number increased or not. We know nothing. A direct confrontation is suicide. We're only two," said Ragnar.

"But you know we can take many of them. You know this Ragnar..." said Olaf, still frustrated.

"Yes, brother, I know. But not all of them. Don't you remember what happened there? Even Eirik was overwhelmed by the guards... You know that this was planned somehow. We don't know what else has been planned nor where Knut is being held captive," said Ragnar.

Olaf exhaled, resigned, frustrated, and hopeless.

We all stayed there thinking for a long time, some of us murmuring the plan before presenting it to the others, but every time we encountered the same problems: We were too few and had no information.

All sorts of plans and strategies were discussed, ranging from a full-blown attack from Olaf as a distraction to Mielikki proposing that she could slip through and free Knut somehow. We only had Olaf and Ragnar as fighters. I was wanted. Thorstein was only a few winters older than me and Mielikki couldn't fight.

The more the night advanced, the more our hope kept extinguishing.

At a given point, late in the night, when Mielikki fell asleep in Ragnar's lap, Thorstein stood up and left into the wild and thick darkness of the trees.

"Where is he going?" I asked, astonished.

"He's gone where he feels more at home," said Ragnar calmly, as if this behaviour was normal.

I looked at Olaf, and he shrugged. He also seemed surprised by Thorstein's behaviour.

We went to sleep with our minds still busy trying to figure out a way of rescuing Knut without dying in the process. I got little sleep. I couldn't stop thinking, but every single plan that came to my mind could be easily countered by the problems mentioned earlier.

It was a sunny and warm morning. The sky was clear; the birds were chirping right outside the house and the noise of the water could be heard clearly.

I helped Mielikki with the house chores and then went outside to train some axe combat with Olaf. He really wanted me to learn as much as possible, just in case. Ragnar worked in the field since his son was nowhere to be seen.

The evening came upon us and still no news from the dark-skinned boy. After dinner, we went outside and shared some other ideas about how to rescue Knut. None of them seemed feasible. Before going to sleep, I couldn't help myself. "Mielikki, where is Thorstein? Are you worried something happened to him?"

"I don't know where he is, Sigurd, but this is normal. Don't worry. He needs alone time in the wild from time to time, especially when he gets stressed," said the beautiful woman.

I was surprised that Thorstein could even be capable of getting stressed. He wasn't the most expressive person around, let's put it that way.

A few days passed. Ragnar and Olaf went to the trading town again, trying to get some more information, but no news came from the south. Thorstein was still missing, and we weren't any closer to having a rescue plan.

We couldn't go back to Norway, to our town, asking for help; because I was still wanted and Olaf presumed dead. We didn't know the extent of the influence of whoever planned all of this. All the evidence pointed towards the chief of Uppsala, Svein, but he wasn't that ambitious nor smart. We couldn't trust anybody right now.

We were having lunch when the door of the house opened. It was Thorstein. He was dirty, with green, brown and black stains on his clothes and a few scratches on his body. He was carrying several rabbits and a couple of birds.

He left the dead animals on the food preparation station, went to his mother, kissed her on the head, nodded to his father and went to clean himself. He didn't say a word.

When Thorstein returned, he grabbed a plate of food and joined us at the table. Still, no words pronounced.

"Son, the perimeter is still clear?" asked Ragnar.

Thorstein nodded.

"And the traps?"

Thorstein stopped eating for a moment. It looked like he was mentally counting or trying to recollect a memory. After a short while, he convincingly nodded again and continued eating.

We all finished eating in silence. We were very frustrated by the lack of a plan to help Knut, a dear friend, family.

While I was helping Mielikki clean, Olaf and Ragnar were preparing to go outside, when suddenly Thorstein, who was still sitting at the table, said, "Sit at the table. All."

Since he had returned, he looked like he was in a constant and intense thinking process, except for the times that he had to answer, so to speak, Ragnar's questions.

Ragnar and Mielikki immediately sat at the table, not out of obedience but of respect. Olaf and I looked at each other. He shrugged like saying, 'I don't know what's going on but let's see what happens', and then we sat at the table.

Thorstein had his eyes fixed on the table. He didn't even look at us directly. It appeared as if he was in a different place.

"We need firstly to scout the town to locate Knut. Most probably, he's being held in the town hall. Then we need a plan to free him. All of these things need to be done without dying in the process," started saying Thorstein, stating the obvious. I was wondering what all of this was about when he interrupted my thoughts by continuing his speech.

"We need silence, stealth, and camouflage to scout the town. Unknown faces in unknown bodies. That's what we need. We'll need to set up a camp close enough to the town but not so close to getting caught. Travel fast and light, by foot. We need to keep out of common paths, crossing the wilderness to get to our camp location."

At this point, we all started looking at each other in awe while the boy kept laying out his plan.

"For the camp location, we'll use the same cave that Sigurd used when he escaped. The entrance point is narrow and some traps can be placed easily. Fires won't be allowed this time."

He directed a quick look at me when he said this last thing. I was about to explain myself regarding the fire that I had lit when I escaped, but he didn't give me the chance. He continued what we now understood was his plan's pitch.

"We'll have the support of my tribe," he continued. Then he proceeded to say some things in another language, Mielikki's language. She looked very surprised at what he said. She quickly replied something. He nodded and continued the explanation.

"They'll join us 'where bears meet' in seven days. After that, you'll go to the cave. I'll join them in the scouting party."

Wait, they'll join us? How did he talk to them? Who agreed to this? I immediately looked at Olaf. He gently put his hand on my arm and closed his eyes with a slow nod. I turned my attention back to Thorstein. I never heard him talk this much.

"We verify Knut is being held in the town hall. That should be our best bet. Then we extract him. We'll need you to be ready for that. We'll bring him to the eastern gate of the town where you'll pick him up and bring him to the cave camp in case he's too wounded to walk long distances. If he can walk, though, you'll need to march north towards here, following a path similar to Sigurd's."

For a moment, he paused. Finally, raising his light blue eyes that contrasted so much with his darker skin, looked at each one of us, seeking for any disapproval sign. He found none, only a gaze.

"Initially, I don't think we'll need help on freeing Knut. But perhaps a distraction is going to be needed at the northern gate, the farthest gate from the town hall. Can you provide that for us, Father?"

"Yes. I can do that. Are you sure you don't need backup?" said Ragnar.

"I'm not sure, but we shouldn't need it if everything goes as expected. In any case, you and Olaf will need to be prepared for battle at the eastern gate. So, as soon as you set up the distraction, you'll

189

need to rush from the northern gate to the eastern gate, where the extraction will take place."

"I can do that," said Ragnar.

Thorstein then looked at Olaf. "Olaf, I won't ask for your intervention unless it becomes strictly necessary. You need to keep being presumed dead as much as possible."

"I understand. But I won't leave you alone. I'd rather die for real this time than leave anybody behind again," replied Olaf.

"What can I do?" I asked, seeing how I was being left out of the plan.

"Sigurd, you won't be in the fight. It wouldn't help us. But you need to be our eyes. You'll be to us what Huginn and Muninn are to Odin. I've seen that you have great eyesight, is that right?" said Thorstein.

"Yes, I do. Father always said that I had an eagle's eyesight," I proudly replied.

"Good. You'll need to go to the hill that is in front of the eastern gate. The same hill that you circumnavigated from the back when you escaped. There is a big beech tree, with good foliage. You'll need to climb it and make sure that the plan is going as expected. If it shouldn't, you're the one in charge of letting every single party involved know. Without you, our success is impossible," said Thorstein.

"Sure. I understand." I replied.

"You'll need to tell Father and Olaf if the plan is going sideways so that they can enter the town and go to battle. If we fail, and you don't warn them to come to our aid, we'll die. You'll have eyes over the palisade and into the town," said Thorstein.

What initially seemed to me like a redundant task to keep me busy and proud of myself just revealed itself to be one of the most important tasks in the plan. Indeed, if something went wrong, Olaf and Ragnar wouldn't know about it until it was too late. I would need to be as sharp as possible.

"Questions? Are you all in?" finally added Thorstein.

He stared at his parents until they answered.

"We are in, son," Ragnar proudly said while putting his arm over his wife's shoulders.

Then Thorstein turned to Olaf.

"I'm in, you little elf..." jokingly said Olaf.

He finally looked at me. Never smiling nor changing his facial expression during this whole time. He was dead serious and focused on the matter at hand.

"Yes, Thorstein, I trust you. I'm in," I said convincingly.

After that, Thorstein hit the table with the palms of both hands, as if he was affirming and sealing everything that had been said, and stood up promptly. He then went directly outside to the crop field and started working on it.

We all returned to our affairs and started going through the plan over and over in our heads. We would need to be rested because the following day, we would depart towards the place where everything happened. A desperate mission trying to rescue the last person who was still alive.

Chapter 23
Remember

It was pitch black. The only source of light was a fire lit in the middle of the forest. I was staring at the dancing flames when I looked up and saw Father's face.

He was sitting in front of me, strong and proud, holding a horn with mead. Sitting to my right, was a strong man with long hair. He also had a horn with mead. His forehead was inked with The Helm of Awe. He smiled and winked at me. Then, he looked at Father and said, "Brother, what a warrior he would have been."

Father sipped his mead, then looked at my uncle Harald and said, "He may still become one, brother. If Odin wishes so."

They clashed their horns and drank. I tried to talk or to scream, but nothing came out of my mouth, no sound at all.

Father then looked at me with his ice-blue eyes and said, "It's time, Sigurd. It's time." After that, he poured what mead was left in his horn on the fire, extinguishing it and leaving us in complete darkness.

I called for him, but he didn't reply. I called for my uncle Harald but still got no reply. Then I started crying for help. Mother, Grandmother, Gudrod... Nobody answered. Suddenly, a powerful arm grabbed my shoulder. "Sigurd!"

I woke up soaked in sweat. It was still very early. The sun was slowly starting to rise. I was in Ragnar's home, and the arm belonged to Olaf.

"Boy, you were having nightmares again," said Olaf with a surprisingly low and gentle voice.

"I'm sorry Olaf, if I woke you up. It was Father, and Uncle Harald, and..." I started explaining.

"No need to explain, Sigurd. There is no need to explain..." replied the red-headed giant as he walked back to his bed.

Shortly after that, everybody started waking up and preparing for our voyage. Ragnar went with Olaf and started packing weapons and camping materials. Thorstein went to the field to grab whatever was ripe and patrolled the traps. Mielikki started tidying the house, packing clothes and preparing some food for the journey.

I walked out of the house. I was still soaked in sweat and kind of sleepy. It was a chilly morning, but it looked like the day would grow warm. Fog covered everything. I could barely see Thorstein in the field.

I stood outside for a moment, feeling like I needed some fresh air to regain my strength and focus again on the task at hand. But suddenly I saw a shape in the fog. It looked like the shape of a man, but I couldn't distinguish it properly.

A small breeze moved most of the dense fog between the shape and me. I could see it clearly now, standing on the other side of the clearing where Ragnar and Mielikki had made their home; an old man covered with a withered cloak holding a walking staff.

His face was half covered. I could only see his big aquiline nose and one of his ice-blue eyes. The moment I looked at his eye, he looked back at me, piercing me with his look. I felt like I couldn't hide anything from him, no emotion nor feeling nor thought.

He then looked at my chest, where Odin's mark appeared in The Great Temple, and it was like my body suddenly remembered the burning feeling that I had when I first got the mark. I grabbed my left chest with my right hand, asking him why.

A word resonated in my head, "Remember."

I kept looking at him, at his eye, as directly as I could, without even blinking. He smirked and extended the arm that wasn't holding the staff, pointing towards the trees behind Ragnar's house.

I followed the direction of the arm, saw the trees and then looked back at him, wondering what he meant. His eye opened and got lit with a white, bluish light, so intense that it blinded me. My chest burnt and my mind heard "Remember" loudly one more time. I fell backwards and landed on my backside.

I looked back at the old man, but he wasn't there anymore. Olaf came to my aid when he saw me on the floor.

"Boy, are you alright? What happened to you?" asked Olaf, concerned.

"Olaf, what's behind those trees?" I asked, pointing towards the trees that the old man pointed me to.

Olaf looked surprised and concerned at the same time. He then started mumbling, "Those... Trees you say? Well... It's been a long time... I would have to ask Ragnar..."

I went directly to grab my axe and marched towards the trees. My chest was still burning and my mind was repeating "Remember" over and over, but it wasn't using my own voice. It was using the old man's.

I passed the house and started heading towards the trees. I heard Olaf running back, calling for Ragnar.

While I was walking, I sensed under my feet that the vegetation, the grass, wasn't as mushy as in all other places. I kneeled and started cutting the grass with my axe. After digging a little, I found stone. It wasn't natural stone but rather carefully placed stone. It was a pathway. Long ago, there used to be a stone pathway heading towards these trees.

I renewed my march and heard that Ragnar and Olaf were close behind me, and Mielikki was right behind them, too.

I arrived at the trees and found nothing. I kept walking, trying to sense the ground and walk on the terrain where it looked like there could be stone under the vegetation and grass.

After a few steps, I encountered an enormous boulder covered in leaves and plants. It was a very tall and oval rock. It had plants falling down from the top. I knew this must have been it. I started cutting and slicing with my axe, pulling down leaves, branches, and vines. Slowly, the boulder was revealing itself. It was hollow.

After pulling several vines at once, a stone face was revealed in the highest part of the hollowed boulder. The face had a prominent nose, a beard and a big scar on one eye. Why was this forgotten and abandoned? Why wasn't this taken care of?

I got enraged. I started pulling vines, cutting branches, kicking trunks and punching moss. By this time, the others arrived and were behind me, watching me.

I uncovered most of the hollowed rock. It was very clear now. It was an oval hollowed enormous boulder with a statue inside it. A stone-carved statue of Odin himself, with Huginn and Muninn on each one of his shoulders and with Geri and Freki at his feet. Both Geri and Freki had pendants hanging from their necks, Geri had three intertwined triangles. The same mark that appeared on my chest and the same one that Father had inked in his. Freki, on the other hand, had The Helm of Awe.

This was an exact replica of the statue in The Great Temple, but it looked older, way older, almost ancient.

"Why Ragnar? Olaf?" I asked while turning around and looking at them.

I was dirty, and bloody because of several scratches that I did to myself while wrestling with the plants and still soaked in sweat, this time from the effort. But most of all, I was enraged. I couldn't understand why this had been abandoned this way.

"Why?!" I yelled.

They all looked at each other, concerned. At a distance, I saw Thorstein was following what was happening too.

"Sigurd, come into the house. It's cold and you're not properly dressed. Clean yourself, eat someth-" Olaf started saying before I interrupted him.

"Why Olaf? I don't care!" I yelled.

I couldn't think straight. The only thing that I had in my mind was rage. Father died protecting this. He died for Odin. Uncle Harald too. These two men, Olaf and Ragnar, were supposed to be the same. They were supposed to dedicate their lives to the service of Odin. They swore it. How can they allow this to happen? Why did the old man have to appear to me for this to be properly tended and not left to rot?

"Sigurd," Olaf started saying with a very gentle voice, slowly walking towards me with his hands raised. "Sigurd, my boy... Let me grab that axe. Let's go inside and I'll tell you everything. But freezing here or getting sick won't resolve anything. We need you in good shape if we want to have any chances of rescuing Knut."

195

Knut… Right. I almost forgot. Olaf was right.

"Olaf, I'll go into the house. Only if you promise me that as soon as I'm washed and dressed you will sit with me and explain everything to me," I said while surrendering my axe to him and walking towards the house.

He nodded and placed his hand on my back. Mielikki did the same from the other side as she gently said "Don't you worry, little one. We'll grab something to eat before leaving. We'll talk about this inside."

I nodded and kept walking. Once we arrived at the edge of the clearing, where Thorstein was standing, I stopped.

"Thorstein, did you capture anything this morning?" I asked.

"Yes. A rabbit in one of the traps. I'll kill it now and prepare it for the voyage," he replied.

"Don't. Let me do it." I said while looking back towards the huge boulder.

Thorstein looked at the boulder and then at me. He nodded as a sign of understanding.

I finally washed myself, put some decent clothes on and sat at the table. Soon enough Olaf and Ragnar joined me. Mielikki was still finishing preparing the food, some cereal porridge with berries.

"Sigurd, I even forgot that it existed. It was a long time ago," Ragnar started saying.

"But why, Ragnar?" I calmly replied.

Ragnar sighed and looked at Olaf. Olaf nodded. Then Ragnar started explaining.

"You see Sigurd, you know that this place was a safe house for The Twelve. But what you perhaps didn't know is that this was the Origin of The Twelve. Here is where it's said that the first twelve warriors swore an oath to Odin himself. As a commemoration of it, they carved the boulder that you saw outside. Allegedly, there were other carved boulders, but they have been destroyed with the passing of time," explained Ragnar.

"And why was this one forgotten and abandoned? I know Odin is not pleased by this," I replied.

When I mentioned this, Ragnar stopped and looked again at Olaf. Olaf smiled and touched his left chest while looking Ragnar straight in the eyes. Ragnar then smiled back.

"I should have known. I didn't want to believe it, even though I knew it deep inside me. After all... You're Eirik's son and Harald's nephew!" said Ragnar with a smile.

I didn't smile much. My chest was still burning, not as much as before, but enough to keep me focused on this.

"Sigurd, this boulder was properly tended the last time that we all served together. The last time that we were all here. But, after the death of Harald, everything started falling apart," Ragnar explained.

"I see..." I answered, hoping that he would keep talking.

"It's strange because we've lost many brothers, but something broke when Harald fell. Especially inside your father. Something broke deep inside..." he replied, almost as if he was talking to himself, immersed in his own thoughts.

"We all scattered after that," said Olaf, "Ragnar and I went with a few others and ended up in Finland, where we met Mielikki. Then I went to The Great Temple. Gudrod went back to his father's estate and then went to Uppsala, too. Knut went to Denmark and raised his family and raided for a living. And the rest... Well, the rest we don't quite know..."

After saying these words, Olaf also seemed to enter a world of his own, inside his own mind.

"This was a path of pain, Sigurd, for all of them. They took an oath, but that doesn't mean that they didn't suffer along the way. Perhaps more than anybody," said Mielikki with a compassionate tone while standing behind Ragnar and caressing his hair.

"I understand. I'm sorry if I..." I started saying when Olaf interrupted me with his usual loud voice, almost as if he just awoke from a long sleep.

"Don't say a word, Sigurd! Curiosity is good, and rage too! If properly channelled. Don't you feel pity for us. We chose this path even if it was already chosen for us. If I went back, I would have done exactly the same a thousand times," said the giant man, while hitting Ragnar in the back with his huge hands.

"A thousand times, old friend!" said Ragnar with a huge smile and renewed energy.

"Well then, I think it's time to 'Remember' those times and never forget," I said.

Olaf and Ragnar looked at each other, then looked back at me and nodded.

"I'll need guidance. I hoped you could provide me with that," I said.

"I would die before abandoning you, Sigurd. I'll do my best to provide you with the guidance and training that you'll need to fulfil your destiny. It'll be my honour," said Olaf.

"And mine," said Ragnar while taking his fist to his chest.

I smiled and nodded gratefully.

"Ok, now eat!" said Mielikki while sitting at the table after she had put a plate in front of each one of us.

We finished preparing ourselves for the voyage that lay ahead of us. We would only use one horse to carry our belongings as far as possible, and then Thorsteinn would send it back here. That horse had memorised several secure routes back home, Thorstein trained it well.

I rushed my preparations so that I could have some time to myself. I went towards the partially uncovered boulder and took some time to remove every single branch, leaf, or vine that was covering the sculpture. I cleaned it with a bucket of water, trying to remove the moss, mud, and dirt.

Once we were about to depart, I asked Thorstein to bring me the rabbit that he had captured. I waited for him, kneeling in front of the sculpture, staring at Odin, Geri, Freki, Huginn and Muninn. I felt his presence. My chest didn't burn that much anymore, but I felt the god's presence strongly inside me. It was like I was at The Great Temple again.

Even though Thorstein was quick in bringing me the rabbit, it felt like an entire day. Everything came back to me, every single moment that led me to that place, to that instant. I saw Father teaching me how to use the axe back home when I could barely walk. I remembered the pilgrimage to get to Uppsala, how he was mentally elsewhere the entire trip, knowing that he would be sacrificed to fulfil his promise to the gods. Grandmother and her tenderness and infinite wisdom. Mother and her love for us. Thrúd, my little sister, so special...

"Sigurd!" said Thorstein, interrupting my meditation.

He had brought me the rabbit. I took it in my arms and moved close to the sculpture. I heard the steps of Ragnar, Olaf, and Mielikki behind me. They were all behind me, forming a semicircle, ready for the improvised ceremony.

I looked into Odin's eye, asking him for guidance, for I never had sacrificed before. I had killed while hunting or fishing, but never did I kill for an offering.

I started asking in my mind, "Give me the strength to fulfil your will, All-father." Over and over. So intensely that I started murmuring these same words. The moment I murmured these words, I heard how everybody behind me moved nervously, perhaps even confused, but I ignored that and kept repeating the words over and over.

Without even thinking about it, I took my knife and slit the rabbit's throat. I wasn't completely conscious of what I was doing. It was like a dream, a dream where I was seeing myself from above.

I then wet my hands with blood and passed them on Odin's face, the ravens' beaks and the wolves' mouths. I passed the blood through my own face, from the forehead down to the chin. I put my hand in the small bowl that I had placed earlier, where most of the blood was falling into, and put it on my chest. Finally, I drank a sip.

I never stopped repeating the same words over and over "Give me the strength to fulfil your will, All-father."

I turned and saw everyone's faces; they were in awe. I didn't pay attention to it. I simply signalled for them to come close to me. Thorstein came forward. I placed my hand into the bowl and put a mark on his forehead, then he drank a sip. Then Mielikki came forward, and I did the same operation.

Ragnar came forward. I placed my wet fingers on his forehead and dragged them down to his chin. He then drank a sip of blood.

Then Olaf came forward, his eyes wide open, his expression was of awe and surprise. I ignored that and continued with the ritual. I marked him from his forehead to his chin, but this time, before he sipped the blood, I placed my right fist on his left chest and then on mine, leaving a bloodstain on both our chests.

He lowered his eyes and gently bowed to me, then took a few steps backwards and joined the others.

All of this was happening, and I wasn't completely aware of why or how. It was like it wasn't me making decisions anymore. I could see myself murmuring words that in my head sounded like a prayer, but I'm not sure that the words that came out of my mouth matched those that I heard in my head.

I turned around and carefully placed the bowl at Odin's feet. Taking a moment to finalise some prayers, I asked him to protect us on our journey and to help us succeed in our rescue mission. I also asked him to guide and protect Mother and Thrúd, in the eventuality that they were still alive. And, finally, I wondered why Father didn't show himself to me. Why could I see Odin himself and not Father?

After a moment where all of us stayed silent, in front of the sculpture, I turned around. The moment that I turned around and opened my eyes again, I returned to full consciousness.

I must have had a strange face because Mielikki came running towards me and hugged me. She then grabbed both my cheeks and with an incredibly sweet voice she said, "You're a very special boy, Sigurd. Very special..." and kissed me on the head. I was utterly confused. Ragnar came and hugged me, too. Thorstein stared at me for a while, nodded, and left. Finally, Olaf came to me. He was still visibly shaken.

"How did you...? When did you...?" said Olaf, not being able to finish a sentence.

"I don't understand, Olaf. Could you try finishing what you're trying to-" I started saying in a joking tone when Olaf interrupted me. He was dead serious, which was extremely strange coming from him.

"When did you learn that? Those words?" he asked in a very serious tone while grabbing me by my shoulders.

"Which words? I was just praying, Olaf. Like I always do. Why?" I replied, confused and a little scared.

"You don't remember, don't you? Perhaps you didn't even realise it," he said, pensively.

"Remember what exactly? I simply said: 'Give me the strength to fulf-"

"No! No! Nonsense boy... That's what the words meant, but you didn't use these words..." he said while getting down on one knee and looking me dead serious in the eyes.

"Olaf, you're scaring me..." I mumbled.

Then Olaf started talking in that ancient language that the *völva* used. The same language that I heard Father, Grandmother, and Olaf himself speak whenever they were in the middle of rituals.

In the beginning, perhaps because I was frightened, I didn't understand a word. But Olaf kept repeating the same sentence over and over. Maybe the third time that he said it I somehow understood it "Give me the strength to fulfil your will, All-father."

How was this possible? I never could understand a word of what was spoken in this language...

Olaf read in my face that I finally understood it, perhaps because I was surprised and scared at the same time and, I must say, Olaf's attitude wasn't helping much. He stopped speaking in that language.

He then sighed, looking downwards. I was scared, thinking that something horrible had happened. But while I was navigating in my deepest thoughts of fear, he raised his head again, looking at me. This time, he had a gentle smile and a proud face. He hugged me strongly, perhaps too strongly. He then grabbed my head with his huge hands and put his forehead against mine.

"Sigurd, you're a very special boy, like Mielikki said. Your connection to the gods gets stronger every day. The blood of Odin's Wolves surely runs through your veins. It's an honour for me to accompany you on this journey. I just hope that I'm worthy enough to guide you at the beginning of it," said the red-headed giant.

"Olaf... I am the one who hopes to be worthy, worthy of any of this. I'm blessed to have you by my side taking care of me," I replied while hugging him. Well, hugging his neck that perhaps was as thick as my chest.

"Don't worry, little one. Soon enough, you'll take care of all of us," Olaf replied while patting my back.

We headed back to the clearing. The yield of the field had been collected, stored, and placed on top of the horse. All the tools were placed in the small tool shed near the field. The house was shut and everything inside was tidy.

I really loved this place. It was so unique that sometimes I thought I was in a dream. A small island in the middle of thousands of islands, rivers, lakes and streams. All covered by dense vegetation, a vast forest interrupted only by water. Everything covered but this small clearing on this small island. A house built halfway underground, a field, a tool shed and half a roof for two horses. And now, Odin's sculpture, cleaned, exposed and tended to.

I wondered if I would ever see this place again. I hoped I would, but just in case, I wanted to give it a last look, trying to memorise every single detail.

"Let's go now. We're already very late. They'll be waiting for us," said Thorstein while starting to walk.

We all followed. Our rescue mission had officially started. We would have to walk our way through the wilderness until we got to where I was almost eaten by the bear. There we would meet with the Finnish tribe. I was very curious about this encounter. I still didn't understand how Thorstein communicated with them in such a short time. Hopefully, I could find some answers along the way.

Chapter 24

Transformation

After several days of walking, we finally arrived at a small hill. Thorstein ran up and started scouting the horizon. The rest of us slowly made our way up. Once we arrived at the top, Thorstein pointed towards a forest patch in the distance and said something in Finnish. Mielikki asked him something in the same language. He replied and started walking down the hill. She followed him.

"That's the Bears' Nest," said Ragnar to us before following his wife and son down the hill.

Olaf looked at me, shrugged, and followed the others. I did the same.

We reached the "Bears' Nest" early the next morning. I could barely recognise the place, even though I had been there running for my life in the not-so-distant past. Perhaps I was too weak and afraid at that time.

Before entering the thick forest, Thorstein unloaded the horse and whispered some words into its ear. The horse then started walking in the same direction where we came from.

"He'll get back home. Now we must continue on foot," said Thorstein while splitting the bags into five equal parts that we would have to carry onwards.

We went towards the centre of this dense forest, arriving at a tiny clearing where just a couple of trees were missing. The sun still couldn't penetrate the tree canopy. Most of the tree trunks were covered in lichens or moss.

Thorstein then said something in Finnish to his parents, dropped the bag and took off into the thick wall of green.

Since we left the house, Thorstein didn't pronounce a single word, except for some short sentences in Finnish to his mother. He looked extremely focused, blending into the wilderness, behaving more and more like an animal and less like a person.

"Let's sit down. We'll be here for a while now," said Ragnar while putting down his bag and sitting on a dead tree trunk.

"We should make camp, Ragnar," said Olaf while also dropping his bag on the ground.

"No. We wait," said Ragnar.

"Wait for what? Wolves? Bears?" I asked, concerned.

"We wait for Thorstein to come back," said Ragnar calmly.

We all dropped our bags and sat on the tree trunk. We waited for quite some time. Ragnar laid down and fell asleep. Mielikki wandered close to us, picking up leaves and some mushrooms. Olaf sharpened his axe, and I carved a piece of wood, making a small sculpture of Odin, or at least trying to.

Olaf was grumpy. He didn't understand why we couldn't make camp and light a fire rather than wait for Thorstein to come back. He was impatient because of Knut, fearing that any more delays would cost his old friend's life.

Suddenly, out of nowhere and without making a sound, Thorstein appeared. He had stains of dirt and mud everywhere. He headed directly towards his father and gave him a small kick on the leg to wake him up, not pronouncing a word. Ragnar woke up.

"Are they here?" Ragnar asked while opening his eyes.

"Soon," said Thorstein.

The dark-skinned boy then climbed the nearest tree and lay on a big branch. I never actually saw him in the wilderness. I always saw him coming and going, but never in it. This was really his home, where he felt most comfortable. I understood that now.

We waited for a little longer. Suddenly, Thorstein imitated the sound of an owl, signalling something. We looked around and couldn't see anything.

"What? What is happening?" asked Olaf impatiently.

"They're here," said Mielikki while looking at a tight group of trees and nodding with a huge smile.

I looked at Olaf, and he looked even more confused than I was. Ragnar stood up, dusted off the dirt from his pants, and prepared to meet our guests. I still couldn't see anybody.

Mielikki raised her voice and said something in Finnish as if she was talking to the trees.

Then we started to hear several animal noises. An owl from one direction, a wolf from another, even a squirrel noise from a different direction. I was looking everywhere and couldn't see anything.

One of the trees moved. What seemed like another tree trunk covered in moss was a person. He entered the small clearing and stood there for a moment, looking at Olaf and me. He was completely covered in green paint, with plants attached to his clothes and body. If he closed his eyes, you wouldn't even think of him as human. He had a short sword in what looked like a belt and was carrying short spears, amongst other items that I couldn't quite identify.

Mielikki spoke to him again, this time with a lower voice. The man bowed to her and yelled what sounded like a command.

From everywhere, men started coming into the clearing. All of them seemed to be there, almost in plain sight, and none of us had seen them, except for Thorstein.

The first men that came into the clearing were completely covered in paint, plants, moss, animal horns, and all sorts of things that made them look like moving plants.

Thorstein jumped from the tree and stood in front of the first man that came out. These men were very short in stature but very strong. They had very developed muscles. Thorstein was as tall as their chieftain. The man grabbed the boy from the nape and said something to him. Thorstein briefly replied, then he started greeting all the others, one by one, and they were thrilled to see him; even though they didn't seem to display many emotions.

Mielikki and Ragnar greeted them while Olaf and I stood back. Then the man came to us. He was taller than me, but considerably shorter than Olaf. He looked at Olaf first, then at me. The man said nothing, and neither did we. This situation lasted for a while. I was feeling studied and, honestly, threatened.

Mielikki said something in her language with a very sweet and kind voice. The man immediately smirked and relaxed.

"My name is Piru," said the man with a deep voice.

It surprised me that a man of his short stature would have such a deep voice, but again, Father and Knut also had deep voices and weren't gigantic men like Olaf. Having said that, Father would look like a tall man near Piru.

"My name is Olaf," said Olaf with an even deeper voice and a serious face.

Piru looked back at Thorstein and asked him something in Finnish. Thorstein nodded. Then the man looked back at Olaf.

"It's an honour to meet 'The Bear'," Piru said with a very thick accent while respectfully nodding.

He then looked at me. I looked back at him, straight in the eyes. Piru was an intimidating man, now that he was so close I could see past the paint, moss, and other camouflage apparel; he had very strong and developed muscles; his body was covered in scars and greenish ink with many symbols. He had a huge scar crossing the top right of his face, interrupting his eyebrow. And another one going from his left eye all the way to his mouth. The entire upper lip was scarred, too. He had a thick beard with beads and some small bones; also covered in green paint.

"You look for the soul, boy?" asked the man while staring deep into my eyes.

He strangely had black eyes. All the other men from his tribe had clear eyes, but he had the darkest eyes I've ever seen.

"Soul?" I asked, confused. I never heard that term before.

"It's what southern men call the spirit that inhabits each one of us. What makes us talk, think and feel," said Piru without moving an inch.

"In that case, sir, I'm not sure you have one," I replied.

I don't even know why I said those words. They just came out. Somehow I felt that this man was dark, not only his eyes but his spirit. I felt darkness in him.

The man smirked. He then said something in Finnish in a deep but loud voice so that everybody could hear it, still without breaking eye contact.

"It is an honour to meet you too, Sigurd, son of Eirik," said Piru while placing his firm hand on my shoulder.

He then turned and started giving commands to his men, after which they started moving quickly. Some of them made more animal noises and others went running into the wild.

Shortly after more men arrived, these were not wearing the same amount of camouflage that the first ones did. It must have been a party of around thirty men. After the initial greetings with Thorstein, Mielikki and Ragnar; we sat down and ate together.

We went over the plan again. Ragnar, Olaf, Mielikki, and I would go to the cave. Thorstein would join the tribesmen and scout the town. We would sleep in the cave and at first light, the extraction would happen. The tribespeople would sleep in the forest that is in front of the western gate.

After eating together, we packed again and prepared to resume our journey. We would arrive at the cave close to dark.

Mielikki hugged Thorstein and spoke to him in Finnish. Then Ragnar grabbed his son's head and spoke to him.

"May Odin guide your wisdom, son. May you have the strength of Thor and the cunning of Loki. May the skill of Tyr guide your hand, and may the *Metsänhaltija* guide you through the wilderness. May your enemies swiftly meet Kalma in Tuonela."

Thorstein nodded energetically, joined his forehead with his father's almost in a headbutt, and then left with the tribespeople through the trees.

I didn't understand the last part of what Ragnar told his son. Tyr was a skilled warrior, perhaps one of the most skilled among the gods. Thor was undoubtedly the strongest, Loki the most cunning, and Odin the wisest. But I had no clue who *Metsänhaltija* and Kalma were and what Tuonela exactly was.

We resumed our journey towards the cave. Mielikki was visibly worried about her son. Ragnar looked more proud than worried. After some time walking in silence, immersed in our thoughts, I took my chance to look for answers.

"Ragnar, who is *Metsänhaltija*?" I asked.

"I was expecting your questions way sooner, Sigurd!" replied Ragnar jokingly, "*Metsänhaltija*, in Mielikki's culture, are forest spirits. They protect the forest and all the animals within it."

"Oh, I see. And Kalma?"

"Well, Kalma is a spirit of death. She's the goddess of decay and rotting flesh. It is said that her stink alone could melt your nose. And, before you ask, Tuonela is where she lives, the underworld," Ragnar patiently replied.

"Thank you, Ragnar. And do you believe in all of this?"

"Why not? Why not give Ukko the same credit that we give to Odin or Thor?"

"I don't know. It doesn't feel right."

"With time, Sigurd, you'll see that what feels right or wrong changes over time."

"Ukko..." Olaf murmured while giggling.

"What's the matter Olaf?" said Ragnar, visibly annoyed.

"Nothing. Nothing. It's just a funny name..." said Olaf, still giggling.

"You're incorrigible..." added Ragnar with a smile.

The day passed, and we travelled with no incidents. In front of us, we could see the town in the distance, the hill in front of the eastern gate, and the bigger hill where the cave was.

Now the time for jokes and relaxation was over. Any wrong move would mean death or worse. We needed to be alert and focused.

We headed towards the bigger hill, towards the cave in complete silence, hoping that Thorstein and the others managed to get to the other side of the town safely, probably they were scouting the town at that very moment, hidden in the ever-growing shadows.

Ragnar was leading the way, behind him, Mielikki; I was behind her, and at the tail was Olaf. We were approaching the big hill by the east, making sure that we always stayed in the woods and outside any paths or roads, and also keeping an elevated terrain between the town and us. We couldn't get spotted. If we did, the plan would immediately fail.

While we were getting closer, I suddenly heard a scream behind me, a scream of desperation and agony. I turned around and saw Olaf down on one knee, gasping for air, groaning. It was like he had been struck by lightning.

"Silence! We'll be heard!" ordered Ragnar.

"Olaf!" I yelled while running towards him.

He raised his eyes to the sky, and I saw his face, a face of desperation. He was looking at the sky in despair, demanding answers from the gods.

He kept moaning, shouting and groaning in pain, even though no visible wound could be seen. He clenched his fists with such strength that blood started pouring out from between his fingers.

We approached him, trying to find out what happened to him. We also wanted to reduce the noise that might lead the guards from the town in our direction. None of us dared to touch him, not even Ragnar, who also was a big and strong warrior.

The pain inside Olaf continued. He grabbed his left chest with his bloody right hand. It looked like he wanted to rip it off. The red hair that was previously tied got loose and fell over his downwards-facing face.

"Olaf…" I murmured while getting close to him to grab him or console him somehow.

"Not now," Mielikki gently said while stopping me by placing her arm over my shoulder and hugging me.

Olaf stopped screaming. Now he was growling in pain and rage, breathing exceedingly quickly and deeply.

Even though I knew it was Olaf, I felt scared. Me not knowing what was happening, his huge and strong body on one knee, his growling, not being able to see his face anymore, just red sweaty hair dangling in front of his darkened face, his bloody hand grabbing and almost tearing apart his chest, the other hand closed in the strongest of fists buried in the ground by the weight…

I looked at Ragnar, wondering why nobody was helping him. But to my surprise, he wasn't looking at Olaf anymore but rather was facing towards the town. He stared at the town for some time and then looked back at Olaf and sighed. He deeply exhaled while lowering his head. Ragnar understood something that escaped my comprehension.

Olaf started slowing his breathing and his growling intensity started decreasing until it eventually stopped. He now was breathing deeply and slowly, a huge contrast to what was happening instants before.

Finally, his right hand released his chest. Blood stains appeared on his shirt due to both his bloody hand and his wounded chest. He stood up slowly, still looking downwards, with his hair in front of his face. Both his fists were clenched strongly at his sides. He slightly raised his head as the last ray of sun hit his eyes and I couldn't recognise them. A frown and evil eyes composed now his face. He looked in our direction, but not directly at us. He looked beyond us as if we didn't even exist.

Mielikki released me, but I didn't dare get close to him. I was genuinely afraid of him. It was like a monster from the underworld. I couldn't recognise Olaf in this man. He started walking with decisive, long and fast strides towards the big hill, completely ignoring us.

"What happened?" I asked while looking at the back of Olaf getting farther away from us.

"I'm not sure… But it's best to leave him alone for now. Don't bother him unless he talks to you first. Understood?" said Ragnar with a very serious tone while still looking at the town and then back again at Olaf.

We continued our way towards the cave in the big hill, lagging behind Olaf's accelerated march. With the last light of the day, we reached the cave. The sun was almost buried, and the moon shone high in the sky.

The cave was empty, except for Olaf. He was at the furthest part from the entrance, where it was almost pitch black. He sat close to where I slept the night that I spent there. His knees were up, his arms resting on his knees and his face looking downwards with his hair falling in front of it.

We ignored him, as Ragnar suggested. We prepared some beds with the furs and hides that we brought with us and also some branches and leaves that we picked up from outside.

Right before first light, the rescue mission would start. We needed to be rested and focused if we wanted to have any chances of rescuing Knut and surviving.

I prepared another bed for Olaf and then went to my bed and prepared for sleep. Olaf hadn't moved since we first saw him.

What happened to him? I wondered while lying down on the uncomfortable bed. What did Ragnar see? Why would Olaf react this way? The pain? The growling?

I couldn't remove from my head the image of the giant redhead growling in pain and desperation, apparently for no reason. But, if something these past moons have taught me is that the truth reveals itself when it is ready to be revealed. I simply had to be patient and wait for the answers to come to me, or wait for the right moment to ask the right questions. For now, I simply had to rest. I needed to be as sharp as an eagle for the mission. My eyesight could make the difference between rescuing Knut or Thorstein dying.

I couldn't sleep properly, at least not completely. I could still hear the wind whistling outside the cave, the tree branches moving and the nocturnal animals making their presence felt.

Suddenly, I heard a movement from within the cave. It was Olaf. He stood up and walked out of the cave. It was almost pitch black, but I could still see him thanks to my eyes being accustomed to the darkness.

I followed him at a distance, in complete silence. Once I got out of the cave, I saw a clear sky, a huge full moon and a raging wind hitting the trees mercilessly. I looked around and couldn't find him anywhere until I heard a noise of stones moving and rolling down the hill.

I started climbing the hill in the noise's direction, and as soon as I climbed over a protruding boulder, I saw Olaf. He was standing on a big flat rock. It looked almost like a terrace from which you could see the entire landscape. He was shirtless. His facial expression hadn't

211

changed since the last time that I saw him. When I saw his eyes and his face, death was the only word that came to mind.

He didn't see me. I was careful enough to remain hidden and silent. He never looked in my direction. He stood there for a while, looking towards the smaller hill that was between Uppsala and the big hill where we were standing. The moonlight exposed all of his scars and inked inscriptions, it also revealed even further his powerful muscles. I never saw him like this, not even when he came prepared for battle rescuing Father at the *Thing*, not even after Grandmother had been brutally murdered.

He looked more than a warrior, more than a berserker, more than one of Odin's warriors... He looked like a god! I couldn't stop admiring him in awe, when, to my surprise, he raised his hands towards the sky and started murmuring some words that I couldn't hear properly nor fully understand.

After a while standing in that position, he started beating his chest, arms, legs, and head. Then, he bent over and reached for a bowl that he had brought with him. He drank the content of that bowl, and then with his fingers grabbed some of the remaining stuff inside it, and ate it. All of this was done while still murmuring words and, from time to time, growling like an enraged animal.

I didn't know if I should've stayed or not, but I felt I needed to leave and let him do whatever he was doing in private. I didn't know if he saw me and ignored me or if he genuinely didn't notice my presence. But this was something that he had to do alone. That I knew.

I descended as silently as possible, entered the cave again and, slowly, found my bed. I was pretty sure that what I saw was Olaf preparing himself for battle, but I never saw him like this. Olaf was barely recognisable in that man.

I tried my best to fall asleep. It wouldn't be much longer before we would have to prepare for the decisive moment.

Chapter 25

Invasion

I was having a dream about being on the beech tree's branches on the small hill, watching over the eastern gate and seeing how Thorstein and the Finnish tribe rescued Knut and everything worked out fine. I was conscious enough to know that I was dreaming, but I was asleep enough to allow the dream to play itself out.

Ragnar's hand on my shoulder finished waking me up. "It's time, Sigurd."

Mielikki was already awake and preparing some food that we brought with us. Ragnar had already eaten his ration and was going back and forth making sure that everything was in order and that we were still hidden from external eyes. Olaf was nowhere to be seen.

I ate accompanied by Mielikki near the firepit that I had lit the time that I was there, but this time we didn't light any fires nor made any noticeable noise. Nobody knew we were there.

With the morning light slowly entering the cave, we could better see the interior. The sacrifices' remains and symbols in the walls... This place had been used for dark purposes, and Mielikki could feel it since we entered it the previous night.

"The sooner we get out of here, the better," she said.

"Isn't it late already? The stars are disappearing and the light is gradually increasing..." I asked, concerned.

"Ragnar has been awake for some time now. No signal from Thorstein. Probably they want the day to start so that the guards can move on and empty the main building where, most probably, Knut is being held," she answered, visibly worried.

"Are you worried that something could happen to Thorstein?" I asked.

"I'm worried that something could happen to any of you, Sigurd."

We finished eating in a hurry and prepared ourselves for whatever could happen. I had my knife with me, like always. I had my axe too. Well, my new axe. The last time that I saw my old axe was buried in the announcer's throat, whoever he might have been.

Ragnar returned to the cave in a hurry. "It's time. Let's get moving."

We immediately stood up and walked towards the entrance of the cave. The sun had still to fully come up, but now the light allowed for a clearer view outside. The stars were almost hidden. It was the first light, and we were ready to rescue Knut, finally.

"To your positions now, hurry!" commanded Ragnar.

I ran down the big hill and upwards to the smaller one. Once I was almost at the top, I started silently walking through the vegetation until I found the big beech tree facing the eastern gate. The same tree where Father had stopped and leaned against when we first arrived here.

I swiftly climbed the tree and cut several branches to clear my view of the town. Ragnar rushed towards the northern gate, ready to create the distraction that Thorstein and the tribesmen so desperately needed for the plan to succeed. Mielikki stayed back, behind some dense bushes, so that she could help carry Knut into the cave or directly home if his health allowed it.

Ragnar reached the northern gate and passed my vision range behind the wooden walls. I could see neither Thorstein nor the tribesmen. I was sweating and my belly was hurting like never before. I never felt so nervous but, at the same time, so alive.

After some time, I started to see smoke coming up from the northern gate. That was Ragnar's distraction, a fire. Soon enough, I started seeing flames rising high. The entire northern gate was on fire. I would discover later on that he and Mielikki spent some time before the first light placing sticks, straw and wood piles against the northern gate, right before waking me up.

A tremendous commotion and chaos sparked in the town. I could see guards running towards the northern part of the town, people running around with buckets of water and everybody shouting. I also saw Ragnar running from the northern gate to the eastern one, just in front of me, and hiding inside some thick bushes. Olaf should have been there with him, but still no sign of him.

I started focusing on the western gate, on the opposite side of the town, to see if I could identify Thorstein or the tribesmen. I could only see the gate closed, no guards, and past the gate, the thick forest of trees.

But soon enough I saw, in the distance, how some of those trees started multiplying and moving. It was the tribesmen. They hid in plain sight and were getting out of the forest and heading towards the western gate. Now my task was easy but essential: sound the alarm if they should get in trouble.

The tribespeople threw reindeer horns over the wall. These horns were tied to a rope that they would use to climb the walls. One of them climbed the wall at each side of the gate, and once inside, they opened the gate just enough to let the others in.

They started moving between the houses, streets and paths of the town in such a way that nobody within the town could spot them. They were always covered by either a house, barn, pantry or any other type of building. Their movement was flawless, synchronised and, simply put, perfect. They really had spent time scouting and planning this invasion of the town. Now I could understand why Ragnar and Mielikki were so confident in giving their son to these people. They truly were masters of their craft.

Promptly they reached the *Thing*, the biggest building of them all. Several guards were still guarding and patrolling this area, it was clear that they had somebody important under custody inside the town hall.

Once the group of guards patrolling got further away from the main building, also being distracted by the fire situation on the north side, Thorstein and the tribesmen started the attack.

There was no actual fight or confrontation. They silently moved towards the back of the guards that were standing still and they slit their throats. They did this in a coordinated way so that the bodies falling would not alert the guards next to them. Sometimes three guards at a time, sometimes five, other times one guard only. Soon enough, all the standing guards were on the ground with their throats cut.

When the patrol came back and saw the bodies on the floor, they started shouting, but to no avail, for five spears pierced their chests before they could even utter any proper sounds.

Around twenty guards were dead and the way into the *Thing* was now clear. Thorstein and approximately twenty other tribesmen ran into the town hall while around ten or twelve other tribesmen stayed outside guarding the building, hidden behind buildings, carriages, hay mounds and any other visual obstacle that could be used for coverage.

The fire in the north gate seemed to have consumed the entire gate, and it started spreading on the walls and some houses near the palisade. More and more people were being drawn towards the fire, trying to put it out. It didn't rain for several days, strangely enough, so this fire was having a bigger impact than initially expected.

The wait time seemed an eternity. At any moment, anybody could realise that there were no guards at the *Thing*. The tribesmen did a good job at hiding the bodies but still, no guards were in sight, and this could trigger the alarm and shift it from the fire towards the town hall.

Ragnar was visibly impatient. He was staring at me, looking for any sign from me that would indicate that his intervention was needed. I could see he was eager to help his son in rescuing his dear friend.

Finally, I saw some movement. Piru was the first one to exit the building. He was covered in green paint, attached plants, and plenty of blood. Then several other tribesmen came out and finally, I saw Thorstein and other two tribesmen dragging a bald and robust man, covered in blood. It was Knut.

I signalled Ragnar. Immediately, he made several owl sounds. These sounds were heard by one of the tribesmen that had positioned himself near the eastern gate and he swiftly opened the gate, allowing Ragnar to get into the town. He sprinted towards his son and helped him carry Knut from the southern-centre part of the town, where the *Thing* was, towards the eastern gate.

After they made a few steps carrying the wounded companion, a dozen guards came out of the house that was nearest to the *Thing*, blowing their horns and hitting their shields with their swords and axes. They promptly blocked access to the eastern gate. Thorstein, Ragnar and Knut had to stop right where they were. They started running in the opposite direction, but the western gate was now closed and blocked by guards who had heard the alarm horn and came back to their post, killing the tribesmen left behind to guard the gate.

The townspeople, in a joint effort, managed to put out the fires in the walls and the houses but were still struggling with the gate's fire, for it was so big that the flames were two times taller than the tallest building.

All the guards that were initially trying to put out the fire were now heading towards the *Thing*, delegating the fire problem to the townspeople.

Ragnar, Piru, Thorstein, wounded Knut, and the tribesmen that had entered the *Thing* were getting surrounded. From the west the few guards that returned earlier and killed the remaining tribesmen, from the north all the guards that were initially drawn to the fire, from the east the dozen that had just come out from the house and, finally, from the south they had the *Thing*.

They started looking around and started moving slowly towards the *Thing*, perhaps hoping to use it as a fortress for a final and desperate attempt at resisting such a force. But, from the town hall, ten guards came out and blocked the entrance, then started moving slowly towards them.

Apparently, Thorstein and the tribesmen didn't clear the entire building but rather stopped as soon as they found Knut and rushed outside with him.

The number of guards probably doubled our number. I didn't know what to do to help. I was holding so tight to the branches of the tree that I felt they were about to break. But I couldn't wait there anymore, these people were the closest thing to a family that I had left,

I wouldn't allow them to die without me trying to help, even if I couldn't fight grown men, but at least I could distract them.

I jumped down from the beech tree and rushed towards the gate, fully opened it and took out both my knife and axe. I was ready to join Father in the halls of Odin.

Some guards that came out of the house turned around when they heard me open the gate and started giggling when they saw me.

"A boy? You expected to successfully invade us with a group of dirty trolls and boys?" said one guard, referring to the tribesmen, Thorstein and me.

One guard that came out from the *Thing*, the one in command judging by the quality of his helmet, shield, weapons and armour, moved forward, close to where the tribesmen were cornered.

This guard was quite tall, big, and strong. He had a clear brown, almost blond beard, light blue eyes, and expensive clothes.

"What is this, Ragnar? How dare you defy the lord of Uppsala and his allies? How dare you kill my men from behind, like the coward that we all know you are?" said the guard while staring at Ragnar, Thorstein and Knut, who had fallen to the ground.

"Bjarni, why am I not surprised to find you here? Are you tired of slaughtering unarmed villagers? Or is it that the pay was simply greater here?" replied Ragnar calmly, almost as if he wasn't in a desperate situation.

"Ah, yes, I forgot. Your love for these trolls from the woods. Tell me, old friend, is that your son?" Bjarni said while drawing his sword and aiming it at Thorstein.

Ragnar didn't answer, he jumped in front of Thorstein and pushed his son back.

"I see... So you got your way with that troll whore. Tell me, Ragnar, she was the daughter of a chieftain, right? For how much do you think I can sell her? Is she here with you?" said Bjarni, looking around.

At these provocations instead of Ragnar, was Piru who reacted. He moved forward and put himself in front of the chief guard. The guard was quite taller than Piru, but Piru looked as menacing as a

218

person can look. He almost didn't look human. His dark eyes pierced Bjarni's confident look. His body was covered in green paint, blood from the slaughtered guards, dirt, and attached moss. The scars made him look even scarier, and the parts without scars were covered with many inscriptions and symbols.

"Who's this? The chief of the trolls? How old is he?" said Bjarni jokingly, at which all the guards laughed.

Now the tribesmen were completely surrounded, but somehow the guards didn't notice the hidden tribesmen.

Piru stared at the man, steady, without ever breaking eye contact nor moving a muscle. Bjarni stopped laughing and started taking Piru a bit more seriously now. He looked him in the eyes. This lasted for a moment, but it felt like an eternity. Bjarni was looking into Piru's eyes the same way as someone looking at the inside of a well. Suddenly, Bjarni's face changed expression. He was afraid and surprised at the same time. Piru finally smirked.

"What... are you?" murmured Bjarni, who looked both terrified and intrigued.

Piru's evil smirk grew in size. His dark eyes seemed to have conquered Bjarni's heart.

"I'm death," Piru said with the deepest voice ever heard, still without breaking eye contact.

Bjarni took a step back. It seemed as if these words had hit him like a rolling boulder falling from a mountain slide.

Seeing the fear on Bjarni's face, three of the guards that were accompanying Bjarni moved forward and attacked Piru. The Finnish chief threw his spear at the first one, with a demonic speed. He then dodged the sword from the second guard and amputated his hand with a swift and strong sword slice. Using the same movement from that slice, he fully turned and extended his sword towards the third guard, slitting his throat.

In what was essentially an instant and two flawless movements, he had eliminated three guards. Everybody, except for the tribesmen, Thorstein and perhaps Ragnar, held their breath in awe.

While everyone was trying to make sense of what had just happened, especially Bjarni, Piru grabbed the second guard, the one with the amputated hand that was now standing on his knees on the ground; and slit his throat slowly and methodically while staring at Bjarni. He then moved towards Bjarni as if nothing had happened, as if this had been the most effortless thing that he ever had to do and with his face dripping blood from one of his recently slaughtered enemies, he smirked while looking again deep into his eyes.

"Now... What are 'you'?" asked Piru with a deep and mocking voice while pointing at Bjarni with his blood-dripping blade.

The tribesmen started giggling after this. It looked like they were enjoying this, almost as if they were hoping for this to happen. The guards looked around and noticed that something wasn't adding up. Soon they realised they were hearing more laughs than people were accounted for. The hidden tribesmen came out of their hiding places with a smirk and a challenging attitude. Confidence was pouring out of these people.

The guards started looking around nervously. They were big and strong men; they were also considerably outnumbering their foes, but Piru's display seemed to have made an impression on them.

Finally, Bjarni shook off the fear and regained his composure.

"What am I? I'm a Norwegian. I'm a Viking! I raided your lands, took your women and burnt whatever was left. I'm the last face your kinfolk saw before leaving this world, and I'm the last face you'll see today before I carve your eyes out and feed them to the ravens!" said Bjarni in a battle cry.

The guards yelled and started bashing their weapons against the shields. They started walking closer towards the cornered tribesmen. Some guards faced the newly discovered Finnish warriors. Combat and slaughter were inevitable.

"Stop! Stop this! There is no need for this!" yelled Ragnar.

Everybody, including myself, was surprised by these words. But before we could make sense of them, Ragnar continued.

"Bjarni, even if you win, you'll lose many men. It's not worth it. Let us leave. Remove your men from the eastern gate. Let us leave and you'll never see us again. It doesn't have to end this way," implored Ragnar.

Bjarni looked at him with contempt and then gave the command that nobody expected.

"Kill the boy!" he yelled while pointing at Thorstein with his sword.

Several guards launched themselves towards Ragnar and Thorstein. Simultaneously, several tribesmen rushed to protect them. Piru and the bulk of his force faced the guards from both the *Thing* and the western gate, and some that came from the north. The guards that were blocking the eastern gate engaged in combat with some tribesmen that were hidden and that had recently come out.

The fight was fierce. The guards were trained warriors, coordinated in defence and attack, well-armed and armoured. The tribesmen were fast, skilled and precise but weren't wearing any armour.

Blood, screams, body parts and guts invaded all my senses. I couldn't move, nor could I scream or help. Fear paralysed me.

Ragnar transformed himself into the fiercest of warriors. He slew any guard that came near his son. Thorstein's primary concern was defending Knut, who was on the ground half-conscious. Ragnar swung his axe and shield as if they didn't have any weight, slicing, blocking, hitting and maiming anybody that dared come close to him or his son. The more he engaged in combat, the more he was becoming the man that he had left behind, an animal of prey, a man possessed by rage and death.

His facial expression started changing from concern, alertness and focus into satisfaction and even happiness. A smirk started slowly appearing on his face each time he was lightly wounded or hit an enemy. His eyes glowed. Thorstein looked at his father. He couldn't recognise the man standing near him fighting off waves of guards. Growling, laughing, yelling and taunting.

I looked at Bjarni and he was also a very skilled warrior, focused and precise. He was fighting against the bulk of the tribesmen while Piru was slaying guards left and right, biting, slicing, head-butting and laughing. He was truly a madman. There was something dark deep within him.

I got so immersed in deeply studying how Ragnar, Piru and Bjarni fought that I didn't realise the guards from the eastern side had killed all the tribesmen that were there and were headed towards me. Only five remained, but still… I was about to die. I prepared myself to face them. I knew I would die, but at least I wanted to kill one of them and try to tilt the balance of the battle in our favour. Father would be proud.

They were just a few feet from me, charging at me with a smile on their face when I heard a whistle near my ear and saw an arrow hitting one guard in the chest. He immediately fell. The other four guards stopped their charge to assess what had just happened. They looked at me and then at the dead man with the arrow in his chest. Another arrow flew near my other ear, whistling towards the enemy. It hit another guard, this time in the belly. He fell on one knee screaming in pain.

I looked back and saw Mielikki with a curved bow, half her body coming out of the bush where Ragnar was hiding earlier. She shot another arrow. This time, it landed on the wounded man's throat. The remaining three guards closed the formation and clinched their shields together, forming a shield wall, and started slowly advancing towards me.

I moved backwards slowly. I didn't want to run away because I wanted them focused on me and not the major battle, and now I wanted to keep them in Mielikki's range so that she could keep firing arrows at them.

A couple more arrows were shot, but they were blocked by the shields. This time, I was doomed. One guard launched at me and attacked me with a quick sword vertical attack. I don't know how, but I managed to place my axe in a blocking position and deflected the blow to the side. My axe went flying in the air.

Luckily enough, this deflection made the guard slightly lose his step, which created an opening. An arrow came right into his chest.

Now I understood who taught Thorstein to shoot a rabbit in the eye from a distance. It wasn't the tribesmen; it was Mielikki.

The two remaining men, seeing that I had lost my weapon, kicked me in the chest and charged towards Mielikki, the real threat. I landed on my back, but I got up quickly. Father had kicked me ten times harder while training me. I rushed behind them and stabbed one of them with my knife in the back. I stabbed him twice before he turned around and hit me with his shield. Luckily, he hit me in the chest and arms and not in the head.

The other guard turned around to finish me, seeing that I was closer and still had a weapon. He charged his arm and prepared to strike me. I was on the floor and trying to get up, but the shield hit me so hard that I struggled to breathe.

I saw the sword coming down and immediately thought of Father and Grandmother. I would finally see them. Finally, I would be hugged again by Grandmother, and my eyes would meet Father's ice-blue eyes again.

Right before the stroke was about to hit me, the sword jumped from the guard's hand. The point of an arrow appeared from the guard's throat in an explosion of blood. He had received an arrow in the scruff. I dragged myself out of the other guard's range, as he was wounded but still could reach me. When he was about to stand up again and reach for me, Mielikki appeared behind him and slit his throat.

The eastern gate was now clear. The escape route was open again.

Chapter 26
Wrath

The more the fighting went on, the more Piru seemed to enjoy himself. A dark cloud surrounded him, or so I felt each time I laid eyes on him. The tribesmen were ferocious and skilled warriors, but Piru was like a creature from another world. His speed and precision were unmatched. While a guard attacked once, he had already attacked twice and hit the most vulnerable points of his opponent. Something similar happened to Ragnar. I could barely recognise him. He was covered in blood, several superficial wounds all across his body, and a smirk on his face. His hair was soaked with sweat and blood, his dark eyes gleamed at the sight of death. This man was a gloomy version of the sweet man that I had met until that moment.

After Mielikki had verified I wasn't seriously hurt, she stood near me. I looked up at her and saw how she froze when she saw her husband. Thorstein was lying on top of Knut, protecting him from harm. But Ragnar was completely taken over by rage and battle. Whenever he had disposed of an enemy, he would find new foes and slay them, too. He would scream, growl, taunt, and laugh.

"Ragnar…" murmured Mielikki.

The dark-skinned man was now attacked by another guard. He blocked the sword's blow with his shield, headbutted the guard, and kicked him in the chest. Right at this moment, another guard attacked him from the rear. Right before the blow could hit him, he spun around and hit the second guard with his shield. He hit him with such force that the shield broke into pieces and the guard's helmet flew in the air, revealing his broken skull. He then threw the broken shield away, looked at the sky, and roared the fiercest of battle cries. The first guard started running away from him, but Ragnar tackled him, sat on top of him, reached for a helmet lying on the ground nearby and started hitting him with it until his skull was completely crushed.

Most of the guards that came from the northern and western parts of the town were defeated by Piru and his closest men. The eastern path was clear. Now a handful of guards remained, led by Bjarni.

Piru and Bjarni fought relentlessly until they finally met in battle, surrounded by wounded, maimed and dead bodies. The moment their eyes met, the world seemed to stop. Bjarni launched a menacing battle cry. He looked fierce and unbeatable. Chain mail, shield, helmet and axe. He was covered in blood and mud. The more I looked at him, the less I could see any weak spots. He had slain many tribesmen.

Piru was standing still, gasping from the battle and the excitement. His green body paint had merged with the red blood of his enemies. The small plants and moss that he had attached to his body as part of his camouflage had fallen off. His muscular body, covered by scars, symbols and inscriptions, was more visible than ever.

The dark and sinister eyes of Piru met Bjarni's light blue eyes. The Finnish tribe leader grabbed his spear from a nearby corpse, and with the speed of lightning, threw it at Bjarni, without a warning. Bjarni managed to barely block it, but it got stuck in his shield, forcing him to dispose of it.

Most of the peripheral fighting had stopped at this point. Everybody was spectating the duel between the two leaders. It could very well mean the last duel of the entire skirmish.

Once Bjarni threw the shield with the stuck spear, Piru's dark eyes gleamed even darker. He then opened his arms and smirked mockingly.

"Finally, you meet death, warrior," said Piru with a deep voice.

Bjarni charged fiercely. He swung his axe with great speed and force, but Piru dodged or blocked all the blows. After dodging one of the blows, he did a half-turn and cut Bjarni's leg with his blade.

Bjarni didn't seem to notice or care about that wound. He was a seasoned warrior and a wound like that would not matter to him anymore.

"Shield!" commanded Bjarni.

One of his guards launched a shield at him. He grabbed it and positioned it in a defensive stance. Once more, he looked unbeatable.

Nothing could pierce his thick armour, his perfect skill with the shield and axe, his experience and battle knowledge.

This changed Piru's expression. He now started getting enraged. He wasn't smirking anymore, but clinched his teeth and started growling. His dark eyes lit with fire. He started running at full speed towards Bjarni. The chief guard placed his shield high and strong, but right before reaching him, Piru jumped high in the air and hit the shield with both feet.

They both flew in the air. Bjarni flew backwards and Piru fell in the same spot where Bjarni had previously stood. As soon as Piru hit the ground, he grabbed the shield and threw it away with demonic speed. He had dropped his own sword, but it didn't seem to bother him. He now jumped on top of Bjarni. The chief guard, as soon as he made sense of what had just happened, threw a blow with his axe at Piru.

Piru lowered himself, putting his head against his opponent's chest, almost hugging Bjarni, and used the blow's force to roll over, completely controlling the arm wielding the axe. They both rolled and in the end, Piru was on top again, but this time he had a knee on Bjarni's chest and a foot stepping on the arm that wielded the axe. He quickly removed the axe from his opponent's hand and threw it away. Bjarni tried to stand up but Piru started elbowing him repeatedly, then he removed the guard's helmet and started head-butting him in the face.

Blood was squirting after each subsequent headbutt. Piru looked as if he had been possessed by one of Loki's monster-children. He moved at such speed and had no compassion at all.

During this moment, the guards were looking nervous but without intervening. The tribesmen surrounded the combat area, proudly.

When the head-butting ended, Bjarni had his head cracked open. Piru stood up with blood cascading all over his face and dripping from his beard. He then looked at Ragnar, waiting for a command.

I never saw anything like this. Perhaps the only thing that I remember could be similar to this is when I saw Father in the tent with the traders, how he looked like an animal ready to destroy his opponent, no matter what. An unstoppable force.

Immediately after that Piru had stood up and exposed Bjarni's dead body, the rest of the guards placed themselves at the *Thing*'s door and defended it. I thought it was strange considering that we had their prisoner, but perhaps they realised that right now the numbers were even, and they had lost their leader.

Mielikki rushed towards Thorstein to be sure that he wasn't harmed.

"Let's go! The eastern gate is clear!" shouted Mielikki while grabbing Knut by an arm and dragging him with the help of Thorstein.

Ragnar didn't move. He was looking at Piru and at the *Thing*. It seemed like his interest wasn't saving Knut anymore.

"Ragnar!" yelled Mielikki in desperation.

Ragnar turned and looked at her. He then looked at Knut, Thorstein, and finally at me. I was standing midway between the gate and the battlefield, which was the clearing in front of the *Thing*.

"Take him to safety. Only death is left in this place," said Ragnar with the deepest of voices.

Mielikki and Thorstein froze. They didn't understand. The mission had succeeded, Knut was rescued, and we could run to safety before reinforcements arrived. Why was he staying there defying the guards defending the *Thing*?

"How much more blood do you want to spill, Ragnar?" yelled Mielikki in a crying voice while looking around at the battlefield.

Right in front of the *Thing*, where the fight had happened, there was a clearing where all the paths converged. It was now soaked in blood, mud and urine. Body parts and entrails spread all across the place. Maimed bodies, weapons, shields, helmets, eyes, fingers, hands... The view was only worsened by the stink. I know I should have been disgusted but, for some reason that I couldn't fathom, I liked it. Something inside me, that rage that I always felt growing inside me, craved it.

Ragnar also looked around, but his expression wasn't of disgust and sadness like Mielikki's, it was of pride. He then looked dead in Mielikki's eyes with a very grim expression.

"Run away. Now. Take Thorstein, Knut and Sigurd with you."

Mielikki looked confused, hurt and afraid. She dragged Knut with the help of Thorstein. As soon as they got close to where I was standing, I helped them out until we got to the gate. Once there, I let them go and started heading back into the town.

"Where are you going Sigurd? Come back!" said Mielikki, desperate.

"I'm sorry, but there is something that is not right here. I feel it, Mielikki. I won't put myself in danger, but I know I can't leave. Something tells me I can't. There is more to this, to what's happening here, but I can't explain it," I replied.

She looked at me in awe. She moved towards me to grab me and perhaps force me to come with her, but Thorstein grabbed her arm and shook his head, signalling her to let me go.

They dragged Knut up the small hill until they reached Mielikki's initial hiding spot. They rested there while they saw what would happen in the town. I went back in and hid behind a carriage near the battlefield.

Ragnar moved towards Piru's position, right in front of the town hall. They talked to each other in the tribe's language, perhaps assessing the situation. The tribesmen gathered in a semicircle in front of the *Thing*.

Right when Ragnar and Piru started talking, the guards moved away from the door of the *Thing*, as if they were about to let someone in or out. Everybody stood still, not knowing what was happening when suddenly a man came out of the town hall.

He was a tall man, taller than Ragnar, and he was strong, strong like a bull. He was wearing a shiny chain mail, a sword and a shield decorated with a blue background and a stag's head in yellow. He had a very blond and long beard tied in a braid, and he was completely bald and had a helmet in his hand.

He looked around, almost ignoring Ragnar, Piru, and his men. He looked far north at the smoke and the flames still consuming the gate. His attention shifted towards the western gate from which the invasion had happened. I could see how he noticed the ropes tied to the reindeer horns. Then he looked east, where Mielikki had just escaped with her son and Knut.

He was clearly assessing the situation. The *Thing* was slightly elevated from the ground and had a couple of steps, so this man had a superb view of the battlefield and the town. Finally, he looked in front of him, but no surprise could be found on his face.

"You...?" said Ragnar, surprised.

"It's been a long time, Ragnar. But finally, our paths cross again," said the powerful man.

"How do you even dare enter Uppsala, where The Great Temple is, where the gods speak to men!" yelled Ragnar, challenging.

"I was invited. You, on the other hand, have just invaded the land that you profess to be sacred," replied the man, taunting Ragnar.

"Hjalti... You snake..." said Ragnar filled with rage.

"Still holding grudges, Ragnar? Have you not learnt anything? Your fragile group of purists disbanded as soon as Harald, that madman, died. How strong was your bond if the death of one man brought everything crumbling down to pieces?" said Hjalti with a smirk on his face.

"You betrayed us. We came to fight at your side, and as soon as we finished saving all of your people you betrayed us... You poisoned everybody against us... But today, you'll pay," Ragnar said while doing his best not to launch himself into an enraged attack.

"Yes, well, we'll see about that," said Hjalti while signalling one guard at the door.

The guard rushed inside, and after a few moments, he came out with another dozen guards. We could not believe it. All these guards had the same shields as Hjalti.

"I knew eventually you would come, Ragnar. But I never thought you would come accompanied by these... 'people'. I must admit, I wasn't expecting such a force. Bjarni should have handled this better..." said Hjalti while looking at Bjarni's corpse near the *Thing*'s steps.

So Hjalti was expecting Ragnar? This was a trap! But, if it was a trap... Why did they let us take Knut? Perhaps the target was to kill Ragnar, and they used Knut to lure him in. Still, something didn't add up.

"Gudrik, Ingvar, Kalf, Snorri, Bardi, Rognvald... We fought side by side in many battles. Why this?" said Ragnar pointing at some of the guards that had just come out of the *Thing*.

Indeed, they didn't quite look like regular guards. They looked like experienced warriors, of which Hjalti was the most experienced and accomplished.

"Indeed, Ragnar, we fought side by side. But 'Odin's Warriors' always took the glory. All of our blood got spelt, but it always seemed that it was 'The Twelve' who tilted the balance in our favour on the battlefields. Well, let me tell you a secret: We all worship Odin. And today, we'll kill the last of The Twelve. Knut will die from his wounds anyway..." said Hjalti while signalling his men to attack.

Ragnar, Piru, and his men were now clearly outnumbered. Only a handful of tribesmen survived. Undoubtedly, as Ragnar had said moments before, only death was left in this place.

Hjalti's men started advancing when suddenly a horrendous battle cry was heard. It sounded as if the skies were opening and all the animals in the forest cried out loud. Everybody froze. Hjalti looked out north, in the direction from which the battle cry came, but couldn't see anything.

"It can't be... It surely cannot be!" Hjalti started saying while looking at two of his warriors.

The battle cry was heard again, closer, stronger, ever more menacing. Hjalti's jaw dropped as a godly figure jumped across the shrinking flames in the northern gate. The townspeople fled from the presence of the colossus that had just entered the town, leaving the fire unattended.

The giant started making his way through the northern path towards the *Thing*. Redhead, shirtless, blue body paint all over his scars and inscriptions. He was wielding a huge battle-axe. The top of the hair was tied in a small ponytail, and the rest of the hair flapped after each step.

"You told me he was dead!" reproached Hjalti to his warriors.

Once the giant was close enough, two of the warriors charged against him.

"Stop! No! Don't!" yelled Hjalti to no avail, for these were probably the warriors who gave the news of Olaf's death, thinking that he would have died from his wounds.

Olaf didn't seem disturbed or worried seeing these warriors charging at him. He still had that grim expression on his face. As a matter of fact, now that he was closer, I could see an even darker and more frightening look in his eyes.

The warriors charged with all their strength, but Olaf kicked one of them in the shield, sending him flying backwards and threw a horizontal blow with his massive battle-axe to the second one. The blow was so strong that it destroyed the edge of the shield and managed to hit the warrior. The warrior's belly had been slit open and his entrails started pouring out.

Olaf then moved towards the first warrior, the one he had kicked, and swiftly delivered a lethal blow to the head, inserting his axe deep into the skull. He then stepped on the warrior's face and pulled his axe out of the skull.

He kept walking towards the *Thing*, unchanged, as if nothing had happened. His eyes fixed on Hjalti.

I remembered when I saw him the night before, on the big hill, preparing for this moment. He now looked even more godly than the night before. He had the face of death. It seemed as if nothing in this world could stop him.

The tribesmen stood aside and lowered their heads in a sign of respect. Piru smirked and also made way to the giant. The guards formed a line in front of the *Thing*'s steps, where Hjalti was standing, astonished. Hjalti still had the numbers advantage, but he looked paralysed by what he was witnessing.

Olaf finally stood in front of the *Thing*, he looked at the warriors one by one in the eyes. The hate and despise in his look could be felt at a distance.

"You'll pay for Rognvald and Snorri..." said one of the warriors while advancing towards Olaf.

Another two warriors followed him. Soon all the warriors launched themselves towards the redhead giant. Right when the fight was about to start, a loud command was heard.

"Halt! Halt!" commanded Hjalti.

The warriors stopped and took a few steps backwards, forming a defensive line protecting the entrance of the *Thing* again.

"Enough... Let's solve this the old way, Olaf. Let's solve this with a duel," said Hjalti while going down the steps of the *Thing* and positioning himself in front of his opponent.

"This time there is no army nor king to protect you... Nor the secrecy of your treachery. You're still willing to engage in single combat?" said Olaf, taunting him.

"I've seen death many times, Olaf. You don't scare me," said Hjalti while preparing himself to fight the giant.

"Yes, you've seen death, Hjalti, but you've never faced me..." replied Olaf while signalling Hjalti to attack him.

Hjalti threw the first blow, a powerful vertical blow with his sword that Olaf blocked with the handle of his axe. Then Olaf countered with a horizontal strike that was strongly blocked by Hjalti's shield. The sound of that axe impacting the shield sounded like thunder.

They continued attacking, defending, and blocking for a while. Their skill was incredible. Hjalti was truly a master with sword and shield, but Olaf and his battle-axe looked like one for such was his skill with that weapon.

Suddenly, Hjalti managed to hit Olaf in the mouth with his shield. Olaf stood still with his head turned from the impact. Hjalti saw an opening and went in with the killing blow. Right when the sword should have hit Olaf's neck, the giant quickly turned and grabbed Hjalti's arm, the one wielding the sword. His mouth and beard were full of blood and his eyes were wide open. He looked like he had lost his mind.

Olaf then head-butted Hjalti, making him lose his step and lower his shield a little. Without releasing Hjalti's arm, Olaf started hitting Hjalti in the face with the other hand, the one wielding the enormous axe. Hjalti countered by finally hitting Olaf in the chest with his shield.

They both got separated from each other. Both their faces were covered in blood, especially Hjalti's. Olaf's breathing sped up, his eyes got bigger and bigger as a stream of blood poured from his mouth, soaking his beard. Suddenly, he threw his axe at Hjalti's feet, distracting the warrior, and making him look downwards. As soon as Hjalti looked upwards again, he saw how Olaf had launched himself against him with his fist coming towards his face.

Hjalti tried to react, covering himself with his shield and striking Olaf with his sword but the giant knew what he was doing, he adjusted his left arm to block Hjalti's sword arm, and he changed his right arm from launching a punch to striking with his elbow downwards. The blow was terrible. Hjalti fell backwards. His sword flew from his hand after Olaf's forearm had strongly hit his wielding arm. He tried to get up quickly, but, while doing so, his face met Olaf's huge knee, making him fall again and making his helmet jump out from his head.

The warriors made an attempt to save their leader, but the tribesmen, Ragnar and Piru, immediately positioned themselves between the warriors and Hjalti.

"It's single combat!" yelled Ragnar.

The warriors stood still. Their morale must have been depleted after seeing their fearful leader fall at the hands of such a warrior as Olaf.

"You called for our help…" Olaf started saying to Hjalti while bending to grab his battle-axe.

"You benefit from our spilt blood…" said the giant, while walking around the fallen enemy.

"And then... You betray us for silver and glory..." said Olaf right before kicking Hjalti's face.

"You're responsible for Harald... And that, Hjalti, you'll have to pay for..." Olaf said while raising his battle-axe.

"I was just a pawn, and you know it, Olaf... We all were..." murmured Hjalti with huge difficulty while coughing blood and looking at his men for help.

"Still, I have to start somewhere," said Olaf an instant before strongly lowering his axe and severing Hjalti's head from his body.

The warriors looked at each other nervously until one of them took a step forward that was met with Piru's spearhead an inch from his face. The warrior then threw his sword and shield and raised his hands in a surrendering position.

"Lower your weapons. Everybody! Lower your weapons!" shouted the warrior nervously.

First, his fellow warriors threw their weapons on the ground, and then Piru slowly started lowering his spear while Olaf positioned himself right in front of the surrendering man.

"Olaf... It's done. Hjalti deserved it. There is no need to-"

"Gudrik. Where is he? Tell me now and maybe you could still keep your miserable life," said Olaf with the deepest and most menacing voice.

"Follow me. Everybody, stay outside," said Gudrik while entering the *Thing*, followed by Olaf and giving his men the command to stay put.

Chapter 27

The Fallen

While Olaf was inside the *Thing*, Ragnar started questioning Ingvar, one of the warriors left outside.

"Ingvar, who knew that we were coming?" asked Ragnar, still soaked in enemy blood.

"Ragnar, they knew. That's all that I can say. They knew you would come for him," replied the warrior.

"But why keep guarding the *Thing* after we rescued him?" asked Ragnar, intrigued.

I could see that Ragnar suspected something. Maybe that's why he stayed there instead of escaping with Knut, Mielikki and Thorstein, as we had planned. Perhaps his suspicions had something to do with what happened to Olaf the day before.

"Who? Knut? Ragnar, you must know it already. You know Knut was simply a fortunate coincidence..." replied Ingvar with a smirk.

Ragnar's face lightened up. He changed his facial expression, struggling to believe and make sense of whatever he had just discovered. But soon enough, he returned to his focused and menacing face.

"Why is Chief Svein not here? Why didn't the *völva* come out of The Great Temple after all the chaos that we unleashed upon the town? Tell me everything or you'll die slowly, Ingvar," said Ragnar while Piru started poking Ingvar with his spear.

"Ragnar, you don't have time to torture me, but I'll tell you nonetheless. I was never fond of this plan. No chief nor earl is in Uppsala right now. We knew you were coming. The *völva* was threatened. If she left her temple, we had the order to burn it down," calmly replied the warrior.

"How dare you threaten her? How dare yo-" Ragnar started reproaching when Piru interrupted him by questioning Ingvar himself.

"Why did you let us slay Bjarni and his men? Why didn't Hjalti and his men come out sooner?" asked Piru while getting closer to Ingvar, intimidating him with his dark eyes and his grim presence.

"We… Didn't know that 'you' were coming. We heard nothing until you started fighting Bjarni's men in the open, thinking Bjarni would have been able to defend the *Thing*. The order was to guard the most valuable-" Ingvar started stuttering, scared to death at Piru's penetrating look, right before interrupting himself at the presence of Gudrik who had just come out of the *Thing*.

Gudrik came out of the town hall and positioned himself near the entrance with the other warriors. Right behind him, Olaf came out. He was carrying a body over his shoulder, covered with a blanket soaked in blood. He came down the steps, found a place that wasn't tainted with blood or mud from the battle, and gently placed the body on the floor.

Olaf proceeded to uncover ever so gently and slowly the blanket from the body's face, which I couldn't see from my hiding spot. The moment that Olaf uncovered it, he screamed so loud and so profoundly that it seemed that his entire throat had shuttered. He then launched himself, enraged, against the warriors.

"Cowards! Cowards!" yelled the giant while punching, kicking and head-butting the warriors.

Ragnar and Piru got closer to see the body and, the moment they laid eyes on whoever it was, they froze. Ragnar fell on his knees right beside the body. Piru started cursing and murmuring in his language while closing his fists and yelling at the clouds.

I understood nothing. Who was that body? And why did they invest so much effort and men into protecting it? Indeed, it looked like Knut was simply a decoy.

Everything started moving slowly in front of me. It was as if time had stopped. A gentle rain started falling, but the raindrops seemed to be falling slower than feathers do. I could see Olaf's brawling, Piru's cursing and Ragnar's despair happening extremely slowly, almost stopping in time.

Suddenly, behind all of this, I saw an old man walking about. He seemed to have come out from behind the *Thing* and heading towards The Great Temple. He stopped in the middle of the path and looked at me.

Aquiline nose, white long hair, white long beard and a missing eye with a huge scar… I recognised him immediately. He had a serious look on his face, almost as if he was angry. His eye penetrated my body and looked right through me. He then extended his arm and pointed it towards the body, just like he did at Ragnar's house, pointing at the carved boulder. I looked at the body, but still couldn't see the face from where I was standing, then I looked back at the old man and he smirked.

Why did he do that? I looked back at the body and nothing changed, still couldn't recognise who it was. When I looked back, the old man was gone. But a feeling struck my heart, a strong feeling.

I jumped out of my hiding spot and sprinted across the battlefield towards the body, dodging blood puddles, body parts, entrails, helmets and broken shields. While I was running, the feeling grew ever stronger in my heart, and the time seemed to speed up again, returning to a normal speed the closer I got to the body.

I jumped and landed beside Ragnar, hitting him in the shoulder. He was distraught and now very surprised, not expecting me to drop out of nowhere and land almost on him. He immediately covered the body again, tried to grab me and take me away.

"What are you doing here? You're not supposed to be here! Go back to safety!" yelled Ragnar while trying to pick me up.

"No, Ragnar! No!" I yelled while strongly pushing him and looking him deep in the eyes.

"Sigurd…" he murmured, still visibly affected by what he had just seen.

"No Ragnar… I have to," I replied while gently pushing him aside and kneeling beside the body. Ragnar reluctantly moved.

I stood on my knees near the covered body and took a deep breath as I felt my heart coming out of my mouth. I was convinced of what I was going to see. In my heart, I knew it. I gently lifted the blanket from the body's face, revealing who it was.

A bitten-off ear was revealed. Then I noticed a head with the sides shaved and covered in sacred inscriptions. I turned the head, and I saw the scar on the side of the face and the beard decorated with beads. It was Father.

My heart exploded. Everything inside me seemed to have exploded. I felt my gut boiling with rage, my heart crying out loud and my head going at the wind's speed. My eyes filled with tears that started dropping over his blood-stained face.

He had been beaten, cut, pierced with nails and who knows what else.

I turned my head, looking at the men responsible for this, the warriors that had previously fought side by side with Father and that now did this. Olaf was still beating them uncontrollably. The tribesmen were trying to prevent Olaf from getting killed by separating him from the warriors, which was proving to be an arduous task.

At a certain point, the tribesmen got hold of the giant by blocking his arms and legs. One of the warriors seized the moment, grabbed his sword from the floor, and proceeded to strike Olaf's chest with his sword. But right before the metal could contact the berserker's skin, the warrior was punched unconscious by Gudrik.

"Enough! Go to the western gate and stall them! Now!" yelled Gudrik.

The warriors grabbed the swords and shields from the ground, ran towards the western gate and closed it. Gudrik then placed his hands on Olaf's face, forcing him to look straight at his eyes, which Olaf wasn't quite willing to do while being possessed by rage.

"He's alive, Olaf! I couldn't. I just couldn't do it. Hjalti asked me to do it, and I wouldn't do it. I wouldn't dare, Olaf. You know this," said Gudrik.

The more these words resonated in Olaf's head, the more he calmed down.

"Olaf, they're coming. The bulk of the King's forces are coming. Svein is just a pawn, the same as Hjalti. They're coming,

Olaf. Grab Eirik and run away. We'll try to stall them even if it costs us our lives," said Gudrik while still strongly grabbing Olaf's face.

"Why now? Why help us now?" asked Olaf while still trying to digest the fact that Father might be alive.

"Enough... I've had enough, Olaf. I've strayed from the right path for far too long. It's time for me to meet my fallen brothers with honour..." said Gudrik, filled with shame.

Olaf was then freed from the tribesmen that were holding him. He placed his own hands on Gudrik's face and his forehead on Gudrik's forehead.

"To Valhöll, Gudrik, to Valhöll..." whispered Olaf.

"To Valhöll, brother..." replied Gudrik right before leaving in a rush and heading towards the western gate, where he joined his fellow warriors.

"Grab him and run! Reinforcements are coming!" commanded Olaf while running towards our position.

The moment Olaf uttered these words, a horn blew in the wind from the west. It was the reinforcements getting closer to the town. Ragnar and I looked at each other when suddenly we noticed a slight movement in Father's chest. He was breathing!

"He's alive? He's alive!" yelled Ragnar, incredulous.

"Father!" I yelled in an explosion of tears.

The overwhelming happiness was interrupted by Olaf, who came and grabbed Father like he was a bag of bones and started running towards the eastern gate.

Piru then gave a command to his tribesmen, and they all ran behind Olaf. Some of them stopped by the dead bodies of their kinfolk, grabbed some weapons and belongings, and also murmured some fast prayers.

Ragnar and I joined the tribesmen and ran alongside them. We closed the eastern gate behind us, blocking it from outside with a few logs planted in the ground. Then we continued running up the small hill until we reached Mielikki, Knut, and Thorstein. They came out of their hiding spot, Thorstein and Ragnar grabbed Knut, who could barely walk, and we continued running towards the bigger hill, the one with the cave.

At the top of the small hill, I looked back at the town. To my surprise, the reinforcements had already arrived. While we were running uphill, the reinforcements breached the gate and slew all the warriors but Gudrik. He was on his knees, surrounded by the newcomer force. Right when I turned to check on the town I saw how one of the warriors surrounding him landed a fast blow with an axe, decapitating him, and then showing his head as a trophy and, probably, as an example of what happens when someone betrays them.

Perhaps he took part in what happened to Father and my family, but perhaps he didn't have a choice. What I knew is that he died fighting with honour and that he would dine with Odin in Valhöll that night.

We ran past the cave and continued our way towards the north. We would run until we reached the Bears' Nest. There, the wilderness should provide us with enough cover to stop and rest.

It was an exhausting and hard journey. Knut kept falling, and sometimes Thorstein or Ragnar would fall with him. They had their knees full of blood. The tribesmen and Piru, after exchanging some words with Ragnar, Mielikki and Thorstein in their language, left and went their own way. I'm guessing that was to travel in smaller numbers and have better chances to go unnoticed.

We stopped near a pond, Olaf couldn't carry Father anymore. He was struggling to breathe from the immense effort. Ragnar and Thorstein were almost fainting from carrying Knut. Father still looked like he was unconscious, or even dead. Knut could barely breathe and stay somewhat awake.

We freshened ourselves up near the pond and quickly ate some dried meat that Mielikki had prepared before leaving the house. I took this chance to clean Father's face and reveal the rest of his body that still we hadn't seen. He had several fingernails pulled out or cut open. They had cut his left pinkie, which now made him have four fingers on each hand. He also had deep cuts all over his arms, chest, and legs. His back was filled with wounds from lashings. He was completely unconscious, but at least his chest moved, and I could hear a slow heartbeat if I placed my ear next to his wounded chest. I took care of him as best as I could while Olaf rested and Mielikki tended Knut's wounds to the best of her ability. But we quickly resumed our hard journey. We needed to get to the relative safety of the Bears' Nest as fast as possible. If the reinforcements followed us, they would move twice as fast as we were.

The journey from the pond to the Bears' Nest was hard, especially for Olaf, Ragnar, and Thorstein. But we managed to get there safely. We went to the same clearing where we stayed with the tribesmen the day before.

As soon as we arrived, Mielikki rushed in looking for wild herbs that could help in treating Father's and Knut's wounds, Thorstein ran into the thickest wilderness, and Ragnar went for water in the nearby stream. Olaf lay down, exhausted from carrying Father on his shoulders. And, finally, I stayed near Father, trying to clean his wounds and see if he would wake up. I couldn't believe that he was alive and that I was touching his flesh. I couldn't let him go. He had to survive.

We stayed in that place for the entire evening and were preparing to spend the night. Mielikki had put some smashed herbs into the wounds of the fallen warriors. Ragnar had prepared a small fire pit, but he didn't light it yet, he was waiting for something before doing so.

Thorstein popped out from some bushes with a dead rabbit in his hand and said something in Finnish to his father. Ragnar immediately lit the fire. Mielikki grabbed the rabbit and started preparing it for cooking.

After a short while, Piru and his men appeared from behind the trees. I didn't hear nor see them until I had them right in front of me. Piru had a brief conversation with Ragnar, Mielikki, and Thorstein. He then came towards where Father was lying down. He bent over, squatting, and placed his hand on Father's chest. It looked like he was making sure that Father's chest was properly getting filled with air and then emptied. He then whispered some incomprehensive words into his ear and stood up, looking at Olaf, who was lying down right near Father.

"You carry the wrath of the gods inside you. Now I understand Eirik's words about you, warrior of lightning," Piru said while placing his right fist on his chest as a sign of respect. Olaf did the same and nodded.

Piru then looked at me and took a few steps to get closer to me.

"Your flesh is young, but your spirit is old and dark. You're no stranger to death and blood, you crave it. It was an honour meeting you, young cub. Never forget what we did," said Piru with a deep voice and a dark and intense glow in his eyes.

I did the same that Olaf did. I placed my right fist on my left chest and nodded.

"I will never forget, Piru, embodiment of death," I said without thinking.

Olaf and Ragnar immediately turned their heads towards me, concerned about my daring, but Piru smirked and nodded. Then the tribesmen finally exchanged some kind words with Thorstein, who was deemed as one of their own, and finally left into the darkness of the forest.

"Sigurd, why did you say that to him?" asked Olaf once the tribesmen were far enough.

"I don't know. It simply came out of my mouth that way..." I honestly replied.

"You don't talk like that to someone like Piru!" reprimanded Ragnar.

I was about to respond, but Mielikki was faster than me. "Stop it! Ragnar, didn't you see? Piru liked the boy. He wasn't offended by that. Stop it with the formalities..." said the beautiful woman while changing some bandages on Knut's wounds.

Ragnar exhaled and didn't reply. To my eyes, it looked like something broke between them. He was a caring and loving man, but what we witnessed in the town... It might have changed how his wife now saw him. One thing was to know about his past and to see him as a simple raider that saved her. Another thing was to see him transformed into a death-seeking warrior. Be it as it may, I was convinced that the love they had for each other could overcome anything.

We stayed in silence for some time. We ate what Mielikki had prepared, and we lay near the fire. Darkness surrounded us. The noise of the leaves and branches moving in the wind and the water streams nearby were only interrupted by animals' nocturnal calls.

I kept thinking about why Olaf and Ragnar got so concerned about what I said to Piru. I also couldn't remove Piru from my mind. The feeling that I had in his presence was a disturbing feeling at times, but especially his dark eyes… Staring at those eyes was like staring at death itself. I needed to know more.

"Ragnar, who is Piru?" I finally asked, breaking the silence.

He sighed, looking for an answer, and then turned his head towards his wife. "We know little about him, except for some stories…" replied Ragnar, still staring at his wife.

Mielikki, who was lying down, sat up and while staring at the flames from the firepit, started addressing my question.

"My grandfather once told me that many creatures lived in the forest, many of them are good, others… Not that good. He told me that folk had entered the forest and encountered a demon who challenged them, assessing if they were worthy of the forest or not. The ones deemed not worthy never returned…" explained Mielikki with a calm but disturbed voice.

Olaf, who also was lying down, sat up straight and started paying more attention.

"Legend has it that this demon owes allegiance to no one but the forest. There have been people who tried to recruit this creature but to no avail. It has no interest in gold, lands, or titles. Whoever tried defying it died from the most horrible and painful death," said Mielikki, still staring at the flames.

I could sense how we all had chills from what she was saying.

243

"Grandfather once told me that a local chieftain wanted to either recruit or destroy this folk myth. He gathered a party of his most skilled and loyal warriors to enter the forest and confront the darkness. Days passed, but there was no sign of the chieftain's warriors. When the townspeople and the chieftain himself went towards the forest to see what happened, they were horrified by what they saw. At the edge of the forest, they found the warriors that had been sent by the chieftain. Impaled, hanging from branches, maimed, decapitated, gutted... It was a scene worthy of the darkest of nightmares."

A tense silence reigned for some time. We took some time to visualise and process what we had just heard.

"Needless to say, this demon that Grandfather was referring to was named Piru," added Mielikki after a while, creating an even more disturbing and tense silence.

We were all sitting straight, staring at the flames dancing in the firepit. Many unanswered questions, many thoughts flowing like water flows in a waterfall: Fast, constant, in copious amounts, and without ever resting.

"Oh well, enough with the fairy tales. I'm going to sleep. Tomorrow is going to be a tough journey back home," said Olaf while lying down and covering himself with furs.

Ragnar looked at Mielikki. They had Knut's body between them, but he looked like he was expecting some sort of comforting words from her. She stood up, went to check on Father's wounds, then did the same on Knut's wounds and finally went to sleep without saying a word.

Ragnar also went to sleep. Thorstein was missing but, at this point, I wasn't worried nor surprised anymore. I needed to rest for the day after we would have to travel back to Ragnar's home carrying two heavyweights.

I closed my eyes, but sleep wouldn't come easily that night. My mind was racing: Father was alive! But why torture him? Why torture Knut? Piru? If these stories that Mielikki's grandfather told her were true, how old was he? And why help us? Why did the Swedish king want to harm us by sending Gudrik, Hjalti and the others? Who was really behind everything that had happened? And why?

So many were the unanswered questions I had in my mind that I finally exhausted myself to sleep.

Chapter 28

Home

"Is he breathing? Is he breathing?" I heard in my sleep.

I opened my eyes and saw Mielikki, Ragnar, and Olaf around Knut, checking if he was breathing. It was still very early in the morning, judging by the lack of sunlight.

"What happened?" I asked, still under the furs, trying to make sense of what was happening.

"Knut... He fell into a deep sleep," replied Olaf with a worried tone.

Mielikki and Ragnar were still trying to check if he was properly breathing or not. I stood up and rushed towards Father. He was slightly breathing, even though still unconscious. He was getting too weak. We had to hurry.

"Knut is breathing. He just fell into a deep sleep. We need to rush home, for both of their sakes. We don't have the proper herbs here. Place them on the stretchers, let's go at once!" commanded Ragnar.

I saw that there were two stretchers made of branches near our camp. Ragnar and Olaf carried Knut on one of them and tied him with some rope. Then did the same with Father. I rushed to help them carry him. I didn't want them to drop him. He was too weak.

"Where did these stretches come from, Olaf?" I asked, intrigued.

"Thorstein... He left them there for us," replied Olaf while carrying Father and placing him gently on the stretcher.

"Left them? Where is he?"

"Probably went home to make sure that it's safe. You want to waste time asking questions or taking your father to safety? Hurry!"

I rushed and grabbed all the furs. It wasn't much. We had left a few furs and utility items in this place before heading towards the cave, just in case we had to come here in a rush, as we eventually ended up doing.

We immediately departed, heading towards home. Olaf pulled Father's stretcher and Ragnar pulled Knut's. I was concerned by the urgency of the situation. Perhaps Ragnar verified that either Father or Knut were fading into the realm of death.

The journey was silent and hard. Olaf and Ragnar were exhausted from carrying such heavyweights through the wilderness, having to lift the stretcher for crossing rivers, and streams, or simply avoid rocks and other imperfections of the terrain.

Like everyone else, I walked in silence. I would watch my feet, immersed in my own thoughts. The journey that took me to these lands was on my mind, with Father, Mother, Grandmother and Thrúd. I remembered when Father asked me to sit and talked to me about The Great Temple, the *blót*, Uppsala... I remembered when Thrúd would play with the ashes from the fireplace. I visualised Grandmother dancing in Thor's temple, laughing and drinking with Olaf.

Without realising it, I was leaving a trail of tears along the way. Perhaps Mielikki noticed it. She slowed to reach back at me, placed her arm over my shoulder, kissed my head, and kept walking.

Not long after that, we saw someone in the distance coming towards us. It was unusual, for these paths were not widely known. We hid behind some thick vegetation and waited. But as soon as the person got closer to us, Ragnar jumped out of the hiding place.

"It's Thorstein! He brought the carriage!" yelled Ragnar filled with pride and relief.

"Oh! May Odin bless your son Ragnar... Well, with that wit of his, I must thank Mielikki!" yelled Olaf, while laughing.

Ragnar and Mielikki looked at each other briefly, but as soon as their eyes met, Ragnar went back towards the hiding spot to pull Knut out of there. Soon enough, Thorstein arrived and jumped down the carriage. Ragnar hugged him, and so did Mielikki. He truly had saved the day. Then he said something in Finnish and helped us carry the wounded warriors to the back of the carriage. I hopped on the back and sat near Father. Olaf joined me and Mielikki too, which was strange considering that she always travelled in the front, driving beside Ragnar.

The journey luckily went by with no incidents. We were home, finally.

As soon as we arrived, Mielikki jumped off the back of the carriage and rushed into the house. We carried Father, the weakest of the wounded, into the house and placed him on one of the beds. Then we carried Knut and placed him near Father.

"Undress them and clean them. Be careful, we don't know what exactly happened to them," Mielikki said to Olaf and Ragnar. Then she said something in Finnish to Thorstein that ran out of the house into the wilderness.

"Sigurd, come with me, help me prepare the herbs," she gently said.

"I want to help clean Father, please," I asked.

She looked at Father and then at me with a sad expression. I could see she was trying to protect me from suffering further.

"I need to do this, please," I insisted.

She then looked at Olaf, who deeply sighed and nodded. She nodded back at me, so I joined Olaf and Ragnar in the task.

Ragnar placed a large bowl filled with water near the bed. Then he started cutting with a sharp knife the clothes off of Father. It was a hard task, for in many places the clothes and the wounds had been in contact while fresh, and now the hardened dry blood made it difficult to remove the cloth without further harming him.

It took us a lot of time and patience, but we slowly revealed his tortured body. They had burnt his left chest, exposing the flesh and expunging any trace of the mark of Odin that he had inked there. He had his pinkie cut off, which we had to cauterise with a scorching blade. They had pulled off and cut several fingernails. He had lashes all over his back, with lumps of flesh falling out. They even had iron nails hammered into his arms. We had to pull them out one by one. He also had cuts all over his chest, arms, and legs. We had to cauterise all these wounds, and he still didn't wake up.

248

"The bastards knew what they were doing. They knew perfectly how to inflict pain without killing him. That's why he's alive. Thank Odin that Gudrik refused to finish him…" said Olaf with watery eyes.

The rage and hate in my gut were so strong that I thought it would kill me. The unanswered questions, Grandmother, Mother, Thrúd, Gudrod, Knut, Father… It was too much to handle. I couldn't take it anymore.

After we finished cleaning and properly tending to Father's wounds, I rushed out of the house in tears. Tears of rage, tears of hatred. From deep inside me came an impulse to scream, and so I did. I screamed like I had never done before, feeling my throat tearing, my gut emptying, and my strength leaving me. I found myself on my knees, vomiting, in utmost despair, when I felt a gentle hand on my back.

"Let it all out, child. Let it all out…" said Mielikki gently.

Once I finished feeling sick, I raised my eyes and saw Thorstein standing in front of me, looking at me. He then came to me and offered his hand for me to stand up. I took it and stood up, feeling weak. I looked upwards, for he was not only older but also taller than me, and he smirked and moved his head, signalling the boulder with Odin's statue.

I started moving in that direction when I felt a firm hand on my belly. I turned and saw that it was Thorstein who had placed his hand there.

"Embrace it," he said in a deep and serious tone. Then he let me go and gave a basket filled with plants and herbs to his mother, who rushed inside again, followed by her son.

I headed towards the boulder, still wondering what Thorstein meant by "Embrace it." Once I arrived at the boulder, I felt chills running through my body like thunder running through the sky. I fell to my knees.

"Odin, All-father, thank you for bringing back both Knut and Father. But why all of this? Why must our fate be of suffering, blood, and death?"

My words were met with silence. Only the stream that surrounded the small island where Ragnar's house was built broke it. In despair, I grabbed my left chest and insisted.

"All-father, please save Father. Awake him. I need him. Please All-father, I'll forever serve you."

More silence. Until suddenly a deep voice interrupted it. "You're already destined to serve the One-eyed."

Where did that come from? I looked around, and behind me, saw Olaf leaning on a tree.

"Olaf? What about Knut?"

"Ragnar and Thorstein are tending to his wounds. He's in a much better state than your father."

"I see... Olaf, what do you think he wants from me?" I asked while pointing towards the statue.

Olaf sighed and took a moment to think about his answer.

"Everything, Sigurd. Everything..." replied while turning his head towards the house, where Father was fighting to stay alive.

We stayed for a while in silence. I kept looking at Odin's marvellous stone statue, asking for Father's fast recovery and guidance. I could still sense that Olaf was there because I could hear him breathe strongly, sometimes deeply exhaling.

"Is it worth it?" I asked, breaking the silence and the meditative atmosphere.

"Serving the All-father? Dedicating one's life to defend our ancestors' ways, people and country? Every single drop of blood is worth it, Sigurd. Without sacrifices like these, there would be no Norway, no Sweden, no Denmark... There wouldn't be an Odin or Thor. We would be forgotten like this boulder was forgotten before you arrived here," replied Olaf convincingly and proudly.

Before I even had the time to digest what Olaf had just said to me, we got interrupted by Mielikki's voice in the wind.

"He's awake! He's awake!" she yelled from the house door.

We ran towards the house and rushed inside it. To our surprise, Knut was sitting up straight, with his eyes open and holding a bowl with some hot beverage.

An immense joy of seeing him awake got mixed with disappointment from not being Father the one that awoke. But I still trusted in Mielikki's healing skills and Father's inner strength. We immediately sat around Knut. Except for Thorstein, who kept his distance sitting at the table near the fireplace.

"How are you feeling, brother?" asked Olaf.

"I've been better…" said Knut, who could barely talk.

"Who's behind all of this?" asked Ragnar.

"Why are they doing this exactly? What did they want to know?" asked Olaf.

"Have you heard about Mother or Thrúd?" I asked.

Knut started mumbling, trying his best to answer, but nothing comprehensible came out of his mouth. His head started falling to the side and his grip on the bowl with the beverage started getting weaker.

"Enough! All of you! Let him rest! You'll get your answers whenever he feels better! Off you go!" said Mielikki while removing us from around Knut and pushing us out of there.

She was right. The man had just recovered from being tortured for many days. We had to give him as much time as he needed. In the meantime, we would work on our chores, which were plenty.

Thorstein checked all the animal traps on the island. He came back with several rabbits, birds, squirrels and some fish. Then he started tending the field. Ragnar and Olaf went to the toolshed near the field and sharpened and oiled the tools and weapons. I went to cut some wood.

Later that day, while I was walking amongst the trees collecting some sticks for the fireplace, I heard a voice praying.

"Father, Oh All-father! Please guide me. Forgive me for abandoning the path that you had set for me, but please guide me to regain Mielikki's trust. I thought I wasn't, but I'm still the man that I was once. Please guide me back to Mielikki's heart like you once did…"

I was near Odin's statue and had just heard Ragnar's cry for help. I was about to leave to continue my stick-gathering task when I heard Mielikki's sweet voice.

251

"Ragnar, oh sweet Ragnar. You'll always have my heart and my trust. Never will I depart your side..." said Mielikki while hugging the kneeling man.

He put his head on her belly, and while hugging her, he continued his plea for mercy. "I'm not that man anymore. Not always, at least. You have to understand that-"

"Ragnar, that's who you were, and you are. There will always be a part of you that will crave blood and death. But there is another part of you too, the one I fell in love with. That's your curse, the same for Olaf's, Knut's and the others. I've always known what you were. Seeing it made me need some time to adjust," she replied with a sweet voice, reassuring the desperate man.

I started moving away from there as silently as I could, but I stepped on a stick that cracked.

"Come on Sigurd. I saw you there the moment I arrived. Let's go home, you two, it's getting dark," said Mielikki with a smile. I came out of the bush that I thought was hiding me and joined them back home, feeling stupid and ashamed.

I checked on Father, placed the small Odin sculpture I had carved during the last trip near him, and started the fire with the sticks recently gathered. Mielikki fed Knut, who was feeling better, and then prepared our dinner with Ragnar's help. Thorstein wasn't in the house. As usual, he must have been somewhere outside in the wilderness.

We were sitting at the table to have dinner right when Thorstein entered the house carrying another basket but, this time, he had very few plants. He gave them to Mielikki, went to clean himself and joined us at the table. After we had finished, we finally sat near Knut, who was feeling better.

"How is the pain?" asked Mielikki.

"I'll manage. They started with me once Eirik fell into a deep sleep. It wasn't long before you rescued me," replied Knut with more strength than earlier that day, but still struggling.

"What can you tell us?" asked Ragnar gently.

"Right now everything is confusing... But it was the Swedes. The Swedish king was behind it all..." started explaining Knut with great difficulty.

"Can you tell us which king?" insisted Ragnar.

"Don't remember the name... King... Swedes..." mumbled Knut.

We looked at each other, both surprised by his answer and concerned about how weak he was feeling.

"Who could it be, Olaf?" asked Ragnar.

"Hmmm... any of them, really. In one way or another, we've had some conflict with most of them. But if I had to bet... It would have to be King Orm," replied Olaf, thinking out loud.

The moment Knut heard that name, his eyes opened wide. "Orm! Orm! Orm!" he repeated.

"Alright, alright. We'll continue tomorrow. Rest now, old friend," said Ragnar while calming Knut and ensuring his wounds didn't open again.

He wasn't in as bad a shape as Father, but still, he was cut, burnt, lashed and had nails in his arms, too. He needed to rest, perhaps the day after he could reveal some more details about what had happened.

We went back by the fireplace and discussed this new information.

"Why would King Orm attack any of you?" asked Mielikki.

Ragnar and Olaf looked at each other, exhaled, and then the latter started explaining.

"During the prime of The Twelve, we were tasked with defending Norway from an invading force: King Orm's men. At that time, he wasn't a king yet, he was an earl. He gathered an enormous force and decided to make a name for himself. Invading Norway sounded like the best way of doing so..." said Olaf.

"The *völva* got a clear sign that we had to defend this aggression, which was against the gods' will. So we went to King Harald's father, who was king at the time and offered to fight for him in this battle. He agreed..." added Ragnar.

253

They weren't fully committed to recounting what had happened for some reason.

"And then?" I insisted, losing my patience with these long pauses.

"Then, Sigurd, we destroyed them. We annihilated almost all of his men. He survived because he jumped on a horse and fled. That left a stain in his name that, until today, remains. The only problem is that he took all his lands by force in Sweden and now he rules with an iron fist," replied Olaf, somewhat annoyed.

"But, if he was so heavily defeated, how could he take by force anything in Sweden or anywhere?" I asked.

"There is a reason he's called 'The Snake', of course, only behind his back. He poisoned his brother, who had a vast estate in the south of Sweden and took over. He then started taking by force all adjacent estates. And that's how he got to power, by either assassinating or paying off whoever stood in the way," replied Ragnar, visibly disgusted.

"Do you think that would be enough to pursue such a fierce and expensive vengeance campaign?" asked Mielikki.

"Well, he always made clear that he hated the fact that a group of warriors 'commanded by Uppsala', as he called us, was responsible for his biggest shame in battle," replied Ragnar.

"While living in Uppsala, I was mostly minding my own business, but Gudrod would always tell me that something wasn't right. He sensed that the atmosphere in Uppsala was changing, especially in politics, and he said to me once or twice that he thought King Orm could have something to do with it. But I never paid attention to politics, so I never dug deeper. If I only had listened more to him..." said Olaf while shaking his head in despair.

"Olaf, brother, nobody could have anticipated what happened. Nobody, not even Eirik saw it coming..." said Ragnar empathetically.

We sat in silence for a while, each one of us immersed in our thoughts. Some dwelling on the mistakes of the past, and others wondering what the future would hold.

254

"We all need some rest," said Mielikki, breaking the silence. "Tomorrow we'll be able to gather some more information. We'll also need a trip to the town, Ragnar. I need some things to heal the wounds. Do we have something to trade with, Thorstein?"

Thorstein nodded. Then we all stood up and went to sleep. I was desperate for the next day to come as soon as possible. I wanted to see if Knut could remember something else. Perhaps he knew what happened to Mother and Thrúd.

I could feel Mother's arms around me, hugging me, and I could hear Thrúd's laugh while playing with Grandmother. I don't know what I would have done to see them once more. With these thoughts in my mind, finally, I fell asleep.

Chapter 29

Rings of Fire

The following day I woke up and helped Mielikki tend to Father's and Knut's wounds. We forcibly fed Father by pouring some fish soup down his throat. Then I started helping Thorstein with other chores, such as setting up fish traps in the nearby streams and working on the field. The constant travels and lack of consistent work on the field almost destroyed the crops.

Ragnar and Olaf went to the town to trade hides and furs for some bandages, rare herbs and other materials that Mielikki requested.

We didn't ask Knut many questions. If he talked, it had to be when everybody was there. He rested the whole day. I spent my day learning how to build and set animal traps. Thorstein was an expert.

The daylight started to fade and soon enough Olaf and Ragnar arrived from their trading trip. As soon as they had hopped off the horses, they rushed into the house and called us in. Thorstein and I followed them inside.

"Hurry! Come!" urged Olaf, who sat near Knut.

"Sit! Hurry! We have news!" insisted Ragnar.

We sat around Knut as quickly as possible. Mielikki and Olaf helped the wounded Dane sit up straight.

"We were at the trading post. And as we were buying the herbs that Mielikki requested, we heard a man that was complaining about everything that happened down south, at Uppsala. So we asked him to tell us about it, and he told us about the conflict that led to Knut's being captured and Gudrod's death. We asked him and he wasn't there, but he arrived there a few days later. He approached Uppsala from the south!" said Olaf, overwhelmed with excitement.

We all looked at each other without knowing how to react. These weren't news, but a simple reminder of when everything dear to me had been lost. I didn't understand the excitement and, by the looks of it, Mielikki and Thorstein didn't understand it either.

"Olaf... I think you skipped the important part..." said Ragnar with a smile on his face while shaking his head.

"Ah! Yes! Sorry! Sigurd! You'll love this! Knut! Your boy!" babbled Olaf who couldn't contain the joy.

"My boy? Do you have news from Björn? How is he? Where is he?" said Knut while moving.

"Ragnar, for the gods! Please tell us already! Olaf is making no sense and Knut's wounds will open wide if he continues like this!" said Mielikki, while trying to calm down Knut and force him to stay still.

"You're right. When the trader was approaching Uppsala, a couple of days after the conflict, he told us he saw something very strange. He saw a young boy, around twelve winters old, on a horse, riding south and-"

"Björn! For Odin, that's my boy! Björn! He's tough as nails! He's going to Denmark! He's returning home! He's alive!" yelled Knut, jumping on his bed.

"That's not all, my good friend..." said Ragnar while helping his wife hold down the proud father.

"The trader said that riding with the boy there was a small girl, no more than four winters old... Wearing a silver Mjölnir pendant! Gudrod's pendant!" said Olaf, while looking at me, exploding with joy.

"Thrúd..." I could barely say, astonished.

I was so overwhelmed with emotions that I couldn't even think. She was alive? And she managed to escape with Björn?

"I asked for more details and, apparently, the direction they came from was the clearing right outside the town, in the southern part..." said Olaf while smiling and staring at Knut.

"Where they met... Thrúd must have run to the place where Eirik and I made the introductions. They met there. After that, Björn said he would go to Olaf's house to meet his new brother-in-law!" yelled Knut with watery eyes.

"He came to meet me? That was the day where I was cutting wood and he told me he would marry Thrúd..." I said while thinking out loud.

I remember I had been rude to him, because I wanted to protect Thrúd, and now my sister's life was in his hands. Now 'he' was the one who would need to protect her with his life.

"You hear that, Eirik? Your daughter is alive!" Olaf yelled in Father's ears, interrupting my thoughts and maybe impairing Father's hearing.

"He's in a deep sleep, not dead! You brute!" reprimanded Mielikki while pushing Olaf away from Father.

I jumped near Father and hugged him with care.

"Father, Thrúd is alive. You are wise, and you knew Björn was a good match. He saved her life. His father, Knut, is an honourable man. I should have trusted you. But now I need you to wake up. We need to find Mother. We need to help Thrúd and Björn and avenge Grandmother. We need your help, Father…" I whispered in his ear.

No movement or reaction happened. His body was warm, and his heart was beating, but his eyes were shut.

I noticed how everyone went silent once I started whispering. Perhaps the joy of knowing that Björn and Thrúd were alive made them momentarily forget Father's state. I stayed right next to Father, perhaps if he felt my constant presence…

"This is great news. Thank you for this… But I remembered more while you were away…" said Knut, lowering his head in shame.

"What did you remember, brother?" asked Olaf, now with a serious expression and a deep voice.

"When I was tortured, they told me many things. They were convinced they would kill me, as they were convinced they would eventually kill Eirik. So they felt they could tell me anything. Some things I heard while captive, others they told me to make me fall into despair…" said Knut with a thread of voice.

"Go ahead, brother, tell us what you know," gently said Ragnar.

"King Orm had planned everything. He started a long time ago. As soon as he crowned himself king of his land, he started planning his revenge, not only against us but against The Great Temple too. He started investing sizeable sums of silver, slaves and goods in Uppsala.

Eventually, he bought the earl, who's been a puppet ever since. But that's not all..." said Knut, who now needed some rest after talking for so long.

He was still recovering from serious injuries. His breathing was still difficult and the pain was hardly bearable. Besides, a couple of wounds started bleeding again after his agitation with the news.

"Chief Svein a puppet? It didn't seem like it, especially at Eirik's trial..." said Olaf, incredulous.

"Svein has been doing King Orm's biddings for a long time but he's still a man who respects the old ways. He became difficult to control," replied Knut.

"Became?" questioned Olaf.

"Orm had him killed. He placed another of his trusted men from his estate in his place," replied the wounded man.

"Killed? When? Another man from his estate?" asked Olaf, visibly confused.

"He killed Svein in front of me. It was a form of intimidation, I guess. And he placed a new earl in Uppsala, a puppet by the name of Olaf 'The Ox', from his hometown," said Knut.

"But, who was the other man that he had previously placed there, Knut?" asked Ragnar.

"Egil 'Quick Tongue'..." replied Knut with a disgusted face.

Olaf and Ragnar looked at each other and then looked directly at me.

"Who's this Egil?" I asked while wondering why they were staring at me.

"He's the announcer at your father's trial, Sigurd," said Ragnar.

"The one to whom you showcased your axe-throwing superb skills, I might add..." said Olaf proudly.

"Egil was behind everything that happened. He was behind the traders that ambushed Eirik and he was behind... Well... Helga..." said Knut with the saddest expression that a muscular, strong and fierce warrior like him could ever have.

"I knew it! I always knew it..." I said, thinking out loud.

"That snake… He got what he deserved…" said Olaf, visibly angry.

"Orm wants to control The Great Temple. He wants to remove the *völva* and destroy any old tradition. But before doing that…" continued Knut, who was feeling increasingly more tired.

"Before doing that, he first needs to kill us all. For he knows what could be unleashed if he assaulted The Great Temple…" convincingly said Olaf, pumping his chest with pride.

"Why didn't this snake king attend the *blót*?" I asked, intrigued.

"Probably because King Harald was already there, and he's a constant reminder of Orm's biggest shame and defeat, apart from being his biggest historical enemy," replied Ragnar.

"What's our next move? Ragnar? Knut?" asked Olaf, still proud and ready for battle.

"Well, we lost Gudrod. Knut will need quite some time before he's fit to fight. And Eirik… Who knows if he'll ever come back…" said Ragnar while looking at his wounded friend immersed in the deepest sleep.

I looked at him, and he truly looked dead. If it wasn't for the warmth of the body and the pumping chest, I would think that he was in Valhöll feasting with Uncle Harald.

Mielikki, Ragnar, and Olaf started discussing what to do next. Mielikki suggested hiding and living in peace. Ragnar suggested bringing Björn, Thrúd and even the *völva* there to protect them. Olaf suggested finding King Orm and killing him, perhaps ambushing him while he was travelling.

The conversation started escalating. They went back and forth with their theories on how to bring Björn and Thrúd back safely, and how to get rid of King Orm. The conversation soon became a discussion and after that, noise.

I stopped paying attention to it. I gently placed my hand on Father's chest and closed my eyes, feeling how the hand went up and down while his chest got filled with air and then it got released.

The image of Father alive, strong, enraged and killing the traders in Uppsala popped into my head. I started then imagining how it would be to see Uncle Harald alive, fighting alongside Father. Then Olaf came to mind, how I saw him completely transformed, fighting to rescue his best friend, his brother. He looked like a god, like Thor. Ragnar also came into my mind, how he was a complete savage, a blood-seeking animal on the battlefield.

I could barely hear the arguing now. It was little more than background noise. I could only picture a battlefield with Father and Uncle Harald at the front. Olaf, Knut, Gudrod and Ragnar right behind them. And other six silhouettes at their side. Six black and unknown silhouettes, forgotten brothers.

"What about the others?" I heard myself asking, breaking the discussion and creating a breathtaking silence. They looked at me and each other without pronouncing a single word. I couldn't even hear them breathe.

"Out of The Twelve, I only met five. Uncle Harald died before I was born. Why not track down the other six?" I insisted.

"We wouldn't even know where to start..." said Ragnar still with a surprised face.

"I don't even know if they're alive..." said Olaf.

They kept looking at each other. I could see how their heads were spinning, going at the wind's speed. Either it never occurred to them or they perhaps thought it was an insane idea. In all of this, Knut kept avoiding eye contact and lowering his head. Initially, I thought it was because he was tired, but now I could see either shame or fear in his face.

"Knut?" I asked, staring at him.

Olaf and Ragnar immediately turned their attention towards him. And now also they saw the same that I saw in him.

"Knut, is there something that you didn't tell us?" asked Olaf.

"Olaf... Some things I didn't tell. Either I lacked the courage or I forgot," said the ashamed man.

"Well, go ahead then," said Ragnar with a serious tone.

"I may know where some of the others are, at least two. I never said it because they asked me to swear that I would never reveal their whereabouts," confessed Knut.

"Why would they want to hide from us?" asked Olaf.

"They're leading different lives, Olaf... Very different lives..." replied Knut.

There was a brief silence. Ragnar and Olaf looked at each other as if they were asking themselves what to do next. But, despite having confessed this, Knut still looked ashamed, like hiding something.

"There is something more that I haven't told you... I only remembered it this morning, but I couldn't bring myself to tell you..." said Knut with a thread of voice.

We all looked at each other, wondering what it could be. We trusted him with our lives so we knew he never betrayed us but, what could this secret be? Why was it tearing him up like this?

"Knut, you're our brother. You know that. You can tell us anything..." said Olaf with a compassionate voice.

Hearing this, Knut moved his head and looked at Father. He then looked like he was struggling with himself, finding the courage to pronounce the words that he was about to speak.

"Eirik... I'm sorry. But, I did hear about Thora..." he started mumbling.

The moment he said that Olaf stood up in a jump, I looked at Father and hoped that I would hear good news even though, by the looks of it, it would be unlikely.

"During my torture, right before you passed out..." continued Knut, addressing his unconscious friend, "one of the guards told me they found Thora. She went hiding with your daughter. In an effort to save Thrúd, she started running and was captured..."

Knut interrupted his recount. He started swallowing what seemed like a knot in his throat. I noticed Father's chest pumping slightly faster. Tears were dropping from my face on his chest. The rage inside me was too strong to contain, but there was nothing I could do.

"The guard told me that killing her would be an act of mercy and that they only regretted that you were dead. They thought you were, brother... But finally, they told me they sold her as a slave to a Swedish earl from the south..." said Knut with a broken voice, lowering his face in shame and frustration.

I heard Olaf's grunting, enraged, kicking and punching the wall. Mielikki crying and Ragnar cursing. But I wouldn't raise my eyes, for some reason, I needed to stare at Father. I needed to connect with him somehow, even if he was unconscious.

His chest started moving faster and faster until it completely stopped. I felt chills all over my body. I started feeling strength, rage, vengeance and a godly power. But these feelings weren't coming from within me, but rather from Father himself. These emotions increased until, suddenly... Father's eyes violently opened wide.

His eyes glowed like never before, charged with hatred and rage. The blue icicles were surrounded by raging rings of fire. The eyes of a god. I heard Mielikki's acute and loud scream.

Father awoke. I didn't know what would happen next, but I knew one thing for sure: Our enemies would forever regret allowing Eirik Helgasson, the last of the Ulfhednar, to live.

Only Odin could save them, but, as we all know, the All-father was on our side...

Dear Reader,

I want to express my deepest gratitude for joining me on these pages. Writing this book has been a labour of love, and your support as a reader means the world to me.

Reviews are the lifeblood of any author, especially for someone like me who has chosen the path of self-publishing. Your honest opinion can have a tremendous impact on the success of my book. So, if you've enjoyed reading this story, I kindly ask you to take a moment to leave a review on Amazon.

Moreover, if you're interested in staying connected and being the first to know about the latest Born a Viking saga updates, I invite you to sign up for my newsletter. By subscribing, you'll receive occasional updates regarding the next book release, exclusive insights, and behind-the-scenes content. As a token of my appreciation, you'll also receive the first chapters of my second book in PDF format, completely free. Follow this link to subscribe: riccardopolacci.com/born-a-viking/berserkr.

I can't wait to share this new adventure with you!

Riccardo

Printed in Great Britain
by Amazon

41173598R00158